Acclaim for *Inside~Outside*

‘Claire’s writing is taut yet supple, bursting with exotic images . . . She’s sharp as a scalpel, and compassionate too. Instruct your bookseller to order one for you and a dozen for the shop.’
Time Out

‘A vertiginous, unsettling read.’
Scotland on Sunday

‘Never insipid, full of imagination.’
TLS

‘The writing is elegant and crafted . . . an assured and unusual voice.’
Chapman

‘A most impressive first volume.
Books in Scotland

The Beauty Room

Regi Claire

Polygon

Polygon
An imprint of Edinburgh University Press Ltd
22 George Square, Edinburgh

Typeset in Galliard by Hewer Text Ltd, Edinburgh, and
printed and bound in Great Britain by
Creative Print & Design, Ebbw Vale, Wales

A CIP record for this book is
available from the British Library

ISBN 0 7486 6322 3 (paperback)

Parts of this novel were first published in *Shorts: The Macallan/Scotland on Sunday Short Story Collection*, vol. 1; *Neonlit:* Time Out *Book of New Writing*, vol. 2; and *(Mole): A Journal of Short Fiction*, Burrow One.

The Publisher acknowledges subsidy from

THE SCOTTISH ARTS COUNCIL

towards the publication of this volume.

Many thanks to the following people for their help and support: Sarah Allan, Alison Bowden, Marie Bremner, Ron Butlin, Dorothy Harrower, Carolyn Lambert, Roger Quin, David Rice, Louise Boller, Eduard Eugster, Stefan Gossweiler, Maja Michel, Martin Vrock, and my family in Switzerland. Any errors are my own. Hölloch Cave as described in this novel is partly fictitious.

I would also like to thank the Department of Education and Culture of Thurgau Canton (Switzerland) for awarding me a bursary.

for my mother and Ruth and Ron, with love

'SMACK HER! Smack her!'

Inside the Roth home at Anders, Celia had just been made to stand on her head. Seven years old, half-naked and choking.

With the shutters pulled to, the lounge had a dim underwater feel. The white carpet, seared here and there by sunlight, glimmered pale as sand. The casement window was open; the curtains hung stiffly, baked solid in the ovenheat of another Swiss summer. Celia's new polka-dot bikini clung to her bottom as if she'd been swimming.

'Smack her, for goodness' sake!' she heard her mother scream again, high above, and she felt herself being lifted bodily and shaken, her scalp and elbows scraping the floor as her mother's grip around her ankles kept slipping, chafing her skin.

'It's all my fault, my fault. I gave her –' The voice of her grandmother was heavy with self-reproach but she didn't come any nearer, her sandalled feet tiny and furtive between the two armchairs.

'Well then, do something! Smack her, hard, that's the only way to get it out!'

Chair legs and sofa legs, coffee-table legs, human legs shuddered and swam before Celia's eyes, turning into a mangrove of changing shapes, bloated and stick thin and impossibly twisted, splintering, disintegrating . . . Her face was running with wet. She retched, and retched. Her head was about to explode, her ears had gone deaf. She was breathing lungfuls of dust but no air. No air –

'SMACK HER!'

The sandals got suddenly bigger: her grandmother was bending down, her sea-green eyes reduced to dark pools of distress, her Cupid bow lips drooping, her old woman's fingers twitching as they reached out towards her, claw-like . . .

Ever afterwards it wasn't the exquisite lips and eyes Celia remembered, only those hands, every single knotted joint of them. As soon as her grandmother held something out to her, a thickly buttered bread slice perhaps, or a piece of homemade apple tart, a new nightdress even, she'd see those misshapen knuckles and her mouth would go dry, her throat constrict into a compulsion of swallowings.

The fingers had hardly hit Celia's back when the dust in her nose released itself into a body-racking sneeze. With a final retch her throat unclenched, expelled – and she slumped free, on to the carpet. Free and alive.

As she lay there heaving and clutching at her throat, she tried to focus on the sweet an arm's length away. Banded red, white and brown like a large marble, it was covered in swirls of blood and slime, matted with hairy fluff where it had rolled across the carpet. Celia moaned, closed her eyes. And allowed herself an extra moan because for once in her short existence it was her, and not her brother Walter – five years older and five years more loved and adored – who was centre stage.

'I didn't mean to hurt you, little one. I'm so sorry,' her grandmother said.

'Didn't I tell you, Mum? Smacking's what's done the trick. Thank God!'

Then the weight of a hand on her shoulder. 'Are you all right now?' Already her mother's tone had cooled to the detached proficiency Celia had learnt to equate with affection.

Quickly she let her lids slide open. Her bikini top was askew, exposing two pale-pink nipples like blind eyes. She ignored them. Gave her aching throat one last rub, and grimaced. No use prolonging her ordeal. Something itchy had started to trickle along her spine, down her thighs and arms, a mixture of sweat and old carpet freshener, traces of moth repellent, the ghosts of unwashed feet. She was glad to get up.

'I shall never buy the boiled sort again, never ever, don't you worry,' her grandmother vowed gently, but the words felt like smacks.

All Celia wanted now was to go to Lake Constance as they had planned and not lose any more time, in case Walter arrived home early with his pail load of slimy tail-thrashing trout from Uncle Godfrey's fish farm out of town. Her mother and grandmother would fuss over him no end. Praise him as the man of the house, the mighty hunter – as if scooping up fish with a hand net was such a big deal. In a diffuse way, though, Celia knew their fussing had a lot more to do with the fact that her father was no longer around.

Let's go, she lisped to herself, Let's go, pleasepleaseplease. She pictured the afternoon hours spread out like the shimmering surface of the lake, with herself in the middle splashing and paddling, or licking a triple ice cream on the hot shingle.

A hiss of running water sounded from the kitchen down the corridor, then her mother returned with a small plastic basin and a rag to clean the blood trail off the carpet.

Walter came wheeling his bicycle round the corner just as they were getting into the car, his pail swinging precariously from the handlebars. Celia saw his damp brown curls glisten in the sun, far superior to her own 'rat's tails', and she wrinkled her nose, trying in vain to snuggle herself into the garage-cool upholstery of the back seat. She couldn't help watching the cleft in his chin widen as he laughed – couldn't help touching her own lower jaw, which leaned out of her face like the witches' in her Grimm's Fairy Tales.

For a while the boiled sweet featured as Horror Exhibit Number One: suitably rinsed and wiped, it was displayed in a cork-stoppered jar on top of Celia's chest of drawers.

She showed it to everyone. Her friends Lily and Nita giggled and asked to have a feel. Walter smirked and Auntie Margaret, who wasn't a real aunt but Lily's mother and her own mother's best friend, called it a 'dreadful monster'. Grandfather simply nodded his moonfaced head, then carried on polishing the furniture in his antiques shop. Uncle Godfrey and his housekeeper inspected it with puzzled smiles. And her mother's clients fled to the safety of the Beauty Room.

One day Celia took it into the yard to let Charlie, the black labrador that belonged to old Frau Gehrig from upstairs, have a sniff. He wagged and grinned civilly enough (or so she thought), his lips pulled back a little further, his velvety red tongue flopped out a little more . . . and his eyes blinked shut in ecstasy. Then he ambled off to his kennel, leaving nothing but a slobber on her palm.

1

NOW THAT HER mother is dead, Celia has all the time in the world. No more trips to the nursing home night after night, announcing her name to the security camera and waiting to be buzzed in. No more smells forcing her to strip and wash endlessly. No more anguish, doubts or guilt. From now on she'll sleep undisturbed, eight hours of bliss, and rip each day from the next in one clean tear.

Celia glances at her watch. Ten to ten: the man will be here soon. She strides over to the lounge window and yanks aside the net curtains for a better view of the street. A cold February day, the sky sullen above the tall apartment block opposite. What's left of the snow has frozen over again, forming a thin crust of white on gardens and rooftops. A red Fiat slows for some patches of black ice the salt lorries must have missed, then accelerates away down the side street. The ash tree out front is waving its soiled-looking branches at her.

Nothing doing, it seems to say, *nothing at all.*

She scowls in reply. Schildi, her neighbours' tortoiseshell cat, is stalking through the snowdrops around the tree base, tail in the air, squinting up at the suspended wooden bird feeder where three sparrows and a robin are squabbling over their morning's ration of sunflower seeds. With its snowy slanting roof and the arched openings on each side, the feeder reminds her of a miniature house – or an oddly peaked skull whose eye sockets are grey with snowlight. She stares at it. Until the tree is shaken by a squall that scatters ice crystals and twirls the feeder on its cord like a merry-go-round. Celia smiles to herself, then turns away from the window, curiously relieved.

But her cheek has grazed the bunched-up night curtains and the sensation makes her flinch. She'd always loathed those curtains; their texture's too grainy, their colour too much like putrid skin. 'Silver Sand' was what they'd been marketed as in the catalogue, and her mother would stubbornly insist on the term.

Celia fancies she can hear her voice even now, a harsh whisper from the sofa which sets the air around her trembling:

Celia, please, it's getting dark. If you didn't mind drawing the silver sands?

The silence afterwards is interrupted by her own rapid breathing as she begins to raise a hand, then hesitates in mid-reach. Whatonearth is she doing? It's light outside. And her mother is gone. GONE. Sealed inside that box of polished wood and brass and satin, two metres underground. No need to obey her requests and demands any longer.

Moments later, though, Celia lunges out with both arms. 'Yes, I know what I'm doing!' she cries and pounces on the curtain folds, grabbing fiercely. The cloth gives with a shriek. There's no stopping her now; she wrenches off the metal hoops with the last few putrid-coloured tatters. The net curtains are child's play by comparison; their weak plastic rings break like a sudden wave and she collapses in a heap of fabric and dust, laughing herself into a sneezing fit. One clean tear, she thinks. A start of sorts.

No voice had tried to restrain her. No one. Dabbing at her eyes with the hem of her aquamarine silk blouse, Celia glances at her watch again: three minutes to ten. Better get rid of this mess before the man appears.

Time, of course, isn't the only thing she has in abundance now.

There's the money, too.

And space. Perhaps that most of all. With her mother's death, space had exploded around her, expanding indefinitely until she could hardly see the corners of the room she happened to be in, as if the sharp winter sunlight had obliterated them, abandoning her in the vastness of a desert.

Eventually, a good week after the funeral, she'd rung up a decorator.

'You won't believe your luck,' exclaimed the woman who'd answered the phone, 'someone's just cancelled a contract job.' The men could start pretty much immediately, she said, and would it suit if Herr Lehmann called round, now let me see, on Tuesday?

No, Celia didn't believe the woman's spiel, not one word of it. But, yes, Tuesday did suit.

Seven minutes past ten: Lehmann's late. Celia stands on tiptoe and stretches hard, her fingernails scrabbling at the metal of the empty curtain rail ineffectually. For an instant she feels like a small girl again, trying to prove she'd grown up so her mother would be happier with her, the way she used to be with adults, and Walter – until he left home. Celia groans, caught up in emotions she'd thought were buried as deeply as contaminated waste. Her body sags against the window sill. Outside everything is hushed: not a single car in sight, the branches of the ash tree frozen into stillness, Schildi and the birds scared off. Even the apartment block and the half-timber farmhouse next to it, behind the fenced-in rows of vegetable beds, seem to have sunk into hibernation.

Several seconds pass before Celia rallies herself – forgodsake, woman, you're nearing forty! She tugs open the window and leans out, willing the man to materialise. She hopes his van will be emblazoned, 'Painters & Decorators' splurged in large rainbow letters all over its sides to let the whole neighbourhood know that she, Celia Roth, is beginning a new life.

This is the first time she has made a decision that's bound to leave a mark. To change things. Things as opposed to ideas. Things are visible; ideas and opinions can be hidden away. At last she'll be able to mar those pastel walls – those fleshy pinks and creams, those flaccid greens. New paint will stick and so will the paste under new wallpaper. Even steaming won't ever return the place to its previous state of unholy insipidness. Something will remain. And that something will be hers, and hers alone.

All at once Celia notices how naked the window has become without the curtains, like an enormous peephole inviting others to pry – strangers, neighbours; Rolf and Carmen from upstairs, old Frau Müller in the farmhouse, the shabby tenants of the apartment block. You've got nothing to hide, she reassures herself, nothing to fear. And anyway, there are the outside shutters. They clank closed easily enough.

'But don't say later I didn't warn you, Frau Roth.' The decorator is dressed casually in shirt sleeves, no jacket, and sounds a little petulant.

Celia smiles at him – words of caution no longer have power over her. Instead of smiling back, he regards her with a mixture of distrust and tired belligerence. Since he set foot in the flat his professional pride has been hurt over and over – a room at a time, as it were. He swallows another Kambly *caprice* biscuit, washes it down with his coffee, then slicks a blond-bleached curl behind his ear.

'More?' Celia asks. She has snatched up the coffee pot and the liquid can be heard sloshing about inside. She feels suddenly uneasy, wonders whether she is trying to placate Lehmann after rejecting his suggestions earlier so gracelessly. Or whether she's simply pandering to his good looks. He is in his mid-forties, she'd guess: a man in his prime. With thick curly hair almost down to his shoulders, the way she remembers Walter's before he had to get it cut off for the *Rekrutenschule*, his compulsory five-month stint in the army; and a freckly round face like a boy's, confused a little by the thin nose, sharp teeth and Vandyke beard of the grown-up. His eyes are unwavering – pin-prick pupils in a softness of blue – and they unsettle her. He is wearing a wedding ring. Celia is holding the pot slightly tilted above his cup, ready to pour. 'More?' she repeats, feeling increasingly exasperated, and guilty. 'Or have you had enough?'

His eyebrows, lashes and the Vandyke are black, his natural colour presumably. Just like that hearse-style van he'd arrived in, quarter of an hour late – jet black and waxed to a gleam, with the firm's name curlicued discreetly, far too discreetly, in gold on both doors.

'No, that'll do. Thanks.' Alex realises his hand has covered the coffee cup as if the woman had proposed strychnine. Of course he isn't afraid of her. She's a bit screwed up, that's all. Kind of sleek and wide-eyed, unnerving with that wet-gel straight hair right over her breasts which swell so unashamedly against the water green of her blouse. Like he used to imagine mermaids when he was a kid. But Christ, what a nightmare of a colour scheme for her flat! It's always the same story: first the I-know-what-I-want rashness of choice, then – with the wallpaper still blistered and the paint not yet dry – the stunned silence, finally the murmurs of regret, shrill complaints and acts of sabotage (usually involving some phantom pet that just happens to be moulting).

Not to worry though. The woman's old enough. And once she's put her name on the dotted line, well, what the heck . . . He starts gathering his brochures and sample files while Celia reaches for the order form on the coffee table, signs and dates it, her face glazed with obstinacy. Having fetched a bundle of notes from the rosewood bureau in the corner, she relaxes at last. She smiles to herself, aware of his gaze travelling up and down her front, and counts out the money.

'I'll pay five hundred francs now if that's okay,' she says. 'The rest on completion of each room.'

'Fine by me.' Alex is careful not to shake his head as he detaches the Client's Copy from the form. Her signature is an almost-scrawl: *Celia* Roth – *psychedelia*, more like! He throws the electronic measuring tape into his briefcase, on top of the files, and snaps the locks extra hard.

Celia has stood up. It's twenty past twelve. For a moment she pictures his wife, probably petite and pretty in a tight-fitting apple-green apron, waiting for him. Maybe she has already laid out their lunch on the table, the steam condensing greasily on pan and porcelain lids. Maybe he's even got children. Boys, girls, babies. No doubt he would. And they'll be clamouring for their food. So hungry. Always hungry, always clamouring.

Suppressing a shiver, Celia points to where a small metal tape-measure sits like a snail under the rim of his saucer: 'And don't forget that.'

'Oh, thanks.' He smiles. For the first time he seems gratified, not in a hurry any more. He clicks the briefcase open, then shut again with a gentle roll of his thumbs, saying, 'I've got a longer tape in my jacket pocket, you know. Much bigger. Only I lost a button on that jacket and there's no spare. So now *all* the buttons need changed. But my wife . . .'

After an apologetic cough and a dismissive gesture which erases any lingering impressions of petite apple-green aprons from Celia's mind, Lehmann strokes his Vandyke, raising mournful black eyebrows.

This would be the perfect opportunity to offer womanly help and understanding, but Celia can't quite believe him. He sounds too glib, relies too much on his looks: the male of the species strutting his stuff. And if this wasn't enough, she absolutely hates sewing. Sewing of any kind – buttons, splits, relationships.

Alex gives her five seconds to express a little sympathy. Then, when she doesn't, he slaps the biscuit crumbs off his trousers. What else did you expect? he admonishes himself, irritated at his feelings of disappointment. A job's a job, and that's that.

Getting up he casts an eye round the lounge, pausing for a moment on the unscreened window. A bit risky, he'd have thought, with that big apartment building right opposite. Or does she like the idea of being on show perhaps? None of his business, at any rate. A week from now the room they're in will be purple, various shades of purple, to be precise. The woman made sure of that, flicked back her long hair challengingly every time he tried to object. Lighter tones for walls and ceiling; the centre rosette, cornice, skirting, window frame, door and fireplace surrounds a nuance darker; the radiators and door darker still, with the inside panels near black – like madly diminishing perspectives into a private hell.

It's the middle of the night and Celia is awake. She forgot to pull the curtains and now the moonlight is all over her. It's soaked into the bedding on top of her, underneath her, soaked into the folds around her head and feet, along her sides, making the sheets cold-heavy.

She can't move, not even her little finger, just lies there and stares out at the huge frosty disc which has forced itself on her and stolen her sleep. Not a face, certainly not a friendly one, whatever people might say. She can't think clearly because every so often the disc becomes a gigantic white eyehole that's trying to suck her into its brightness.

After a while she begins to feel dizzy. She still can't move but seems to have shrunk and is being turned roundandroundand-round within those hardened sheets. To steady herself she concentrates on the cloud shadows floating across the disc. Then sees them dissolve very slowly into a ring of refracted light. A gigantic iris – orange, red, violet, indigo, blue, green and yellow – to go with the eyehole that's started sucking again. Sucking, sucking her inside . . .

Inside the eyehole is her brother raging like a red-ragged bull. And everything is happening all over again.

'Mother's flat is yours now?' Walter keeps roaring, 'Yours alone?'

No point in reminding him of the mortgage which she herself will have to take on. Or his share of the money (the legal minimum, admittedly) and the trusts set up for his boys – he is beyond listening.

And beyond himself, it seems. 'Yours alone? What a bitch! I did whatever she wanted, didn't I? Didn't I?' Definitely beyond himself. 'Bloody BITCH!'

Their mother's last will isn't *her* fault, is it? *Walter* is the one that went away – first, at barely sixteen, to the other side of town for his apprenticeship, finally, having married Lily on her twentieth birthday, to the other side of the globe, to New Zealand.

She is the one to 'have it all' as he puts it. Hasn't she just! Does he really think she enjoyed nursing Mother while working full time? Enjoyed the fuzziness at the edges of days when afternoon would blur into evening, evening into night into midnight then early morning, with those cups of milky coffee, bowls of soup and hot-water bottles dripping and seeping into the few remaining gaps in between? Later the visits at the home, the spongy cancerous growths and bloodstained handkerchiefs, the odours needing smothered in lavender – their mother had been a beautician, forgodsake, could he imagine how she'd reacted to the sight and smell of her own decay? Does he honestly believe she, Celia, enjoyed having to witness all that? All that pain and despair, she adds to herself, without once being allowed to feel the intimacy that must exist, surely, between a mother and a daughter?

She'd phoned Walter as soon as she could after dealing with the most urgent formalities, so he would be able to book a flight before she finalised the funeral arrangements. And five minutes into the call he'd asked about the will. How could she pretend not to know? In the end he sent a wreath. Yellow carnations. Gaudily disdainful, the flowers spoke louder than words, and none of the family flew over. Not even sister-in-law Lily, who used to be her best friend.

When Celia wakes in the morning, her left hand is clenched into a fist. Her knuckles are sore and bone white. She sits up, massages the fingers back into place, joint by joint. Her hand is empty. That something she'd been clasping was less than nothing, she tells herself. A bead of sweat perhaps, dried long since, or a dream she can't remember.

2

CELIA HAD NEVER seen black flowers before, not real ones, that is. Black diamonds, yes – though she'd been shocked at their unexpectedly metallic lustre. Gemstones in most varieties she is accustomed to: they come with her job at Eric Krüger's. But not flowers.

She leans back against her pillow and breathes in deeply, rhythmically. In and out. In – out. Already the smell is creeping up on her. In – out. The raw sappy smell of tulips.

Black tulips. A big bouquet of them, tied together with a ruby-red ribbon, had been delivered to the chapel of rest on the day of her mother's funeral – no card, no name, no nothing.

It seemed perfectly natural to want to take one of them home with her.

Before the coffin was removed into the main hall for the funeral service, she'd walked round it one more time, trying to avoid the stern hollow face which seemed to balance on the plastic chin-support like yet another flower head wired into its wreath. She'd bent down ever so slightly to reach for the tulips in the vase at its foot.

Nobody could have noticed how she nipped off a single stalk, then opened her handbag, to all appearances for a paper tissue. It was done in a second and there weren't many people about. Except for some distant relatives, only Uncle Godfrey, big and bent double over his crutches as he stood mourning his sister, and Margaret, her red-gold hair flat and lifeless under the black lace scarf, as if the death of her best friend had drained away all brilliancy. After quickly wiping her eyes with the tissue, it was easy to rub the sap's clotted slitheriness off her fingers unobtrusively. The ungodly thoughts had come later as she leafed through her hymn book during the service and caught a lingering whiff of that zingy smell.

Celia scrambles off her floor-level bed, determined not to give in to those thoughts now. She sees herself returning from the funeral reception at the Schlosshotel and, scarcely in her own front door, bringing the tulip out for a closer look. But instead of simply looking she'd twitched off a petal, and her heart had jumped with spiteful delight. Every day over the next week she'd done the same – a petal a day keeps Mother away. Till delight turned to disenchantment.

Whatonearth had she hoped to find, apart from observing the progressive states of desiccation? The last two petals were almost transparent and when she held them up to the light, they muted the brightness around her like a thin dark veil.

Once those petals had gone, though, there was nothing to hold things at bay. Walter's angry rejection of their mother began to haunt her, charging the very atmosphere of the house. On several occasions in the past week she'd been unable to stop herself from entering his former bedroom (used as a store room since his departure, musty and crowded with junk-filled solid oak cabinets and cupboards from their grandfather's antiques shop) to check he wasn't lurking among the furniture. Even out in the garden – feeding the birds, coaxing Schildi away from the ash tree, or idling by the letter box to breathe in the delicate scent of the winter jasmine she'd trained around the gatepost – she had sensed a strange vicious iciness in the wind. And doing her shopping at the Co-op up the street, she would suddenly hesitate in front of the fresh-meat counter where she'd intended to treat herself to a veal escalope or an ostrich steak from one of the local producers, as she smelt not the chilled cleanliness, but dead flesh.

Breakfast is a rushed affair today because Celia wants to get the clearing well under way before Lehmann and his assistant drop off their tools and tins of paint in the afternoon. Thankgod the house will feel different soon, liberated from ghosts and spirits. She has put on her oldest clothes, the pair of dove-grey flares and the eau-de-nil turtleneck (both presents from her mother, bought by mail order as a surprise years ago and only ever worn if she'd been reminded).

Passing along the corridor Celia pictures the walls in crimson. That's the colour she'd selected yesterday, quite instinctively and without meaning to offend Lehmann, who'd ended up making an impassioned plea for 'gentle gardenia' and 'the illusion of spaciousness'. Crimson, after all, is more than a mere colour to her, it's an emotion. It's the flush of anger on her mother's cheeks whenever she'd suspected her of loitering after business hours at Krüger's, going for a drive maybe or a visit to the cinema rather than keeping her company. Homecoming *is* crimson for Celia, and always will be.

She pushes open the door to the lounge. Gasps. Recoils. And sinks to her knees. For the briefest of instants she'd glimpsed a figure draped on the sofa, extending an arm towards her.

What would they say at work if they could see her now, so small and helpless, crouching on the floor? She who considers herself the best secretary old Eric has ever had, fearless and brisk behind her bullet-proof office partition? But no doubt they're too busy to spare her more than a tolerant smile – well, well, so poor dear Celia is human like the rest of us – Angelina getting the gemstones on her desk all mixed up again while flaunting her apprentice charms at Handsome Henry, the courier; and Eric, ensconced in his king-size swivel chair in the inner office, dreaming up yet another sales ploy to compensate for the 'January hole'. Only fat little Lapis, Eric's blue-roan spaniel, would be happy to pay her his respects: he'd throw himself on his back, legs in the air, right next to her. Lapis the Fat. And the Faithful.

When Celia dares look over to the sofa again, the figure has vanished. There's nothing but a mound of cushions in its place.

Celia's face feels gritty; her contact lenses itch and bite. She peels off her mother's beige church gloves, soiled now beyond redemption, and lifts back her long hair. She wouldn't have believed that a carpet kept so scrupulously clean, vacuumed at least twice a week, could produce such a flurry of dust and fluff. The room seems to be swirling with it, to have grown darker, more distinct, as if its ceiling, walls and corners had hauled in the space between them, compressing it, like a snow cloud closing in on a winter's day.

She has ripped up a good two-thirds by now, pulling out the carpet staples with a claw hammer. One of them, near the fireplace, stuck so fast she'd lost her balance and staggered back against the sofa; the hammer had missed her thankgod, and instead gouged a hole in her mother's favourite silk cushion. Another of her selfish whims, Celia muses, staring down at the floor: a white carpet (white carpet Mark 3) in a room with an open fire – coal at first, then, following the new regulations on fuel emissions, logs. Getting the lounge radiators installed when she moved back in with her mother five and a half years ago had almost caused a fight.

The original carpet had been fitted shortly after Celia's father disappeared 'in search of a better world', as his sudden absence had been explained. The phrase had lodged in her mind like a precious stone. A little girl of hardly more than six, she used to fantasise about him and the Seven Dwarfs mining for gold and diamonds far, far away beyond the Alps; and ever since, she has been drawn to gemstones. Now that she's been told about the flash flood and can cope with abstracts and ambiguities, she asks herself at times: Once you've lost it, whatever *it* is, how do you know where to start looking?

That carpet. She'll never forget the day of her first real date and how nervous she was, so nervous a big lump of coal fell off the scuttle and bounced a smudge trail across its whiteness, as if to mock her tidily laid-out newspapers. She'd done her best to conceal the marks temporarily – it was an emergency, after all – regrouping the armchairs, the coffee table and the standard lamp, scattering a few school books on the floor, spine up, as if for future reference. Then, dressed in her hot-pink trouser suit with lipstick and eye shadow to match, her hair combed one last time in front of the mirror in the corridor, she was just reaching for the spare set of keys on their hook when –

'Oh, before you're off to meet your friend, Celia dear: I noticed a small mishap in the lounge . . .' Smiling her cleanest most efficient smile, her mother held out a basin of soapy water, a toothbrush and several sheets of blotting paper, pale-blue blotting paper.

'I'm really sorry, Mother. I'll sort it when I get back. Promise.'

'This isn't a coalmine, Celia.'

'Honest, I promise.'

'Which only leaves me then, doesn't it?'

She'd been three-quarters of an hour late and her would-be lover long gone. Still she lingered outside the café in the bitter cold, stood waiting and hoping, and thinking of how Walter had taken Lily's affections away from her two years earlier – until she felt the mascara trickle down her cheeks.

She's hated that bland soggy blotting-paper blue to this day. She never walks to the office if the sky is that colour: she either drives or gets the bus, and welcomes dusk like a caged bird might the spread of a dark cloth.

Celia squeezes her mother's gloves back on, rumbles the furniture over on to the floorboards, into the centre of the room, and sets to tearing up the rest of the carpet, kicking and rolling it into a slumped kind of shape. Even Margaret, who tended to agree with her mother in most things and had a weakness for elegance and beauty, used to call that carpet a liability. It's too heavy to shift, a leaden weight with none of its former springiness left. She'll be glad to see it carried out of the house to be burnt or left to rot. Never mind the cost.

Everything in this country has its price, rubbish not least. 'A tag a bag' is the town council's slogan and, at two francs fifty a tag, people have learnt to recycle fast.

The floorboards and the dirt gaps running straight and black in between seem to give the lounge direction at last. As if the entire room was free to move now and might, indeed, at any moment incline slightly towards the ash tree with its host of hungry chattering birds, or retreat through the Beauty Room and kitchen into the peace and quiet of the frost-wizened backyard.

'That should come off easily enough.' It's late afternoon and Lehmann has slid his knife sideways under the champagne wall-paper next to the door surround. 'See?' He half-turns to Celia, shakes out his blond-bleached locks to get her attention. Then he plucks off a strip, revealing a sea-green mural underneath, complete with whorls of blue, yellow and red like tropical fish. He brandishes it but Celia is no longer interested. She has stepped up to the wall and started tracing the different colours with her fingernail, up, down, left, right, roundandroundandround.

She imagines the roundabout a few blocks away, beyond the Co-op. She loves driving round it with the steering wheel at near-full lock, loves the sensation of ease and security, particularly after fiddling with tiny gemstones for hours on end, weighing and re-weighing them. She'd managed a record seventeen circuits, traffic and all, the day her mother died. If it hadn't been for the strain to her eyes and an unaccountable numbness creeping up her legs, she might have gone on forever.

Dominic, Lehmann's assistant, brushes past with a ladder and some dustsheets, his paint-spattered baseball cap back to front. The woman doesn't seem to have noticed him, and for a moment he watches her finger drawing circles on the bare patch of wall, his eyes hooded from years of guarding against splashes of paint, loose flakes of plaster and wallpaper, and single ladies who want their immaculate flats shredded then re-padded for no better reason than to keep themselves entertained. With a shrewd well-rehearsed glance-and-grin towards his boss he says:

'That green colour's nothing out of the ordinary, Frau Roth, just ancient paint. You'd be surprised at some of the other things we've found under wallpaper. Isn't that so, Alex?' He forces open his lids, raises his voice a notch, 'Like that time over at the rectory, remember?'

Her hand doesn't stop, never even slows down. She reminds him of the black cat he had as a boy and how it used to sit behind the closed door, pawing and pawing to be let in.

Alex has crossed to the fireplace, knife in fist, and stabbed the wall high up, slicing off another strip, expertly, right down to the skirting. He has decided to play along for a bit, not really to humour his assistant nor to tease the Roth woman either – he's not the teasing sort – but because she annoys him, plain and simple. Annoys him standing there, ignoring them like they're a couple of dummies. He looks over his shoulder and remarks loudly:

'No skeletons here, Dominic.'

Dominic laughs.

Of course Celia is aware of being watched and ridiculed, only she couldn't care less. These days she can do what she wants, can't she? She's no longer the kid condemned to write dictation on the blackboard, with her classmates snickering at every mistake. She can turn round and snicker back. Or she can stay where she is, and if she feels like stroking the wall she'll damn well do it. The surface has a waxy sheen that makes her think of skin . . .

Such tasteless jokes, though. What do *they* know about skeletons? Ghosts? About the bones of mice and rats, the shrivelled-up bodies of spiders, beetles, slowworms? That was one of Walter's specialities when he wanted to give her a fright. 'Guess what I've discovered by the garden wall, sis?' he'd ask. The first few times she was naive enough to expect a magic frog that would transform itself into her prince, or at the very least a lizard sunning itself on a stone and, if touched before it could flit off into a crevice, obligingly surrendering its tail.

Celia whips round abruptly. The two men, she notices with a certain *Frauenpower* relish, scurry into action at once, flapping their grubby off-white dustsheets over the armchairs, sofa, coffee table, standard lamp, bureau and bookcases assembled under the ceiling rosette, stacking rolls of paper, tools and tins into neatly useless pyramids.

That done, the decorator smooths and pats his curls, then jerks a thumb at the hump of carpet along the wall opposite the window: 'You're better leaving the carpets until the job's done, lady, or the paint'll mess up your nice clean floorboards.' He throws down some dustsheets.

The assistant stares over at her, pushes back his baseball cap and, still staring, mops his brow and drooping eyelids with the sleeve of his sweatshirt.

Celia turns away; how she hates amateur dramatics! Why can't they go now? It's quarter to five and they promised not to keep her late.

Suddenly a flash of metal catches her eye.

'Excuse me,' she says and stoops to pick up the stripping knife. Its hard rubber grip is faintly warm from Lehmann's hand. 'May I borrow this for a while?'

She'd laughed out loud at the men's sheepish scandalised looks. At the threat-and-concern in Lehmann's voice as he wished her 'a pleasant evening' from the street door half a flight below, his Vandyke thrust up at her. Afterwards, like a good girl, she'd laid the knife back down because she didn't really need it, did she?

Celia leans her head against the coolness of the open lounge door. Her eyes have started to water, she's laughed so much.

'You don't blink enough, that's what's wrong with you,' the optician had told her the previous week, cutting short her descriptions of the bleary featurelessness she'd begun to experience in the flat. He'd wiped his hands on his white lab coat, then noted something down on a filing card, muttering to himself. A sad man *he* must be to want people to blink all the time, she'd reflected, and smiled to cheer him up. In response he'd taken hold of her head, squirted some fluid out of a bottle straight into her eyes:

'Come on, Frau Roth. Blink!' And again, his voice split with impatience: 'Blink! I said. BLINK! BLINK!'

And now, all by herself, Celia is blinking and blinking, and it doesn't help. Not one bit.

The room's a liquidy blur and already the walls are receding. The dustsheets are looming larger and brighter, with an unbearable tint of blue leaking from their folds, as if they had absorbed too much daylight.

Celia wants to shut the door and walk away, but there's that cold-heavy weight again all around her, like last night. Blink by blink the clutter of furniture beneath the dustsheets changes shape, its jagged outlines slacken, level out, merge into one single mass, more and more familiar. And although she knows this is impossible, she can see it just the same, right in front of her: that oblong object, shrouded.

Celia blinks and blinks.

If she blinks long enough, the room will settle down – she's got all night.

If she blinks long enough, the furniture won't pretend to be anything but furniture, and she'll be fine.

She's got all the time in the world.

She blinks and blinks, waiting for the rustle as the sky's turned inside out.

3

BY QUARTER PAST SEVEN next morning Celia is up and dressed. She's trying to rouse herself with some icy-sweet orange juice, a couple of microwaved croissants, and Turkish coffee so muddy it can hold her mother's silver mocha spoon propped up inside the cup – the spiky heraldic handle is a painful reminder of when little Celia didn't 'eat nicely' and had her knuckles pricked with it.

Thankgod those days are over. Glaring at the immobilised handle, Celia starts to lick the buttery pastry flakes off her fingers with small smacking noises. And thankgod she doesn't have to brave the office just yet.

A cloud-ridden greyness seems to be frozen into place, up against the window and the balcony door. The house is on a corner and she can hear the commuter traffic thrumming along the side street which links up with the ring road and accesses the sprawling electronics plant nearby. The headlights of the passing cars and motorbikes are sallow smears in the early twilight.

'Don't come back until you feel ready, Celia dear,' Eric had said at the funeral, his hand on her arm. His bushy eyebrows were drooping in commiseration.

That was two weeks ago. Good old Eric – an unbossy boss. Celia munches her second croissant, then has a leisurely sip of orange juice. She knows she mustn't take advantage of his benevolence. Though, to be honest, he can afford to be generous with her; she's never been off for long periods, has never cost him a penny for any maternity leave and, crossmyheartandhopetodie, she never will.

It's 7.29 by the kitchen clock and the greyness outside melting at the edges when the decorators' van turns into the yard, dead on time.

She buzzes them in before they have a chance to ring the bell. The wooden stairs creak under their tramping men's feet and the wide frosted window between the landing and her corridor tinkles in its frame, the cut-glass garland of roses another fanciful legacy of her mother's. Then Celia opens her door and here they are: Lehmann with a cassette player poking from a green sports bag, the assistant with a big silvery gadget like some futuristic vacuum cleaner – the steamer, probably.

They mumble 'Morning', giving her no more than a cursory glance, despite the nice bright clothes she has put on today. She had bought the gold-yellow blouse and emerald satin leggings at the sales last year, stored them sealed and cellophaned, for best.

As she stands gazing after the men and their slovenliness – paint-splattered overalls concertinaed at the waist – Lehmann suddenly faces round.

'All right if we fill up the stripper in the kitchen?' His sharp teeth are smiling at her.

Celia feels herself nod weakly. 'Sure. Just go ahead.' He calls the gadget a stripper – a STRIPPER, forpitysake. She tries to smile back – he is good-looking, she can't deny. But he has already disappeared into the lounge and the door closes behind him.

Too late to tell them about the new dustsheets and what she'd done to the old ones (though howinhell could she explain, anyway?). Celia forces herself to move off down the corridor, walking calmly, not even allowing her hair to bounce off her shoulders. Past the store room, whose door is safely locked and the key deposited on top of the coat rack. Perhaps the men won't notice the different sheets, won't notice the flannel bedsheets – her mother's – which now swaddle the furniture below the ceiling rosette. Past the upholstered chair, the telephone table. Just as they didn't seem to appreciate her new blouse and leggings. Drawing level with the large oval mirror opposite the Beauty Room, where her mother used to see her clients, Celia tilts her head sideways a fraction in silent appraisal of herself.

After the decorators left yesterday, Rolf and Carmen, the young couple from upstairs, had rescued her quite unwittingly from the trance she'd fallen into. Her eyes had been growing numb and helpless when the street door slammed, shaking the thin pane of the landing window, and their voices flared the house alight.

Celia had stopped blinking, stopped doing nothing.

She'd darted over to the heap of tools, grasped the stripping knife once more. Then, slit by slit, slash by rip and tear, she drained that ghostly blue from the decorators' dustsheets. To reclaim what she knew must be there, really there: nothing more than a sofa full of cushions, one of them spilling stuffing from a hole; nothing more than a couple of armchairs, a standard lamp, a round wrought-metal-and-glass coffee table, a rosewood bureau and three small bookcases displaying the gilt-embossed spines of her mother's historical romances and some grimy volumes on potholing with Walter's name inscribed – the latter ones she plans to rip up page at a time for the next paper-recycling collection. In all, nothing more than silk, foam, wool, wood, glass, leather, paper, brass.

But destruction seldom goes unpunished and Celia had ended up polishing and re-polishing two of the bookcases whose tops had got scored rather badly by the blade.

It was while looking for the teak furniture spray, overcoming her apprehension about the store room and searching with clammy cold hands through her grandfather's various oak cupboards and cabinets, that she'd found the shoes. A dozen pairs of gently bunioned shoes, her mother's. All of them suede.

Celia had read somewhere about the processing of hides and how suede is in fact the flesh side, scraped and scoured till eventually there's nothing left to suggest a body, nothing but a surface, velvet-smooth. She herself had always felt an inexplicable aversion to suede, and now it makes her shudder to think of all those people going about their business in coats and jackets, gloves and boots, like animals turned inside out.

Two pairs of the shoes were hardly worn. Others had had their toes chapped bald from shuffling through long winters of ice and grit, hitting against whole townfuls of kerbs, cobblestones and raised shop entrances. A few were hopelessly old-fashioned (two-toned, with perforated zigzags, check and paisley patterns). But none of them were 'quite done yet', as her mother would have stressed.

Well, Celia couldn't have agreed more. That was to be her job.

She had fetched the mutilated dustsheets from the lounge across the corridor and torn them up completely. Kneeling in the cramped space between the antiques, she'd begun to swathe the shoes in length after length of paint-stained cloth, like so many feet cut off and mummified, when all of a sudden she'd heard a muffled scratching. Someone was tapping on wood, their fingernails scrabbling. Her heart missed a beat. *Scrabble-scrabble,* silence, *scrabble-scrabble,* silence. Was there someone in one of the cupboards? Hadn't she been thorough enough? *Scrabble-scrabble,* silence. Quietly, half-sick by now with fear, she'd manoeuvred her body out into the corridor . . . The scratchings got louder, stopped. The silence dragged. Then a miaow – pitiful, plaintive, and coming from outside her front door. Despite her relief Celia didn't feel like laughing. Schildi miaowed again, more plaintively, before continuing her struggle up the wooden staircase which Carmen had waxed to such treacherous perfection. For a moment Celia followed the cat's slow progress through her landing window, then she pulled the night curtain and finished wrapping the remaining shoes, in a hurry now. Having bagged the bundles, cleared away the cloth tatters and loose blobs of emulsion, she dutifully tagged and dumped the lot in the waste container out in the yard. Back inside, she locked the store-room door – as if this could shield her from the goblins of her memories.

When she caught sight of herself in the bathroom mirror, hours later it seemed, her face was scabby with dirt. Raw red lines ran down her cheeks and the exposed part of her throat, joining together in a ragged horizontal where the turtleneck had kept its stranglehold. Celia marvelled at them. She hadn't been aware of crying.

She had gone to bed soon after, not bothering to mask her window, and slept untroubled by the moon, slept hard and dreamless, like a stone.

* * *

Celia has reached the bend in the corridor. There's nothing to worry about, she tells herself, the flannel bedsheets must have escaped the decorators' attention. A little more confident now, she calls back towards the lounge:

'If you need anything, give me a shout, okay?'

But the men's cassette player has been flicked on in there and 'Space Oddity' erupts in mid-song, Major Tom-ing her like an insult. Of course she can hear them, dammit. Who wouldn't?

Instead of going into the kitchen to drink up her Turkish coffee, Celia veers to the right, flees down the rest of the corridor to what used to be her mother's room and has now become the *spare* bedroom.

Alex and his assistant don't think twice about the door banging shut somewhere at the back of the flat. It's a windy blaster of a morning after all, when even a keyhole is enough to cause a draught, and they've just put on some music to have more privacy. They're inspecting the thick yellowed bedsheets with the handstitched monograms that have ousted their own dust-sheets, making jokes about prissy old maids. Then they place a couple of thin plastic covers on top.

'For ultra protection!' Dominic points out with a grin.

'She'll be getting charged for the old ones,' Alex says.

Still, as he prepares the wallpaper for the steaming, perforating it with the hedgehog which his wife always says looks like a medieval torture instrument, Alex (who for the last few months has woken at dawn, aching for a challenge) can't help admitting to himself that the Roth woman isn't all that unattractive for her age.

Celia has flung herself face down on the bed that's only a mattress now, disguised with one of the rich damask coverlets her grandfather used to sell in his shop. She is tense and agitated, in a fury of frustration really, and has wrenched off the emerald leggings, wrenched them off so savagely her knickers haven't been spared either. Her lovely new blouse, shoved into a crumpled mess around her waist, resembles a piece of discarded peel.

To spite the men, she has switched on the clock radio. But it's still tuned to one of her mother's classical stations, which is regaling its listeners with the loud hammerings of a spindly-sounding harpsichord. No time to retune it, though; Celia's hands have already slid to where she needs them most. All she can do now is bury her head deeper in the damask, shut her eyes and get rid of that soft wet tautness, quickly, quickly.

'Fancy not knowing –' she suddenly hears Lily yelp again, like that afternoon they'd tried to teach Nita, who at six was two years younger and still in kindergarten.

They were lying on Lily's bed, skirts up and fingers inside the thick winter underwear.

'But how? How? How?' Nita whined, her milk-teeth mouth pouting open and closed as if she was hoping for a sweet.

The curtains were drawn, and in the semi-darkness Lily's strawberry-red hair shone with static as her head thrashed from side to side:

'Like this! Like this!'

Her breath was coming in shorter sharper flurries, then she yelped that three-word yelp: 'Fancy not knowing –' and Celia thrust herself back into the blankets, burrowed down, down deep, until the rough hairiness of the wool burned hot against her mouth, searing her skin, while the headboard creaked and creaked and the bed seemed to gallop like an imaginary horse straight into the wall.

Later they fooled around much more wildly than usual, Lily shouting, 'Hey, Nita, like this!' and Celia crying in mock-desperation, 'But how? How?' as they did somersaults, then jumps on the bed, trampolining higher and higher, arms outstretched, towards the ceiling, watching their shadowy reflections streak up and down in the mirror on the opposite wall. Nita gave up after her first few efforts sent her tumbling to the floor. Lips pursed, she stared accusingly before picking herself up and pushing the heavy jersey her mother had knitted down into her sloppy woollen tights extra carefully. When she had finished, the folds of spare material round her middle bulked almost like real hips.

They'd already compared chests and decided there was nothing much to see, except if you arched the small of your back in a certain way, drew in your belly and tweaked your nipples.

But kindergarten Nita was a rebel even then. 'Silly-silly-schoolgirls,' she began chanting, 'silly-silly-schoolgirls,' in between smirks.

To shut her up, Lily started a game of prisoner and guard, chased Nita round the room till she was captured, then hustled her into the wardrobe, trying to keep the door closed with splayed legs and arms. Nita escaped, of course, and resumed her chant, triumphant, a born survivor. In the end they'd all been running after each other, getting thrown into the dungeon and breaking out again. At one point, Celia was slammed into the wardrobe so violently most of the dresses fell off their hangers, the slithery fabrics fumbling at her like hands. She'd fought her way out double quick, and wrecked the latch in the process.

When the game slackened off at last, Celia went over to the window to let in the daylight, and almost gave a scream. During their fun the world beyond the curtains had vanished. Not a centimetre was left of the brown rectangle of the vegetable patch, or the grass. The big cherry tree, the fence, the ploughed fields, the copse where Walter and his friends had rigged up a tree house in one of the sycamores – they'd all vanished. Thick ivory clouds of featherdown were shivering up against the glass: Old Mother Frost had trapped them inside that little-girl bedroom for ever and ever, it seemed.

At times Celia still finds herself in there, cowering among the shoes and grit and slippery clothes in the wardrobe, or jammed into the bottom part of the bedside table which had always reminded her of the clock case in 'The Wolf and the Seven Little Goats'. Or flat under the bed on the cold fluff-strewn lino, listening and listening to those puppy sounds from above. Whenever it snows and she is alone that sense of locked-in-ness catches up with her.

Lying quite relaxed now, Celia is no longer bothered by the music from the radio. She deliberately ignores her mother's 'pride and joy', the magnificent waxplant trained arabesque-style over the far wall, and is watching the clouds scudding past the two corner windows – as though they were racing each other round the house. They are snow clouds, she is convinced.

4

'FRAU ROTH, HELLO? Hello! Frau Roth!'

Almost eleven, godknows how long they've been calling her! She must have dozed off, her bare legs and buttocks have a chill wind-fingered feel to them. For a ludicrous instant she almost expects to be spanked, even the swish of the old cane-plaited carpet beater is in her ears again, cutting through the air. Her mother had often threatened her with it, wielding it above her head, but there was only one time when she'd actually been in earnest, and the soreness afterwards had lasted several days. Celia had been doing magic in her room; she'd heaped some earth, including a small worm and some decomposing leaves, on a kitchen plate, then sprinkled a few of Walter's hairs and fingernail clippings on top, to be ritually burnt with a candle flame while she was singing her incantations: 'Father, come home! Come home! Brother will take your place.' The loud singing was what had betrayed her.

Celia rushes her knickers and leggings back on, pulls the blouse down over her hips as she stumbles out into the corridor, past the blare of trumpets and cymbals from the radio she has the presence of mind to turn off.

'Sorry, I didn't hear you,' she says to the assistant who's been flipping through the art-deco calendar on the door opposite, the door of her own bedroom. Her voice has a gasping edge to it and he looks at her lazily, the hoods over his eyes rolling up and down like shutters in slow motion.

He grins. 'Hope I didn't wake you.'

'For your information,' Celia states, pausing to think of an excuse, 'for your information, I was sorting through my late mother's wardrobe.' She sighs and crosses over to him, reaches out to straighten the calendar that's dangling there all crooked. Surely he can't have guessed, surely not? Her hand has come to rest on the side of her face where she feels a sudden itch. 'What is it, anyway?'

'No offence,' Dominic gives a sly half-shrug at the creases in her blouse and the flushed ridge-patterned imprint on her cheek which she seems to be trying to hide from him, 'just wanted to ask for some binbags and, if it's not too much bother, a cup of –'

But the woman's already turned away and is stalking off down the corridor, her green-clad legs looking as stiff and glossy as two freshly painted lengths of wood. Dominic grimaces after her and raises his cap in silent salute. She's worse than the little old ladies with their rattling trays of cups and saucers and shameless banter. If nothing else, she'll be good for a laugh with his mates at the Bluebeard Club tonight. He'll have a gulp of coffee from his thermos instead.

In the lounge, meanwhile, Alex is kicking limp strips of wallpaper into drifts, whistling along to 'Message in a Bottle' and surveying the damp walls and ceiling. Twelve years at least since the last major overhaul, the Roth woman had said (plus, he'd reckon, not too many young visitors either). The plaster is cracked above the window and the fireplace, and there's the occasional hole – nothing excessive, though. Nothing his All Purpose Polyfilla can't put right. The paintwork won't need stripped. A bit of sugarsoaping, a rub with ammonia to get rid of the ingrained dirt, perhaps a little sanding here and there. The only bugger is the cornice and matching rosette in the centre, same as in that perfumed room next door. Not the usual fleur-de-lis but *tulips*, for God's sake – he falls silent and slowly marches round the room, his head thrown back – all kinds of bloody tulip shapes. With spiky snarls of leaves and pointed petals asking to be sponged one at a time, please, coquettishly threatening to break off at the first touch.

Alex tosses his hair. It'll have to be Dominic's job; he is more patient and, for all his clowning about, more fastidious, a sucker for tricky problems (no wife and kids to rile him, before *and* after work). That's that then, Dominic's the man. Alex starts whistling again and slaps out the rhythm on the covered-up furniture. With the wind so strong today, the place should dry out soon enough and they'll be able to get on to the lining and painting well ahead of schedule.

'Goddammit. Dammit! DAMMIT!' Celia crumples up sister-in-law Lily's blue aerogramme, then her own unfinished reply, three sheets so far of black pen on bright fuchsia, and hurls the fistful at the clockface behind the kitchen table. The paper balls bounce off the plastic casing with crisp dry *pings*, innocuously enough. Never budging from her chair, she watches them skitter across the white-tiled floor towards the open doorway.

She'd received Lily's letter on Saturday, two weeks after the raging-bull phone call with Walter and his aggressive roar: 'Mother's flat is yours now? Yours alone? What a bitch!' Hoping for some kind of apology, she'd found herself trembling slightly as she slit open the envelope. Then she'd read and re-read the cluttered frilly handwriting which said to accept the family's 'deepest sympathy, once again', and gave a 'round-up of our latest news', trying to explain away Walter's outburst as a 'temper tantrum, nothing more', and sending his love (*in absentia*, for he seemed to be on some trip or other to do with his wine-growing business). Not even a hint of an apology. 'GODDAMMIT!'

A pair of feet in paint-spotted Reeboks trample in. 'Everything okay?' The Reeboks continue, right over the scrunched-up bits of paper, before coming to a dead halt. 'Oh, sorry, I didn't see –'

'It's all right, nothing to be sorry about.'

The decorator's hair is dishevelled and matted with dust, his black Vandyke streaked cobweb-grey. He is holding a bucket of scummy water. 'I was just going to empty this in the bathroom when I heard you. Sounded like you were having problems or something.' He smiles with his sharp teeth and takes a step nearer. 'Well, I'm glad to see you're okay.' He makes no attempt to leave. Simply stands there smiling down at her.

Whatonearth does he expect her to do? Celia wonders. Swear some more? But she feels curiously touched all the same. For a moment she blinks up into the blueness of his eyes. They are unwavering, and no mistake. Twin pins that force her to gaze back more steadily . . .

Then there's her mother's voice, from way back in the past: *Watch out, Celia, don't let yourself be caught with a little sugar-coated kindness or you'll choke for real. You remember the last time, don't you?*

Celia starts to cough as something seems to get stuck in her throat.

Alex, who has suddenly become aware of his bedraggled state, tugs at his hair with his free hand. He isn't sure exactly what happened. All he knows is that one minute he was smiling at the woman, the next her body had grown sort of rag-doll limp. Except her eyes, which were fixed on his for what seemed ages. Christ, she was weird! Perhaps his first impression of her wasn't that far off the mark after all: Psychedelia, the mermaid. Either she's lost her fish's tail or else she hasn't quite learnt to swim yet. Not properly, at any rate. For an instant he fantasises about putting his wife into a trance like that, and his sons. Sheer bliss to shut them up at will.

'I've been meaning to ask you a favour . . .' Celia falters.

A favour? Alex begins to feel rather uneasy. She sounds much too pleading; ingratiating almost. He doesn't want things to move so fast. He prefers her more difficult – more off the wall. 'Back in a second,' he says, with affected unconcern. 'I'll sling this stuff out first.' Then he turns on his heel and is gone.

Dirty overalls, filthy hair, stupid beard, bad manners. No-no-no, Celia tells herself as she tries to unsquash the paper balls she's retrieved from the floor, the man isn't worth it. He isn't really her type. No. She is confused, upset in a way she hasn't been since Franz's death.

She hears Lehmann clear his throat before he ventures, 'So, you were saying?'

She barely glances up. Ranged before her on the table are the sheets of her letter and Lily's aerogramme, a little creased and smudged, yet miraculously untorn. The decorator must have had a wash and general spruce-up in front of the bathroom mirror, he's come back with his face gleaming. But she doesn't like him. No-no-no. Doesn't want to like him. And she is the boss. She'll be fine. Just fine.

'Having a wee conference?' The assistant has joined them. He is leaning in the doorway, cap angled back, poking out some earwax with his little finger and grinning his trademark grin. 'Ready when you are, Alex. Ladders and board are all yours now.'

'Well, I certainly won't keep you from your work.' Celia gives an awkward laugh. 'On the contrary, I was thinking of adding to it. That carpet roll in the lounge, would you mind getting rid of it for me? I'll pay the council charges, of course.'

Lehmann is all business now. 'Sure, take it away this evening. Together with the first load of shutters you want repainted. Peacock blue you said, didn't you?'

'That's right.' She smiles rigidly. 'Yes. Thank you. And could you start with the lounge, the Beauty Room and the spare bedroom, please?'

Before closing the kitchen door, the assistant looks back at her over his shoulder, winks, and says, 'A piece of professional advice, Frau Roth: you might try a steam iron.'

Celia doubts he is merely referring to the crumpled letters. But she nods anyway. A minute later she is still doing it, nodding helplessly to herself like one of the tiny collapsible bead-and-string toy horses she used to play with as a child. Desperate now to stave off the moment when she'll have to finish her letter to Lily and Walter, recapturing the conciliatory tone of the first few pages and offering them more of the money her mother had left to her – if that's what it takes to make Walter happy.

5

SHE SPENDS THE best part of Friday morning rewriting that hateful letter to Walter and Lily – with various expurgations of passages she'd scrawled the previous night, after a bottle of Montepulciano d'Abruzzo and some Calvados – and pausing every so often to picture life at the office, enviously almost. Her first twinge of regret at not being back at work.

Fridays are the best days at Eric Krüger's – lazy, chatty and sweet. Lazy and chatty because everyone's there: Angelina, Handsome Henry and Martin, their salesman. Martin is always keen to help with anything as long as he can talk about his 'week on the road', especially the male staff at his favourite motorway restaurants and hotel bars (though he never mentions the jewellers and goldsmiths, Celia has noticed, not even famous Herr Q in Zurich. At fifty, Martin studiously avoids mixing business with pleasure, it appears). And Fridays are sweet. Not just for their delicious proximity to the weekend ahead, but for the more immediate gratification provided by the cartons of meringues, cream cakes and fresh fruit tartlets which Eric never fails to order – 'as a little treat' – from the *Confiserie* three doors up.

Still, the office will have to wait. She needs more time to sort out her mother's possessions.

At midday, the house her own again for the short hour and a quarter of the decorators' lunch break, Celia clatters about in the kitchen, chopping an onion and peeling some boiled potatoes for a *Rösti*. The noise from the side street has died down; the last of the employees at the electronics plant must have driven and biked off, or hurried past in their boots, winter coats, gloves, scarves and hats towards the bus stop. Deli-Doris, the young shop assistant and dedicated cyclist at Bänninger's, the delicatessen on the corner, had told Celia how the plant's management had introduced a 'green programme' that subsidised car-sharing, bus passes and the use of bicycles among the workforce. Celia had smiled and nodded, as required, and wrily thought of the large tax rebates promised by the cantonal government to businesses which adopted environmentally friendly policies.

She's just begun to grate the potatoes into a bowl when the growling starts, far down the main street out of town: a low knocking and thumping and booming, swelling steadily, inexorably, until it becomes a deafening racket of crashings and clashings as the caterpillar tracks roll nearer like thunder made metal, to encroach on the buildings, shaking their foundations, reverberating even in the ice-toughened earth.

Celia stands petrified. A half-grated potato disintegrates in her hand.

Not that the column of tanks particularly surprises her. Anders, with its ancient castle complex on the mound, has always been a garrison town, a centre for the country's artillery; and Walter had been a tank driver in the army. But for a moment she's had a vision of everything around her falling apart.

Then she dashes off, potato and all, into the dustsheeted lounge, straight up to the window. The tanks are still rolling by, back from yet another military exercise. They're monsters, beautiful terrifying monsters, practising to do violence. Compliant for the present, they return to their headquarters on the common, between the canal and the River Thur. Biding their time.

The floorboards are creaking, the glass panes juddering, close to shattering. Some of the putty is lying in thin grey worms on the sill. If the decorators hadn't already re-papered the walls and ceiling and given the cornice and rosette a first lick of paint, the plaster dust would be clouding the room by now.

Celia feels the floor shift imperceptively under her feet. Her whole body is vibrating, her lips are in a tingle.

The tanks' gun barrels have been lowered to an almost level position, like the strained necks of big cats scenting prey. Some of the soldiers are showing themselves in the open hatches of the turrets, revelling in the cold rush of air and their sense of power. Celia remembers Walter's words, reported to her by Lily, that 'there's nothing more exhilarating than racing across rough terrain in a tank – nothing, except sex, perhaps.'

She watches the helmeted heads swivelling about like target seekers. Several of the men see her and wave. She hesitates before raising a hand in reply, sending bits of potato crumbling down on herself.

Later that day, after a long nap to soothe her battered nerves, Celia swings open her mother's shiny walnut wardrobe. And it's like a wave of snakes rearing up. Live snakes hurling themselves at her chest, tails rattling against the inside of the door, vicious and unforgiving. She flinches away covering her eyes. But there's only a faint flapping noise now so she lowers her arms. Blinks. Then bursts into laughter that ripples way beyond her, into the past and the future, and seems to make the waxplant rustle in its corner.

She reaches out and yanks the belts off the rail in a quick succession of slaps, flinging them on to the bed where they straddle each other messily: plain-cloth and patterned-cloth belts, a few cracked and cloud-ringed patent leather ones, all of them bent double as if from constant stomach ache, their colours pale and sickly, drained-looking, down to the very buckles even whose metal is hidden under layers of material, bony to the touch.

Staring at the straggly heap on the coverlet, Celia recalls her mother as she used to be, slim and vain, and how she'd hold her breath for a whole minute if necessary, so the fastener could be forced into the very last hole. In winter the corsets helped; several of the belts were too loose and Walter, the 'man of the house', had to punch additional holes into them. Summer with its flesh-bloating simmering heat caused the past-her-bloom beauty no end of twisting and pulling. And violating. Though Celia wasn't aware of that, not really. Not until a certain Sunday in August a lifetime ago.

The sun had been fierce that day, even at nearly five o'clock. The air nuzzled and clung to her skin like a hot damp furriness. Heat was bubbling up from the street surfaces and pavements, ready to tar her bare feet. She and her mother were walking home from Anders Station – no bus service in those days.

They'd had lunch at Uncle Godfrey's trout farm three stops out of town. Walter had stayed on, eager to lend a hand with stripping the fish of their spawn. Encouraged by their uncle, he'd taken to spending most of his free Wednesday afternoons and weekends there, and was paid a little pocket money because he was 'such an excellent assistant'. But then Uncle was Walter's godfather, and a bachelor at that.

'A boy his age needs the company of a man,' Celia's mother would say to her, repeating the words over and over, like a mantra. Maybe to convince herself and feel less bereft.

The barriers were down at the level crossing. As her mother proceeded down the pedestrian underpass, Celia loitered by the keeper's hut in the blinding sunlight, waiting for the fast train from Zurich to come hurtling round the corner in all its twelve-carriage glory, brakes screaming, the slipstream playing havoc with her hair. She'd have much preferred staying with Lily today. They could have cycled down to the common and chased the hares out of the vast maize field by the canal, then had a swim in the Thur, perhaps picked some buttercups and daisies for weaving into gold earrings, necklaces and bracelets.

The barriers had hardly lifted when Celia felt herself being grabbed by the shoulder. Her mother's face was shining with perspiration, her eye make-up dissolving. 'God, what a nuisance you are, Celia!' she exclaimed and dragged her off down the shadowless empty street. Past the linden tree at the canal bridge where Celia wanted to float some twigs; past the kiosk that sold chilled soft drinks; and past the Frohsinn's garden restaurant which was full of children having sundaes with their parents, laughing and clinking their spoons and twiddling the tiny paper parasols.

Yes, Uncle Godfrey used to dote on Walter. Referred to him as 'the spitting image of dear lost Peter' if he was in a sentimental enough mood. And instructed his elderly housekeeper, who was fond of children and loved cooking, to prepare Walter's favourite dishes.

'Poor Uncle,' Celia whispers now, seizing the broad black patent-leather belt that's hanging over the side of the bed, 'how times have changed.' She must go and visit him again. He had looked so miserable at the funeral. Clomping along on his crutches, with that unfriendly new home-help gripping his arm.

'The woman's the worst cook in the world, Celia dear. I couldn't possibly ask you here for a meal. You should have seen today's chicken fricassee: a mushy swamp of peas, mostly. And yesterday she fried my breakfast egg so long it crackled all the way down my throat.'

These were his most recent 'horror stories'. Celia suspects he invents whole catalogues during the boredom of his aimless days, to liven up their Sunday telephone calls. He always chuckles with glee when she responds by ugh-ing and mygoodness-ing and generally clucking in disgust. Poor old Uncle. The fish farm had been his life. Especially after her father disappeared. And then Walter emigrated . . .

It suddenly occurs to her that Uncle Godfrey hasn't once commented on Walter's absence from the funeral. Hasn't, in fact, mentioned Walter at all in their last few conversations. He must know about the row they had, that's the only explanation. Walter is sure to have rung him, moaning and complaining. But not too much either because he wouldn't want to jeopardise his share of Uncle's property.

Celia sinks down on the bed. She almost wishes for another onslaught of those snakes. The length of black patent leather has come to rest across her knees.

Her mother had been wearing a belt rather like it that hot and cruel August Sunday. As soon as they got in the door of their flat she'd sighed, 'Mm, this feels good,' and unbuckled it. Then her fingers played a silent tune all the way down the front of her sleeveless pale-yellow dress, pressing and releasing buttons. The smooth fabric slid off as if by itself. And revealed a deep five-centimetre-wide red mark, wetly glistening, which seemed to split her body in two. Celia had stood rooted. Tentatively, she'd stretched out a forefinger and ran it along the edges, wincing at their knife-sharpness. 'Mum,' she said in a hushed voice, 'have you got a skin belt now?'

In the coolness of the corridor her mother's face opened up, the worry lines on her forehead and about her mouth filled out like the petals of a desert flower unfurling to the first glitterings of rain. Celia made her hands all narrow to fit into the groove of weeping flesh, then laid them one on either flank and began stroking, gently, to and fro. To and fro. Ever so gently. Gazing at her, still smiling, in just her bra and panties and high-heeled sandals, her mother took a step closer . . . and, moments later, started to shiver and shake, her skin covered in goose pimples. The smile had vanished, the petals were sealed dry and papery again, tightly into place.

Celia's hands had been paralysed; she couldn't lift, couldn't tear them away from the glass-brittle belly underneath. As if they'd become part of her mother once more, bonded now not by blood and oxygen but by a filigree tracery of ice crystals.

'Don't be LIBIDINOUS!'

There wasn't time to inquire about the new word which had exploded in such a tight fury of syllables. Her hands were ripped away – it felt like patches of skin and half her heart line were left behind. Then something swished. Her arm stung. A door crashed shut, and a key grated in a lock.

When her mother walked into the lounge a little later, she was wearing a sacklike dress and her house shoes with the surgical footbed. Her voice was steady, controlled even to the last quavers and quarter-tones: 'Well, Celia, reading again? I wish I still had the patience for that, or the leisure. How about a bite of supper? Some rice salad *à la créole*, perhaps?'

Celia knew what that meant, of course. Yesterday's leftovers chopped and mixed and bashed up together, with a fresh-fried egg thrown in for good measure, the yolk ruptured and bleeding thick drops all over. It must have been the sound of the phrase *à la créole* that appealed to her mother and the glibly exotic chaos it suggested, certainly not any experience of the real thing. Her mother had never travelled far from Anders: the Black Forest to the north, Lake Constance to the east, the beaches of Italy to the south, and Lake Geneva to the west – after her apprenticeship she'd briefly worked in Lausanne, brushing up on her French and developing a more refined taste for beauty and extravagance, before being summoned back to start work at her father's antiques shop, which to all accounts she had hated; hated so much she'd snatched at the first offer of marriage, no matter that the man, an archivist for the council, was ten years older than her and spent most of his spare time down caves.

In bed that night Celia overheard her mother on the phone: '*Innocent*, you're saying?' A pause. 'My God, that's rich coming from you!' Another pause. 'Don't laugh. It isn't funny, Margaret. Not funny at all.' Then, after another much longer pause, the voice had dropped to a murmur and Celia, exhausted by the heat, had fallen uneasily asleep.

Celia's palm hurts; she has been clutching the strip of black patent leather as if her life depended on it. Not much of a snake, is it? Dead and fangless. When she lets go, the belt slithers to the floor. But it doesn't keep still. The end that's not weighted down by the buckle has curled back on itself to where the wardrobe rail has left its pinch, and now it's bobbing up and down. Up and down. Slowly. Obscenely almost.

She crosses her legs. From the lounge come faint frantic scrabblings. More like the patter of mice inside a food cupboard than Lehmann and his assistant rushing to get the ceiling finished.

Mice, yes . . .

Celia had been told that during her mother's last night, she'd rung for the nurse on duty and said, fully conscious: 'Oh, I'm glad it's you, Thommy. I dreamt there was a mouse in my bed. But there isn't, is there?' She'd even managed a smile apparently, while dabbing at the blood from her nose with a paper tissue.

The nurse pretended to check under the covers and pillows,

then he put the drinking straw between her lips so she could sip some tea, and said not to worry, he couldn't find a thing – not a whisker. And anyway, didn't she think mice were really very nice creatures, all soft and bright and lively?

How peaceful to die after hearing words like these, uttered by a hunky male nurse – Celia feels she herself couldn't ask for more when her own time comes.

Thommy had been dressed in white, *spotless* white. Unlike the decorators. Celia idly wonders whether underneath their overalls Lehmann and his assistant wear belts at all. Indulging herself she imagines them in shirts, washed-out blue jeans and heavy silver-studded leather belts – the buckles loose, enticingly loose, pulled down a little by the weight of the metal, and almost level with her face. A bit more daring now, she gets the men to unstrap their belts, slip them from their hips and try on an even broader more substantial variety, the kind that has to be slung a lot lower, with the buckle right over the groin. She has just allowed herself to give Lehmann's buckle an appreciative final tug, remarking, 'Great build,' when his voice shouts from the front door:

'Okay, Frau Roth, we're off! Have a nice weekend!'

Then the door closes, and she's alone.

No, not alone, she corrects herself, not exactly. She's free. And in her superior-secretary voice she declaims:

'Celia, hey, you're free! *I* am free. Free. Free. Free. Like in "trouble-free", "duty-free", "childfree".'

Autosuggestion even works for dogs. Tell a mongrel he's beautiful often enough, and he'll start strutting around on bandy legs, pig's tail and foxy old head held high. So, she decides, she'll go out tonight. Not only go out, but go to the Métropole.

The Métropole. She knows she'll have to return there some day, she can't delay it forever, and now is as good as tomorrow, next week or next month. Another decision made, she says to herself with almost awe and a sense of deep heartaching relief. Life's getting easier and easier.

Then, swiftly, unceremoniously, she stuffs the tangle of belts on the bed into one of the binbags she has brought for her mother's clothes.

The Métropole, on the fringes of the pedestrian precinct between the castle and St Nikolaus's Church, is the café where she and Lily used to hang out after school, watching and gossiping about the passers-by, boys especially, over an ice cream. It's also where Celia first met bearded Franz, her scrawny brawny mountaineer, smitten with him even before she'd seen more than half his face and ponytail. He'd never been quite so smitten with her, she doesn't think. On bad days it had felt like he preferred the lichen on rocks and boulders to her freshly bathed and perfumed skin. After his accident she'd avoided the Métropole. But that didn't stop the nightmares. Not for years.

As she stoops to pick up the patent-leather belt at her feet, Celia's eyes are drawn towards the open wardrobe. The clothes on their hangers are pushed up tight against each other, rubbing shoulders and sleeves in atrophied stillness. For a moment she scans the folds of lilac and light beige, of faded eggshell blue, parched yellow and watery green, of twill and tweed, peau de soie, crêpe de Chine, unbleached linen, Italian cotton. Then she shakes her head. No, she won't be a caring citizen just yet – no Salvation Army for that lot. No salvation at all. They'll have to go the way of the shoes, sorry m'loves.

She pictures them flying off into space, doing a lap of honour at the roundabout by the Co-op maybe, piece after tailored piece: the eggshell-blue skirt with the beige blouse hovering above it untidily, hastening to keep pace, the lilac trouser suit next, girdle aflutter, then the stubble-yellow dress with its buttons down the front stained a darker smellier shade, and all the dull-drab rest of them flitting behind like so many ghosts or angels in disguise, hard on the heels of those bunioned old suede shoes.

Celia laughs softly to herself – she's just seen a pair of oyster-grey trousers overtake a pleated skirt – and strokes her satin-sheathed thighs till she feels the heat on her skin. How she'll enjoy the screech of the hinges when she raises the container lid, the dead-earth *thud-thud-thud* as each bag drops into oblivion, and the metal clanking shut!

6

AS SHE RUNS the few steps back upstairs, empty-handed now and light-headed, Celia pretends to herself she is gate-crashing her own home. Breathless with excitement she bursts into the lounge. And stops short.

The ceiling is a dusky red-purple that seems to float between the darker centre rosette and cornice. Perhaps it's the failing light, but she could have sworn that the tulip shapes, set in relief, had squirmed and quivered just now, looking for an instant like live figures with curiously tortuous limbs. And although the walls appear grey and lifeless, merely lined with paper so far, Celia is suddenly aware of an invisible presence in the room.

'I love you,' she mutters, blowing a kiss. She has no idea what she means, or who, and doesn't care. Then she attempts a cartwheel along the free side, past the window, and half-flops over, giggling at her awkwardness.

Two hours later the spare bedroom has been stripped to an echoing bareness. It'll be its turn for redecoration soon. The damask coverlet and the chartreuse curtains have been shoved into the wardrobe – with the radio clock, a tasselled floral lampshade, some pictures of lake views and various glass ornaments bundled up in their folds, and the lace-trimmed waste-paper basket balancing daintily on top. The waxplant was quite a job to ease off its hooks along the wall and is now draped over the bookshelf in Celia's own bedroom.

She had always marvelled at the artificial elegance of this plant.

Its leaves are dark-green pointed ovals, fleshy and polished to a sheen; its flowers stiff clusters of pink-tinged stars which seem to be fashioned from wax, velvet and a sweet scent that fills the air on summer nights. One hot evening when Celia was small, she'd caught sight of her mother standing with her face almost touching a fist-sized cluster of the flowers. Knowing better than to interrupt and risk being told off, she'd flattened herself against the outside of the half-open bedroom door.

All at once her mother had whispered, 'Pearls of nectar', and the red tip of her tongue darted up against one of the flowers, then another, and another, until the whole cluster, the whole stem with all its leaves, the whole plant even, rasped in fits and starts against the wallpaper.

Celia had quietly tiptoed back to her own room, guilty and shaken to the core, as if she'd just witnessed something unspeakably and intensely wrong.

A few minutes afterwards Walter came home from Uncle's, and the familiar *slosh-slosh-slosh* of his pailful of trout approaching up the corridor set her teeth on edge.

'Anybody in?' he shouted. 'Gabrielle?'

He'd begun to call their mother by her first name and she didn't seem to mind – if anything, she was flattered by it. Which puzzled Celia because when she herself had imitated him, vaguely hoping to charm her mother also, she'd been firmly told off.

'In here, Walter!' her mother shouted back. 'Want a taste of something special?' Her voice sounded sugary from all the nectar she'd had.

As Walter closed the bedroom door behind him, Celia could hear low laughter and the words 'Queen of the Night'.

Now, gazing at the rich foliage cascading over her bookshelf, she vows that when the scarred woody spurs bear the next generation of flowers, their beauty and fragrance will be pleasure enough for her. She'll never want to suck them dry.

On her way to the kitchen Celia has a last glance into the dismantled room. The old walnut bedside table is the only thing she hasn't had the heart to tackle yet. Its single drawer is locked, she tried it earlier. Locked for a reason, no doubt. And there's a time for everything. In the light from the corridor the gold-plated drawer handle resembles a mouth: it curves and gleams and leers.

After some stewed apple and pancakes, quick and healthy, though not the most sensible meal before a night out in the coldest month of the year, Celia is almost ready. She's still wearing the emerald leggings and has given her blouse a steaming-over (heeding the assistant's advice). Her face is made up to go with the clothes: jungle-green eyeliner, charcoal mascara, a dash of Or Baroque on lids and brow bone, coral-red lipstick. Now all she needs to feel complete is her opal pendant. The last time she wore it was at the funeral. Two weeks ago yesterday.

The opal had been a gift from Eric on the occasion of her tenth anniversary in the job, some three years previously.

'Not the legendary pot of gold but the rainbow itself, gathered into a stone,' he'd said. 'That's what Australian Aborigines believe, anyway.' Then he'd turned away abruptly and started to pat Lapis, who was teetering on his haunches, front paws out in pathetic supplication. Celia had to pull her boss round physically for a thank-you kiss on his cheek. The memory makes her smile even now.

Entering her bedroom, she sees her reflection in the antique gilt-edged mirror she inherited from her grandfather. The smile has faded from her face but her lips have remained parted, her eyes crinkled and screwed up as if in anticipation of future delights. How she longs for a *younger* man and *his* presents – perfumes, flowers, chocolates! How she longs to feel beautiful, and desired!

Celia reaches for the white-lacquered jewellery box on top of her chest of drawers, beside the African violet that seems to bloom all the year round in constant vivid-pink celebration of itself, and the jade statue of Buddha (a reject of Eric's due to a fracture on its left buttock – not something that worries her unduly as the figure sits meditating with its back to the wall).

The pendant she wants lies sprawling like an ancient iridescent beetle at the bottom of the box, waiting to be cradled between her breasts – it's rather unusual, designed specifically for the small black opal cabochon whose colours burn like pins of fire: red and green and yellow and blue. She acts with the swiftness of habit. And that should have been that: a simple case of removing the pendant from its box, clicking shut the hinged lid, threading one of the leather bands through the loop, clipping it on, *et voilà* – as her mother would have said. But it isn't enough. Not any more.

Ever since her mother died, Celia has left her gemstone collection alone. She isn't sure why. Unless, perhaps, it's a way of making herself feel sadder at her 'sad loss'. Because *not* seeing or touching her stones for so many days and nights, *not* rubbing the chunk of Russian amber until it releases its secret smell of the past, of forests long been and gone, *not* letting the beads of rock crystal trickle through her fingers like a rosary that's come unstrung, is nothing short of punishment, hurtful to the quick.

Still, Celia has been adamant with herself. She's resisted the temptation to switch on the art-deco lamp with its wide disc of green-flecked white nephrite, another costly heirloom from her grandfather, which stands to attention next to the chest of drawers. She hasn't once taken the key from its hiding place under the African violet. Hasn't once unlocked the lowermost drawer to disclose the inlay tray bought at a discount from Eric's supplier, including the colour-of-her-choice lining, a dusty rose velour she adores, even if it doesn't do full justice to her gems.

But now she can't restrain herself any longer: a flurry of movements and she is kneeling in the nephrite lamplight like a true worshipper. Her penance of self-denial is over at last.

They're all there, each stone in its own cushioned compartment, gleaming, sparkling, glitzing with the concentrated fury of twenty days spent in utter darkness. She catches her breath – it's like being assaulted. The eyes of the bloodstone stare at her, inflamed and angry. The moss agate has flushed dark green from held-in passion, demanding to be lifted into the light instantly, to show off its fibrous innards.

Celia has already picked up the ruby, without thinking and a little too rashly. Because set in the centre of her palm the redness will begin to drip on to her skin again – how could she forget? – and the stain will spread. For a moment she weighs the stone in her hand; real Burmese 'pigeon's blood'. She knows its carats to a fraction, electronically gauged and verified, and her fingers would recognise the slippery-sharp feel of its flawless step-cut anywhere. It's her most valuable piece, after all. And her most hateful.

She is beginning to tremble now, a flutter deep inside. Hurriedly she returns the gem to its compartment; she doesn't want to drop it. Doesn't want to think of her former friend either, the friend she lost to her own brother: Lily aka Ruby.

'Celia's just a short form,' her mother would lecture Celia whenever she'd misbehaved, her painted-on beautician eyebrows furled out of reach. 'Remember that. Short for *Cecilia*. So you'd better be careful. Better watch out for the missing bits. If you ever want to grow up, that is, and become a full person.'

The warning seemed to be uttered more frequently, recited word by word and with a certain gusto, once Walter started secondary school.

But howonearth did you 'become a full person'? The way her mother talked, it must be something deliberate. Like thinking, or doing an exercise. Maybe it simply meant covering page after page with those 'c's and 'i's from *Cecilia* till she got cramp in her hand – plain and spidery letters painstakingly drawn, or slipshod scrawls like so many crescent moons, suns half-rising on the horizon, guttering candles, organ pipes . . . Maybe writing out those letters would be enough and she'd end up complete. A perfect adult specimen.

Easiest, of course, would be to take the 'c's and 'i's from the magnet alphabet on the fridge which was always dayglo-daring her to compose some 'nice little message'. She could put them under her pillow before going to sleep, pray for a magic transformation in the dark, and when she got up next morning, hey presto, she'd be whole. Like Walter.

The only problem was the tooth fairy – whatever lay under

your pillow was hers. Not that Celia believed in such kids' stuff any more. And yet, her tooth fairy couldn't be trusted: sneaking in to leave a couple of pricky pencils behind; then a rubber in the shape of a heart, a curvy pink sweet-smelling heart that gave her headaches and blotted her mistakes all over the page; and last, outrage of outrages, fobbing her off with a dozen ancient ink cartridges, sticky and faded-looking after being kept through years of heat, thunder and rain and dry brittle cold, the ink flowing on to the paper thickly, in milky grey splodges the colour of old people's eyes – nothing like the limpid green she'd asked for.

Eventually Celia decided on something altogether different. It wasn't so much a decision really as a sudden insight. She was undressing when she spotted her new orange top where it had been dumped in the deep-sea shadows under the radiator, turned and twisted and glowing faintly, like a crushed sand star. She'd stopped dead, half in, half out of her dungarees: ALICE – she'd call herself Alice. ALICE! It was her name too, wasn't it? Jumbled up but still her name, and with no letters missing, starting slap bang at the beginning of the alphabet.

She told Lily next day as they were walking home from school. Lily smiled and, with a glance towards the track where some boys from secondary were doing long-distance running, she said, 'AAAAALICE,' caressing the name with her tongue. Then she laughed: 'In that case I'll be RUBY. Red-haired RRRRRU-BY.' For a moment her curls flamed and danced in the early autumn sunlight, in sharp contrast to the grey walls of the new ice rink they'd just passed and which was to open in less than a month. And like dancing flames they licked the side of Celia's face. No mention of ruby *lips*, she thought; despite their secret games.

It was a half-day. Lunch over and homework done, they had the afternoon to themselves. They clunked about on stilts, skipped rope and hula-hooped, shouting out their new names all over the backyard, playing around with echoes, accents, voices – their mothers', Walter's, Uncle Godfrey's, Lily's father's, old Frau Gehrig's from upstairs – and pretend-feelings (clipped chopped-up sounds for anger, excitement or fear, slurred and slow ones for love, or drunkenness).

They threw their names at the sun and the swallows in the sky. 'R-u-b-y! Ruuuuuuuuby! Ruby-by-by-by-by-by-by!'

At the telegraph pole with the Beauty Treatments – Private Salon sign. 'Ali-ali-ali-ali-ali-ali-alice! Alice-ce-ce-ce-ce!'

They catapulted them over the latticed fence and into the side street at cars, children on bicycles, at the sour-faced woman with her yapping black poodle from the apartment block. 'Ru-ru-ru-ru-ruuuuby!' 'Al-al-al-al-al-al-al-ice!'

Kicked them like balls down the slope at the two closed garage doors. Across the yard and into the kennel which had been empty since Charlie's last trip to the vet's in spring – 'Rrrrrrrrrrrrruby!' 'Aliccccccccccccce!' 'Rrrrrrrrrrrrruby!' – flustering the wild grasses that thrived in the tarmac cracks and narrowly missing the border of sunflowers and long-stemmed roses.

Suddenly a balcony door squeaked above them, then Celia's mother appeared round the corner from the Beauty Room and leant over the window boxes of pink geraniums and white petunias suspended from the kitchen balustrade. Her eyebrows had been freshly shaved off; it was her client-free afternoon, reserved for her own personal beauty treatments.

'Alice? Alice? . . . Now who could that be?' The lumps of naked skin seemed to be drawn halfway up her forehead.

'Oh, it's nothing, Frau Roth. Just a game.'

'Well, a game's not nothing, Lily, I wouldn't say that. Nor would your mum now, would she? Games are fun, aren't they? Good games, good fun. And I like having fun!' Her smile was like a bruise. 'So, won't you tell me, Lily? There's a pretty girl . . .'

Purring with persuasiveness, the voice asked to be stroked and petted, and Celia knew her friend was going to fall for it. Ten years old and already menstruating, yet so easily fooled by flattery, it just didn't bear thinking about. Already Lily had taken several steps towards the balcony.

'Well,' she squinted upwards, 'when we play this game I am Ruby. It's because of my red hair, and Mum's got that lovely ring with a ruby. And . . . and she –' here Lily looked over to where

Celia had been a second ago, only now she was gone, '– *she* –' emphasis trying to make up for absence '– is Alice. Not in wonderland, though. Never that, *she* says.'

From her hidey-hole inside Charlie's kennel Celia saw the puffy brows glisten. She felt laughter arch above her, like a cat about to spit.

'Just you watch you don't call her MALICE, Lily. MALICE is the full version, you know.'

There was the gleam of mother-of-pearl as a hand sliced the air, wagging a finger. Then more laughter, loops and loops of it that dropped right round the kennel and got tighter all the time. So tight Celia had to cover her ears, close her eyes.

She pictured her mother back in the Beauty Room. Her face would be almost touching the cool silver sheen of the wall-length mirror, pulling away every so often when her breath became too hot and misted the surface. Her fingers would be probing the swollen skin, tapping it gently, gently, their tips soft and fluffy with her favourite Magic-Pink cream.

Celia squeezed her eyes shut harder. As hard as she could. Then harder still.

7

THE MÉTROPOLE IS only a short walk from the bus terminal on Station Square. It's cold, too cold to snow even, though yesterday's clouds have left a new blanket of white – turned slush turned ice, not exactly inviting. Celia hurries along the discreetly lit façade of Casino Mall. She dodges a few late-night shoppers with bulky Migros bags, then a straggle of young soldiers in uniform who have emerged reeling from the restaurant-bar up ahead. One of them is standing hugging a dwarf cypress tree by the entrance and, on seeing Celia, lurches heavily towards her, pleading for a 'Kissie, kissie'. She swerves past him, round the casino into the side street . . . and straight into the arms of something – a huge lion on its hindlegs. She shrieks. Realising at the same instant it's not a lion, of course, and apologising, feeling a right fool.

'S'all right, love. That's the fun of Carnival,' the man in the costume growls back at her with a boisterous drunken laugh, tossing his shaggy mane before loping off after a small slinky catwoman whom Celia, in her shock-and-embarrassment, had quite overlooked.

The roars and whoops and firework-bangs drifting down from the town centre begin to make sense now. She'd totally forgotten about the *Fasnacht,* the annual Carnival.

At the bottom of the Old Town Steps opposite Blumenliebe, her mother's favourite florist's, Celia pauses for a moment. Over to her left, enclosed by a wall with two ornamental corner turrets at street level, is a terraced rose garden that sweeps down the incline in four wide segments. The garden used to belong to her grandparents, and she and Lily would come here when they wanted privacy. Celia still feels a tug at her heartstrings every time she passes by. Usually she ignores it but she can't tonight, not after meeting the man in his lion costume.

The iron railings are freezing to the touch, like tiny sharp teeth they nip into the flesh of her palm as she starts to climb the steps.

The garden games with Lily had been harmless enough initially: tig, skipping, badminton, 'circus acts' of juggling and tightrope walking, even some 'lion taming' which involved diving through hula hoops and was inspired by the Big Cat Show they'd seen at Plättli Zoo on Cemetery Hill. Later they had devised a course of beauty treatments for animals. Any neighbourhood pets were eligible and dealt with free of charge – but none of them could ever be enticed back, and they soon ran out of clients.

Finally they decided on a bear. A fantasy bear. Fat, hairy, and male. In the guises of Snow White and Rose Red they would play tricks on him, tease him with a stick, roll him to and fro. Then tend to his needs. They'd comb and trim his thick rampant fur, clip his nails, file and paint them; they'd tickle his feet, massage him. They'd imagine him grunting with pleasure, writhing on his lair of fresh-gathered leaves, grass and rose petals, belly up. Smiling, they'd converge over his crotch, palms slick with special depilatory oils . . .

Celia blows on her blue-chilled hands, rubs them better. Perhaps it was for the very reason the fantasies felt so real that she hadn't taken Lily's 'true stories' seriously at first. They were all to do with a great old curly bear that kept hanging around her parents' house, lurking in the bushes and sometimes in the branches of the cherry tree and, on exceptionally dark and windy nights, skulking like a blacker darkness under her bedroom window.

The following year, though, the stories became undeniable reality. One evening as they sat listening to the radio Top Ten in the open archway of their turret, sheltering from a downpour of summer rain, Lily suddenly punched the off-button and announced: 'Saw him again yesterday, Cel, after my piano lesson. He seemed as tame as a dancing bear so I let him catch up with me under the bridge by the canal.' She giggled and leant forward to pull some wet petals from a cluster of overblown white roses. 'But then he kissed me, just like that. And I . . . I kissed him back.'

Celia focused on the rain drip-dropping through the trellised vines outside and sliding like mercury down the stems of the roses, swelling a little as it slipped over the thorns. The grass blades bent and bounced under its weight.

Lily gestured with the wad of petals, defiantly. 'I enjoyed kissing him. He's good at it.'

Celia looked at the strings of silver beads falling all around them.

'Much better than any of you. And so grown up, even his tongue's bigger.' Lily brought the rose petals up to her mouth and nuzzled them, smiling to herself.

That's when Celia knew. Knew beyond a doubt. She was stunned, numb.

Lily began shredding the rose petals into minute fragments and added, 'I'm only sorry he hasn't got a younger brother, Cel. For you. But that wouldn't work, would it?' Then she flung out both arms in an embrace, bits of petal whirling round them like confetti, and cried, 'Oh, what should I do, Cel? What should I do?'

For a long while they sat in their turret, damp and silent, holding each other.

That was almost twenty-five years ago. And now the flowerbeds are frozen, the scattered snow on them like chapped skin, with long whitish scars where ice has formed. The garden lies deserted, a scrawny late-winter wilderness of twigs and thorns and empty vines clutching at the walls, concealing no one.

Whatever her advice then, it would have counted for nothing anyway. Walter had made his choice, and that was that.

Celia puts her hands into her pockets, tries to keep her balance on the remaining few Old Town Steps.

* * *

The café is buzzing with life. People are psyching themselves up for the *Maskenball* at the Festhütte. Celia had no idea the ball was today. Laughter squirts round her, voices somersault and chase each other. Cigarette smoke eddies about the coloured paper festoons, the streamers and lanterns dangling from the ceiling beams. At least she'll be safe in here. Turbans, headscarves, stetsons, wigs nod and bob, toppling off occasionally to reveal baby-soft ringlets, bald patches or a mildewy fuzz. Safe from memories of the dead. Masks everywhere. Some soldiers, incongruous in their black berets and grey-green uniforms. A mixture of earsplitting *Guggenmusik* and techno-rock booming from the back room. The perfect exorcism.

She is sitting cramped in the corner – to her right a radiator that makes her back slide with sweat, to her left a plate-glass window and the car park. In front of her is a *Cüpli* of red Crimean champagne, her third within less than an hour. There's one solitary chair at her small round table of snowy Carrara marble: hers. The other four have been claimed and carried off in rapid succession by a witch, two pirates and a ghost, with an 'Is-this-chair-free-please?' parrot politeness varied only by the degree of stiffness of their plastic grins.

But now that she's here she might as well enjoy herself. Glancing around, breathing with her mouth half open in expectation, Celia attracts the attention of a young woman decked out exclusively in gold – gold-spangled hair, gold-painted face, shoulders, arms and legs, gold lamé dress, gold-lacquered handbag and court shoes – who's just detached herself from a not very suave-looking 007. The Golden Girl stares over quite openly, shamelessly, then winks and blows a kiss from a golden palm.

Celia twists away at once. The woman has reminded her of Angelina, the apprentice at the office. She'll be around here somewhere. Celia can almost picture her: waistcoated to bursting point, with a monocle and stick-on beard, her long hair coiled inside the crown of a straw hat – done up as a dandy to mislead her various boyfriends.

Celia's thumb and forefinger have begun to glide up and down the delicately fluted champagne glass. Up and down. This is the first time in months she's gone out for the night. She takes a lingering sip, letting the champagne prickle the roof of her mouth. Then she lays her cheek against the window pane and closes her eyes.

When she opens them again, a few heartbeats later, *there*'s Henry, weaving his way through the cars parked outside. Handsome Henry, the courier – as if she'd dreamt him up. She's sure it's him, despite the monk's habit. No one else moves like that, sluggish yet springy. She raises her hand in a wave. But already he's been captured by a group of emancipated squaws, trussed up in their streamers. In the days before Angelina started spicing up work at the office, Celia had a bit of a soft spot for Henry. Just motherly feelings, of course. He's too young for her, early thirties at most. *And* he's got a wife and kid. Briefly Celia touches her cheek; the skin has gone all clammy where it rested against the window.

The noise level is rising. She'll have to stand up soon to keep herself from drowning – unlike the group of pirates at the next table, who're happily afloat by now. They slap each other's shoulders, bang fists, practise sea shanties, smoke cigarettes and gurgle beer straight from the bottle, tilting up their masks to disclose tidemarks of soreness along their jaws, nostrils dark and weedy as the insides of dead razor-shells and, in one case, a seal's moustache. Not a pleasant sight.

Celia turns away too hastily and almost knocks her glass over. Raking her fingers through her hair, smoothing it down her face and shoulders, she makes a show of gazing out of the window. But doesn't get beyond a rather intriguing reflection further along: a buxom gypsy girl is adjusting her suspenders, seemingly oblivious of the dark shadow with horns and Tyrolean hat that's watching her, leaning right into her cleavage. Then, just as a second shadow with even bigger horns joins the first, she whips a fistful of confetti from under her skirts and, in a swirl of multicoloured snow, pulls down the front of her top.

'A pair of real devils, no?' she shouts loudly.

From behind her curtain of hair Celia sees the pirates shove aside their masks and eyepatches for a better look.

She has another sip of champagne. A few more drinks, she knows, and they'll all be ready. Ready to be reckless. Once they're inside the Festhütte and the Carnival Ball is in full-flaring swing, the men will swagger up to the women with moist dribbling lips. They'll kiss and suck at the naked flesh of their shoulders, lick off the sweat along the collarbones, their tongues like strips of raw meat poking through the holes in their masks. The women will ease back their heads, expose the silky underbellies of their throats. Their fingers will get entangled in the tunics of Roman emperors and Greek philosophers, squashed up against the paunches of grass-skirted cannibals or lured into cowboys' trouser pockets for a quick grope. Some women, though, will clamp their chins down on their *décolletés*, push the men away and, lips moist and quivering, walk off in search of other women . . .

Celia shifts in her chair; it's a metal imitation of rattan and stylishly uncomfortable. Made for squirming, as it were.

'So you did come, after all.' A gravelly voice, subtly familiar.

Celia spins round. Stares.

The mask is arresting in its repulsiveness. Not a face but the absence of it; no lips, nose or cheekbones, just an oval shape coarsely speckled black and white like granite, with mere slits for eyes, nostrils and mouth, too small to give anything away. She can't tell if it's a man or a woman; black mittens cover the hands, a black balaclava throat and hair, and the boots, big, black and clumpy, might be oversized. The rest of the outfit consists of an almost jaunty-looking carmine robe with padded shoulders, loose enough to hide even the widest hips, fullest breasts, a weightlifter's torso and biceps, prosthetic limbs, whatever.

Celia has taken one–two–three–four swallows of her drink but now the glass is empty and her hand flies up to clutch the opal pendant. She doesn't believe in that old wives' tale of opals bringing bad luck, does she?

'Abracadabra,' the apparition says, flourishing a new *Cüpli* as if from out of nowhere and placing it in front of her.

Celia jerks aside. The back of her chair clangs against the radiator and a sound escapes from her throat, a panting gasp like she's being strangled.

'You don't recognise me? No?'

For a moment the mask is almost touching her face. Underneath the slits, the eyes flash white; perhaps she only imagines the wriggle of a tiny red snake next to the left iris. There's a whiff of what seems like the sharp hot dust-smell of stone, the echo of a low menacing laugh, then the stranger begins to back off, whispering, 'Well, next time, I hope . . .' and is gone. Swallowed whole by the cannibals or spirited away by the witches and gypsies, tossed overboard by the pirates, argued into shreds and thin air by the philosophers.

Celia is still clutching the pendant, the leather band taut against her neck. Her mouth is panting open. Was this a threat? A silly prank? Noise and smoke surge round her, engulfing her. Home, sweet, sweet home; even the huddled unfinished silence of her lounge is preferable to this. Then a sudden thought: the decorator – could it have been him? Or that assistant of his, with the sneaky hooded eyes?

The table's iron base shrieks as she propels herself up out of the chair, snatching the empty glass away from the edge, just. She doesn't give a damn about the full one – some of the liquid has fizzled over its rim and gathered in a thin red pool. Heavenknows what Granite Mask might have concocted for her.

The Carnival throng is at its most riotous near the door and Celia feels rather conspicuous in her ordinary clothes. Over by the coat rack she glimpses her tree-hugging soldier again, his face smeared with lipstick. Ducking her head, wishing she hadn't put on that glitter-bright eye shadow, she tries to sidestep the rattles and streamers and false noses, the hot greedy hands.

'Hey! Where're you off to, darling?' A sheik makes a grab at her, his fat red lips all puckered and wet.

Confetti trickles down her neck, sticks to her sweaty back.

'Going to get changed? Let me help, haha!'

'Wow-ow-ow!' an Apache howls, 'Give us a kiss or –' and he brandishes his tomahawk, messing up her hair.

Roll tongues shrill past her ears. Then she's over the threshold and out on to the pavement.

Someone blocks her path. She trembles inside and for an

instant can't see a thing; not Granite Mask again, pleasegod-please. But no, it's only a harlequin wearing pink-tinted wide-winged glasses.

He pats her on the shoulder in a friendly way. 'No need to look so scared, lady.' His huge mulberry mouth stretches into a grin.

Celia is too nervous to give him a smile in return and buttons up her coat instead. Nodding goodbye she strides off briskly – she's had enough of people for the moment – when the harlequin is at her elbow again. He bows: 'To escort you through the unruly night.'

'Oh no, that's not necessary, thank you. I can take care of myself.' Celia breaks into a run. Laughter echoes behind her, ricocheting off walls and Carnival decorations. Coming after her. Her heels scrunch up humps of frozen slush and coloured paper. Along the short promenade of chestnut trees, half-tripping over the kerb . . . into a lane of shuttered windows, rigid-hanging flags and pennants, and out again . . . skidding across the red cobbles of the pedestrian precinct close to Eric's, the bunting overhead like the strung-up rags of madmen . . . almost smashing into the potted shrub by the *Confiserie* . . . past more soldiers, more masks who whistle after her . . . down a narrow back alley congested with waste containers . . . towards the baroque shadows of St Nikolaus's.

She must have thrown him off; there's no one behind her now. Halfway round the side of the church she slows to listen. Nothing apart from some indistinct shouts battered by buildings and distance.

On her right a dozen or so steps lead below ground to a pool of blackness bounded by a wooden door and a window whose metal bars gleam feebly in the moonlight. She doesn't bother to go down to test the handle but moves on – crypts have a nasty habit of trapping not just the dead, she's heard.

The cobbled path circling the church is mossy and slippery with frost. The black iron railings along the back where the plateau of the Old Town drops steeply towards the former military barracks and Anders Railway Station have a forlorn and insignificant look, as if they've shrunk in the cold. At the foot of the tower with its onion dome, pigeon feathers have got stuck to the ice like tiny tattered sails.

There are portals here, set in an elaborate porch. Locked. Of course they are. And anyway, she isn't the least bit religious. That was one of the sore points in her relationship with her mother, who during the last few years of her active life had taken to attending the Sunday service to say prayers 'for the soul of your poor lost father'. Never 'my poor lost husband'. And never to light a votive candle either – no doubt she thought that too blasphemous under the circumstances, with him having gone missing while he was exploring the Hölloch, Hell Cave, near Lake Lucerne.

Instinctively Celia has retreated to one of the corners behind the church porch. She still can't muster up any true feelings of sorrow, or pity. It happened so long ago she can hardly remember her father. Better to let him rest in the dripstone peace of his cave forever. She shivers. It's freezing out here, especially after the body heat of the crowded Métropole.

All at once she starts shaking, flushes hot and cold, hot and cold. That harlequin. The voice had reminded her of someone . . . As if to jolt her memory, the slabs of stone in the porch wall have begun to sway, pressing into her, then sliding away in a stumble. She tries to steady them with her head, her shoulders. With both hands. The stone feels coarse and sharp and grainy; there's a silvery glint just above her thumbs, the glint of mica – and she hears herself say 'Granite Mask?' in a wondering tone.

Afterwards the questions won't stop. What if the two had been one and the same person? The diamond-patterned costume concealed under the carmine robe, the greasepaint under the hideous facelessness? Was this how the stranger had managed to vanish without trace?

But why the elaborate disguise? Why pursue her like this? Forgodsake why?

Celia's hand is at her pendant again, clasping it till the opal seems to throb alive against her skin. Then, breath by breath, she relaxes. Surely she's overreacting. People enjoy playing games, especially this time of year. No rhyme or reason. She's just not used to it. And she did have several *Cüpli* . . .

It might even have been one of Eric's more eccentric clients, one of the stone-crazy ones. Saw her sitting there and wanted to test her reaction – the voice *had* sounded kind of familiar. Celia is convinced that's all it was: a chance encounter, a coincidence.

A wind has sprung up. It carries the stuttering rush of a train towards her, then the cries of more Carnival-goers, raucous and bone shrill. The crane that juts up into the darkness from among the rooftops, heralding the final stages of the millennium building project at the station, seems to rattle very faintly, like the skeleton of some prehistoric beast. Not enough for them to tunnel into the earth, dislodging tens of thousands of cubic metres for their novelty underground roundabout – they're striving to fill up the sky as well.

Celia turns away. The shaking isn't so bad now. In a little while she'll come out from under the shadows and set off home.

With the window covered up so her bedroom's pitch-dark, and a mere smell of port left in the tumbler on the night table, Celia is about to drop off. When all of a sudden she has the impression of something hovering above her in the black stillness . . . something palely phosphorescent . . . an oval form, purplish and parted across the middle, like a mouth blown up out of all proportion. It seems to be talking to her, only she can't make out what it is saying, even after the message has been repeated twice. She is fuzzily aware she must be asleep already, and dreaming.

Celia had been nine the winter Lily's mother and her own went to the *Maskenball* together. All excited, she'd begged to see the fancy dress beforehand. Had begged and begged, on her knees eventually, in helpless childish supplication.

Her mother had laughed, brushed off her lilac linen suit where Celia's head had left a crease and possibly a hair or two, and said, 'Nonsense, dear. You're too young for this sort of thing. I've promised Margaret to do her face and I'll get changed there. It's all arranged. Now would you please be a good girl and let me get ready? Have something to eat if you're hungry.' And she went into the Beauty Room to pack her vanity case while Celia looked on from the corridor.

A little later Walter's door opened. 'Have fun, both of you,' he called out. 'I'm off to a tree-house party.' His blue sleeping bag rolled under one arm, he fastened some straps on his rucksack which was crammed with Coke bottles, *Bürli* rolls, *Cervelat* sausages and a carbide lamp from his potholing days with their father (Celia had done a little snooping earlier, when Walter was in the bathroom washing his curls).

'Oh, a *party*,' their mother mimicked, emerging from the Beauty Room. She sauntered right up to him, reached out a hand, 'No need for this then, is there?' and tried pulling the sleeping bag away from him.

'Christ, Gabrielle, it's damn cold out. Trees don't have central heating, you know.' He straightened up, flung on his fleece-lined leather jacket and walked out, banging the door.

Celia glanced at her mother furtively. At only fourteen Walter seemed so much more grown up than herself. His behaviour had awakened a vague memory in her of a series of doors slamming shut like a line of dominoes toppling over – her parents' bedroom door, the kitchen door, their front door, the cellar door, the garage door, the car doors – and her father driving off with Walter and a whole bootful of provisions and caving equipment. Exactly like then her mother now stood glowering into space, ignoring Celia, who'd sidled up to her and was doing her best to be nice and make amends by default. Walter had won a minor victory – from that day on, the blue sleeping bag travelled to and from the tree house with him unchallenged.

Having realised there was no hope of ever being shown her mother's fancy dress, Celia decided on action.

Lily was spending the night because her father was away somewhere with the chamber orchestra he conducted, and old Frau Gehrig had been asked to keep an eye on them. Frau Geriatric, as they'd nicknamed her, playing the syllables round their mouths like pinballs, was easily duped.

By bicycle it wasn't too far to the casino where the ball was held in those days. The streets were dry, most of the snow having melted during the week. They raced each other over the level crossing just as the barriers were coming down, then put the bicycles into the stand at the station. There was no Casino Mall yet, no late-night shopping, and the train passengers had soon dispersed. Out of sight from the casino's main entrance they found a ground-floor window which was slightly ajar and conveniently fringed by shrubbery. A few lumps of snow crunched under their boots as they hunkered down. Heavy plum-coloured curtains were drawn across a small recess, almost joining in the middle. Close to, Johnny's Carnival Band sounded fast and brash but slipshod somehow, as if all those feet they could hear stamping, tripping, shuffling and clattering about were treading the music to bits. There were giggles, shrapnels of laughter. The air wafting through was warm and clotted with smoke, alcohol fumes, scents and sweat.

Lily was freezing, and getting impatient; they needed a larger gap to see anything really. She nudged Celia and pointed to a slash of light from a window further up to their left. 'Let's try that one.'

They were about to move when an arm appeared between the curtains. The leafless thicket of twigs thrashed their faces like a Santa Claus birch rod, and ice crystals rained down on them. With bated breath they cowered in chandelier brightness. Then the curtains flapped once more and they were back in the soft plum-coloured dark.

Though not quite. There was a shadowy glow now from above: someone veiled in white layers of chiffon was leaning against the window. Pretending to be a ghost – at least that's what Celia assumed at the time. She shrugged at Lily, who'd put a gloved finger to her lips and was gesturing with her other hand. Slowly, stealthily they hoisted themselves up.

A woman. The Carnival ghost was a woman. She had her back to them and was gripping the sill. Her face – or the little of it that wasn't obscured by a half-mask – shimmered like mother-of-pearl.

Abruptly, as if she'd been waiting for their arrival before she could begin, the ghost woman started to moan, slipping into her role free and easy. Small low moans to spook people, drive them away. Her head had fallen lolling against her shoulder in an uncanny imitation of death. Just as it should be, Celia told herself. But her spine was tingling – whether with cold or fear or disgust or something else entirely she couldn't have said. Then Lily beckoned and smiled in that loose lazy way she had, smiling and beckoning until Celia crept nearer, bent forward beside her.

The woman wasn't alone. Certainly wasn't interested in *them*. Someone three-quarters invisible was kneeling on the floor in front of her. Someone in black knife-edge trousers and narrow shoes with unworn soles was hiding under the filmy whiteness of her dress. And the fabric seemed to be shifting and billowing and dancing to the music all by itself.

Several days later Celia had thrown out some bubble-gum wrappers by mistake, forgetting to peel off the collectable pictures she'd meant to swap at school, and ended up having to sift through the rubbish. Instead of the wrappers, she discovered a mysterious-looking little ceramic pot. It was squarish and matt black, with a silvery lid and silvery writing that curled like a ribbon all round, saying: *LOVEly LUSTre: Shine – at your Own Peril.*

The entry under 'peril' in the dictionary warned: 'serious danger'. But Celia still daubed some of the leftover cream on her hands. And it was only when she saw the skin turn as rainbow silky as the inside of a seashell that she finally let the sob rip out of her. The sob she'd been holding in for days now, stifled to a mere whimper. Seeing that seashell gleam on her own skin, she couldn't deceive herself any longer. Yes, she *had* recognised the woman in the plum-curtained window recess. Had recognised her from the start. Despite the half-mask, the veil and the make-up. As for the person under the dress, well, it didn't matter who it was. It could have been anyone, absolutely anyone.

8

SATURDAY LUNCHTIME Celia is in the boiler room in the cellar, hanging up a double load of laundry. A pale wedge of light is falling through the pivot window above the washing machine, down a shaft at the side of the house. The window is propped open a fraction and the gauzy spiderwebs outside ripple in the draught. When Celia was little, a fat toad speckled the colour of dead leaves used to sun itself at the bottom of that shaft, with a smaller skinnier creature on its back, like a hump. A baby toad cushioned from the hard pebbly ground, she'd thought.

'That's the female lugging about the male,' her mother said, adding after a short pause, 'Just like us humans.'

She'd been baffled. Her father was gone by that time, but she remembered him as a big man. Much too big, surely, to have ever been carried by her mother. And Walter weighed almost forty kilos.

The boiler is sputtering, then growling. Celia feels suddenly hungry. The air has grown so sluggish she picks up the next piece of laundry, a lime-green pillow case, in near slow motion.

She'd spent most of the morning doing her weekend shopping. The town centre had seemed infested with the torn remains of firecrackers, bangers, caps, confetti, streamers, coloured straw and feathers. Crushed and dirty, they clung to the soles of her boots. Encased in iced-over puddles, they glittered at her coldly in the winter sunlight. They even latched on to the hem of her coat, godknows from where.

Having bought some vegetables at the market on the chestnut-tree promenade – no sign of the harlequin, she was glad to see – she'd stepped on to the zebra crossing between the Sämanns-brunnen, the seed-sower's fountain, and the castle with its farmhouse structure of half-timbering and shingle. That's when the bright-red Anders–Wil shuttle came shuddering round the corner, honking harshly, down its track along the middle of the street. A boy leant out from a window like a jack-in-the-box and aimed at her with a silver toy pistol. The shot made her jump.

'Stupid kid,' she shouted before she could stop herself, and he fired a whole volley.

Once the last carriage had trundled by and she was safely on the pavement opposite, Celia scurried up the way instead of down past the central post office towards Station Square. Up along the castle park with its scarlet benches and evergreen plants to the arcaded entrance of the Town Hall, where she knew the large barred window on her right belonged to the offices of the police, 'your friend and helper'. But after a while she'd felt recovered enough to laugh it off: all that boy had given her was a fright for fun. Perhaps the Carnival bunting flittering in the wind between the solid *Bürgerhäuser* of the Old Town had cleared her mind.

Now, stooping for a fluffy striped towel, it occurs to Celia that quite possibly this was what Granite Mask had intended – fear and fun in equal measure. The greater the fear, the greater the fun. The fun always feeding on the fear. Her fear. Maybe if people didn't show any fear, the fun would stop. Or would the threats only get worse? Celia slaps the towel into shape with the flat of her hand, then reaches down into the laundry basket for another piece.

'Oh hi, how're you doing?' Said in a low drawling voice behind her.

Celia's heart clenches . . . and unclenches almost instantly. It's Carmen from upstairs, pushing aside a wet bedsheet and smiling her gap-toothed smile.

'Thanks, I'm fine – getting there, at any rate.' Celia plucks at the clumped-up mass of her new fluorescent-red nightdress and presses her lips together in a grin-and-bear-it grimace.

For a moment they gaze at each other. Celia notes how worn out Carmen looks – violet shadows under the eyes, her usually vibrant complexion slack and dingy. Small wonder, of course, with her working half the night at the Bluebeard Club, then having fun at home. Yes, FUN.

She herself could never be a waitress, certainly not in a place like the Bluebeard, full of schmaltzy music and girls on the stage, run off her feet by a clientele of drunks and clumsy bum-grabbers.

Carmen breaks the silence, 'Good idea to get the painters in. A bit of redecorating can make such a difference. And Dominic's great.'

'Dominic?'

'Lehmann's assistant. He is a regular at the Bluebeard.'

Celia pictures the man with his hooded eyes wide open, like a lizard's, in a clean baseball cap, drinking with his friends and smacking his lips at the dancers every so often.

'Much more approachable than his boss,' Carmen continues. 'Quite vain that one, so they say, and something of a softie.'

'Well, I hadn't noticed,' Celia replies, untruthfully.

'Guess I'd better shut up or I'll be passing on trade secrets next.' Carmen giggles and Celia glimpses her new tongue stud. 'I'm off this weekend, thank God. Carnival's such a hassle. The punters consider it a free-for-all, if you know what I mean.'

Celia nods yes. Doesn't she just!

'Well, if there's anything Rolf and I can do for you . . .' The silver-studded tongue has settled in the gap between the front teeth, full of promise.

Thanking her, Celia can't help recalling the bedroom noises from upstairs. Can't help playing them back to herself. The memory has made her fingers dig into the red nightdress. Hastily she shakes out the cotton material and, on an impulse, lifts it up for Carmen to see:

'How would you like this for a night in?' she asks with a laugh. 'I got it half-price.' She watches her neighbour read the sprawling yellow letters on the front: Babies? – No Thanks! Made in China, it says on the label inside, but Carmen doesn't bother to check.

Her face has changed from an expression of pity (for a woman who has recently lost her mother) to a flush of bewilderment and back to pity again (only now it's for a woman who doesn't seem to want to be a mother, which is another thing altogether).

'Very nice,' she mumbles without much enthusiasm, shrugging at the three-quarter sleeves, the slits up the sides and the low neckline. 'Let's hope it'll keep you, uhh, warm.' She waves goodbye, in a sudden hurry. 'Got to go. Catch the shops before the afternoon rush.'

She departs in the direction of her lock-up section and seconds later Celia hears a key, then the clank of empty glass jars, bottles and tins being thrust into bags for recycling.

Rolf and Carmen are good neighbours really; she ought to be ashamed of herself. They invited her up to their flat on several occasions. Even sent a flower arrangement for the funeral – white lilies, beautifully tied with a black velvet bow.

Of the two, Rolf is probably Celia's favourite: late twenties, sturdy, with shiny quick-glancing eyes and a toothbrush moustache. He works as an engineer at the large sugar factory that crouches like a grey monster on the western outskirts of Anders, stuffing itself with wagonloads of sugar beets and disgorging black sludge and stink. In his spare time Rolf is a biker. On good days he'll service his Harley in the backyard, surrounded by tools, spare parts, oil-smeared cloths, cans and sprays, and a gaggle of children from the neighbourhood – while Celia stands watching covertly from behind her kitchen balcony door.

'Want me to see to your smart little Golf?' Rolf had offered when she moved back into the house. Since then he's done quite a few repair jobs, replacing a broken wing mirror, the fan belt and a windscreen wiper, even crawled underneath to fit a new exhaust pipe. He's a handy man, and very nice.

Several drops of water have plish-plashed to the floor, but Celia keeps staring at the red nightdress spread-eagled in front of her. It feels like she has put herself on the line.

9

But the afternoon doesn't turn out too bad. At Bänninger's Celia buys herself some Valentine treats: a small Tipo di Milano salami, a jar of white asparagus, extra thick, and a bagful of sinfully expensive purple grapes.

Just as she is leaving, Deli-Doris, the plump young assistant, offers her a free massage. 'All over,' she adds, her brown eyes touchingly sincere, 'if you want. It's very relaxing. Soothing.' She pauses, smiles until her dimples show, then asks with the eagerness of a child, 'Would you like to try? I'm pretty good by now. Ready for the diploma course in spring, they said at the evening class.'

Nonplussed, Celia stares at Deli-Doris's hands which are resting on the counter like two soft floury rolls. She laughs quietly to herself and, before the girl knows what's happening, lays her own hands on top, saying, 'That's really, really kind of you. Some time, maybe.'

'I only thought, seeing that your mother – I mean, ah, I'm sorry.' Deli-Doris has blushed pimento-red and Celia, more than a little taken aback, saves the situation: So, were Doris and her friends going to be in the Carnival Parade tomorrow then? What, up on the Valentine Float? That should be fun. Be nice if it snowed some more overnight, wouldn't it?

At that point the shop's glass doors slide open and in walk two of her mother's former beauty clients. They start homing in at once, their overrouged cheeks puffed out expectantly, their richly mascaraed eyelashes ('fly's legs', her mother would have said, cruelly apt) flapping rather than fluttering. There is no doubt in Celia's mind as to what they are after: a detailed account of The End, down to the very last burst capillary.

'Have fun,' she says towards Deli-Doris and makes her escape, her hand lifted in a hurried gesture of farewell. God, she's glad to get out of the place. Out and home. Away from inquisition and the iniquity of kindness.

As she crosses the side street to her house, Celia pictures the half-hour ahead: an instant cappuccino sprinkled with real chocolate flakes, a palmful of grapes and some loud music from the CD still in the player, 'Love You Live' by the Stones. Having seen them at the gigantic rock festival on Anders Common the previous summer, she'd become a belated Jagger groupie – too old now, and perhaps never quite young enough.

A second cappuccino and a double dose of 'Honky Tonk Woman' – then Celia finally buckles down to the cleaning. But before she has vaccumed more than a third of the lounge, suctioning decade-old dirt and slivers of fresh lining paper from between the floorboards, her jeans and the camisole top begin to stick to her skin. That's what gives her the idea. After all it's hot enough; the central heating is going full blast. She strips quickly, with the same urgency and excitement she used to feel during the sun-drenched summers of her childhood with Lily when they'd change into their bikinis behind a tree by the Thur or in one of the sweaty cubicles at the open-air swimming pool. She drops her clothes on to the dustsheeted furniture, then reaches for the extension tube of the vacuum cleaner, looking over to the window for a moment. Snow clouds have gathered into the murk of an early dusk – no one will notice anything different about her in the curtainless unshuttered twilight.

The ceiling casts a purple glow over her naked skin, like a spell, and the tulip figures in the cornice seem to bend their heads in her direction, quizzically, watching her every move. Her breasts swing and slap recklessly, squashing up against her arms and belly, deliciously warm. And every time she stands astride the body of the machine, the hose springs spiralling up between her legs, alive and willing. Suddenly, doing the housework is no longer a chore she's subjected to. It's an act of anarchy. Rebellion even. How her mother would have disapproved! She always wore an overall for cleaning jobs, and horrible yellow rubber gloves to protect her hands.

Afterwards, on the phone to Jasmin, her Zurich friend, they giggle like mad and when Celia remarks, in a flippant undertone, that she is still naked, Jasmin sighs with envy and vows to try it out herself as soon as she's alone at home. 'Or perhaps not alone. Might give my man a bit of a surprise in his study while he's preparing some lecture or marking papers or – hey, Cel, how about that? – video-conferencing!'

Celia stares down at her thighs sprawled out over the seat of the upholstered chair. They're nice thighs, soft without being flabby; smooth and unworn. Unwanted, she thinks, in a rush of bitterness.

The Carmen-story rather amuses Jasmin, who doesn't take Celia's anti-kid stance too seriously one way or the other. 'Live and let live, right, Cel?' is all she advises.

Celia knows better than to bring up the topic of Walter; it would fall on deaf ears as usual. Jasmin refuses to be involved in unpleasantnesses. At the funeral reception she'd actually said, 'Lucky your brother hasn't put in an appearance.' Celia had been too upset and exhausted to be annoyed, and now it doesn't seem worth the trouble. Jasmin has difficulty dealing with conflict, all the therapy in the world hasn't sorted that. Conceived after years of doctoring, she'd been fought over the instant her umbilical cord was cut. Years ago, at a full moon *Walpurgisnacht* Party on Lake Zurich as they were sitting round a bonfire with other women, burning photos of deceitful lovers and, in Jasmin's and Celia's case, so-called loved ones, Jasmin had drunkenly announced:

'You want to hear about me and my parents – well, here goes. If I smiled at Mother, I'd have to smile at Father. If I kissed Father, I'd have to kiss Mother. And so on. I even had to shout and scream at both of them. If I failed, they'd blame each other. Punched each other – often until they were bruised. I felt like the prize in a boxing match nobody could ever win.'

Celia for her part had kept her mouth carefully shut.

She tunes back in to what Jasmin's been saying about a new client at the private clinic where she works as a physiotherapist. 'Old goat. Had to remind him the massage parlour was one block down.'

Celia's laughter makes her breasts quiver. She is getting a little cool now that the surge of frenetic energy has drained away. Her nipples have stiffened, their aureoles the colour of dark wine. Her arm brushes against them as if by chance and the touch conjures up images of herself in the bath, playing with the shower nozzle set at turbo speed. She pushes the pictures from her mind, for the present at least.

Should she maybe tell Jasmin about the masked stranger from the night before? Instead, she ends up asking after Igor Junior, a bright and lively child with the wheat-blond hair and broad Slavic features of his father.

Before they hang up, almost as an afterthought, Jasmin inquires how she's coping and Celia says, 'Okay. Ready to treat myself to your seaweed bath – as the climax of my cleaning coup!'

And now, relaxed after a quick tease-and-release thanks to the invention of adjustable shower nozzles, Celia is having her bath.

Three candles are wax-glued to the tub's enamel rim at her feet. The first one's a creamy white. The middle one is red. And the biggest, on the left, a deep black-pit black. With the main light off and the shadows trembling on the walls, the windowless bathroom resembles a cave, damp and slightly draughty because of the extractor fan near the ceiling. Celia herself is immersed up to her chin, wrapped in a thick layer of Shiver of Sensuality Seaweed from the waist down.

Jasmin had given her a big trial pack for Christmas. 'Our latest hit,' she'd written on the box with a green felt-tip pen, 'freeze-dried and loves to expand. ENJOY!!!' And, in a small PS: 'Igor Junior's just had his first "shivers". His comment: "Great. Almost like mucking about in the playground." – What more do you want!'

Celia moves her legs a little; the loosened rubbery fronds around her body wobble. She smiles, reminded of Deli-Doris: a well-meaning girl if perhaps a bit too trusting for her own good.

Celia flips over on to her right and the seaweed floats off her hip like a badly tucked-in blanket. Shadows chase themselves around the walls and ceiling, past the washbasin, mirror-fronted cabinet, toilet, radiator, door, chest of drawers, towel rack, bath, extractor fan. Zigzagging ghosts.

For several minutes she lies motionless, gazing at the wavering candle flames reflected in the water. Some of the wax has dribbled down the rim of the bathtub, tentacle-like.

She'd come across the red and the white candles in the store room the other night – the night of the suede shoes – while rooting around in the old cupboards and cabinets for the teak furniture spray. They were stockpiled in small cartons behind dozens of dried-up woodfiller tubes, re-touching crayons, tins of furniture wax and bottles of polish. 'Explorers' Essentials' it said underneath some uninspired drawings of grottos. Her mother mustn't have had the heart to use them. But Celia has. After her phone call with Jasmin she'd retrieved the store-room key from the top of the coat rack, then in, seize a carton of red and white candles each, and out again – as if the place was haunted. She'd felt like the little girl she'd once been, darting in and out of their cellar lock-up with its deep dark shelves hidden by curtains, to fetch a jar of her mother's irresistible fruit preserves for herself and Lily.

For the black candle, though, Celia had trudged all over Anders. She'd tried the Co-op, Denner and Migros, Blumenliebe by the Old Town Steps, a craft centre close to Eric's that only sold blocks of unformed wax, and even a couple of artsy pharmacies – until, reluctantly, she'd stopped in front of Boutique Exotique, the letters painted topsy-turvy across the shop window. Under her grandfather's ownership the name Alfred's Antiques had arched in gold relief above the entrance. She hadn't been back inside since then.

Pulling the lengths of seaweed tight over her belly, Celia slips on to her buttocks. She'd hesitated in the door, in the midst of an oriental tinkle, and asked towards the counter did they have candles at all? Black ones? The air was thick with incense. How Grandfather would have hated this – for a moment she could almost see him shuffling around the shop, peering with tired distaste at the wind chimes, the mobiles of brass Indian elephants, wooden birds, shiny metal stars and crescent moons, at the lampshades smothered in strings of coloured glass beads like cheap Egyptian headdresses.

The assistant was friendly enough. Tall and lanky, with luminescent green hair and glittering studs in his eyebrows, he unfolded himself from behind the counter. Had one look at her jeans, poncho-style coat and rainbow silk scarf, and said:

'Black candles, no problem. They're over here. I'd recommend Black Magic. Burns for hours and smells of you-know-what, even makes you feel kind of giddy. Great stuff.' He cocked his head, eyebrows sparkling like exclamation marks, and grinned down into her face.

Instead, Celia had pointed to a sign on the top shelf: 'Black Sugar Loaf – guaranteed hygienic and odourless.'

By the time she'd twigged what the shrink-wrapped stumpy veined candle was really meant for, the man was already rolling it up in lurid green tissue paper colour-co-ordinated with his hair.

This candle is for Walter.

Walter, who will always be five years older than her. Walter with his curls, their grandmother's chiselled lips, and the sexy cleft in his chin.

Walter, who while still in primary was allowed to accompany their father on his caving expeditions – shrugging noncommittally when asked about them, like a conspirator. Every other weekend they went off, the car boot a medley of overalls, boots, gloves, helmets, rucksacks, torches, carbide lamps, foodstuffs. Off to explore the secret treasures of dwarfs and gnomes, Celia thought. Off to 'creep and crawl and prowl in the dirt', her mother said.

Dear brother Walter, the 'man of the house', who made her gifts of desiccated beetles and spiders and the bleached bones of mice. Who netted trout at Uncle's for killing on their kitchen balcony, sprinkling the concrete floor with silvery scales. Who left home at sixteen to train as a chef at the Schlosshotel.

Walter, who lumbered after Lily like a lovesick dancing bear, then claimed her: the bear transformed into a trim young soldier in charge of one of those wall-shaking tanks, seducing her on his blue sleeping bag up in the tree house. Who later took her away for good. Took her away so far she couldn't come running back even if she'd wanted to.

Walter, who now blames her, Celia, for their mother's last will and testament.

Celia feels an icy current on her forehead. Is it her imagination or has the hum of the extractor fan got louder? Almost grinding? The candles flicker. Was that the door of her flat opening – and closing? But she locked it, she remembers. Double-locked it, in fact, to be on the safe side. Something she'd never bothered to do before . . . DAMN THAT MASK!

Then she yells it out at the top of her voice: 'DAMN THAT MASK! DAMN THAT MASK! DAMN THAT MASK!' to rally herself back into a *Frauenpower* mood. She hates Carnival. Hates the way its sweaty drunkenness has seeped into her life, leaving her adrift, and vulnerable. DAMN THAT STUPIDSTUPID MASK!

She calms herself by focusing on the white candle.

This one is for her father.

White like a blank page.

Like stalactites and stalagmites.

She doesn't have many memories of her father, she was too young, barely at kindergarten, when he disappeared. Mostly they are associated with smells, tastes. The butter on her breakfast croissant tainted by raw onion because he'd yet again flouted the house rules, forgetting to wipe his knife as he prepared himself a midnight sandwich.

Or the clear sharpness of white wine from his mouth, smudged with smoke scrolls. Like the time he was telling her a new picture-book story – some adventure of Schellenursli's, the boy goatherd from the Alps – while she was perched on his knees, his twisted cigarillo curling smoke round them like the thread of a silkworm. On the page in front of her a nanny goat is stamping its feet, sneering at the herbs and flowers in Schellenursli's pasture. There is silver paint on the goat's hooves and bell, its brows are pencil thin, the eyes rimmed bluey black and bristling with lashes.

Her father had begun to cough. Doubled over, he spluttered smoke, and she was nearly bounced off his knees. Then she saw he wasn't coughing; he was trying hard to hide his laughter from her, rocking her up and down playfully, up and down, to make her squeal. That's when her mother had stormed in saying, couldn't they keep the noise down, honestly, Peter, you know I'm doing a manicure next door, and he'd snapped the book shut so fast one of Celia's fingers got trapped between the pages.

Once her father was gone, of course, and the dining room redecorated as the Beauty Room, Celia had realised he must have disliked her mother's occupation. She'd felt obscurely pleased, and had loved and missed him all the more – despite his preference for Walter when it came to treasure hunting in caves.

She slides down deeper into the bath now, trawling her arms and seaweed legs through the water to seek out the last pockets of heat. The three flames flare up as one. For an instant they throw a shadow against the door – a figure with an hourglass waist and shoulder-length hair, unmistakably real.

Yes, the third candle is in memory of her mother.

Red: for those final weeks when the thin blood refused to be stemmed and came dripping slowly, steadily, staining paper tissues, pillowslips, sheets and the fronts of her nightdresses.

Red: for the seething fleshliness she'd always kept under wraps – apart from the night of the *Maskenball* and that Sunday afternoon in August, the afternoon of the skin belt.

And red for the pain she inflicted, even on mere things.

The small roll of glass wool had been lying in a skip, only Celia didn't know it was glass wool then – she couldn't have been nine yet. Such a nice fleecy rug it would make for Charlie's kennel, she'd thought, grabbing hold of it. By the time she got home her hand had felt like a pin cushion, and flexing it was torture.

The kitchen door down the corridor was open and she could see her mother, hair over her face, standing at the table. She was stoning cherries. Cherries from Margaret's garden. Her white rubber gloves were stained crimson, her arms spattered beyond the elbows. Spurts of juice were trickling down the fat smile of the ladle-licking chef on her plastic apron, puddling into the sheets of newspaper at her feet. Two large woven baskets were placed on chairs, heaped with fruit from which her mother had already removed the stalks and the odd leaf. With the sunlight trembling over them, the cherries looked strangely animate, fresh and pouting as babies' mouths. The gadget her mother used for the stoning had lost its silvery colour; it was oozing blood and shreds of flesh like a witch's cauldron. The smaller of its two spouts was spitting teeth into a bowl with gravelly shrieks.

Celia couldn't bear to see or hear any more and turned away, crying out as a spasm of pain gripped her hand.

Her mother's hair flew up. 'What on earth –?'

'I wanted it to be a rug. To keep Charlie warm. But now I can't even move my fingers.'

Her mother didn't fuss, she never did. Just glanced from her to the glass wool on the floor, then crossed over to the sink, took off her gloves and apron and washed the splotches off her skin. There didn't seem to be a trace of blame in her words when she said, 'Why not leave Charlie alone, Celia? I'm sure Frau Gehrig is perfectly capable of making him comfortable. He's old and arthritic, you know that. The poor thing'll die one day soon, rugs or no rugs. There's nothing you can do about it.'

While her mother went to get the tweezers from the Beauty Room, Celia wept a little, thinking of Charlie in his bare kennel and how he'd begun to snuffle around the backyard all stiff-legged, dribbling pee on the ground, and how she couldn't help him, ever. Then she was told to sit down next to the balcony door. In the summer sun her palm and half-clenched fingers appeared to be studded with the glitter of pain.

'Don't, mum, please! Let me do it myself, it's less –'

'Keep still now, they're almost out.'

'NOOO! Aow!'

'Silly Cel, don't be such a baby.'

'You're hurting me! MUM!!'

'Almost there, just a –'

'AAAOOOOWWWWWW!!!'

At that moment Walter came in from school. He dumped his leather satchel beside a kitchen chair and surveyed the scene. 'Little sis in trouble again?' he asked. Lifting the glass wool between thumb and forefinger, he dropped it into the bin. Then suddenly yowled, his face contorted.

'Walter?' Their mother sprang up from where she'd been kneeling, 'All done, Celia – go and wash your hands,' and, tweezers flashing, rushed towards him.

'Only joking, Gabrielle,' he replied, coolly. 'Just checking you'd do the same for me. So, what's to eat?'

'*Mon dieu*! You *are* wicked!' Laughing, she had opened the fridge and produced some juicy cuts of *Buurehamme*. Afterwards she carried on with the stoning.

They had cherry tart that evening. The kitchen was filled with a sugary lacerated smell and the last few rays of the sinking sun seemed to bleed all over its cupboards and walls. Celia, her hand salved and bandaged for the night, ate slowly, trying to ignore the looks of complicity and amusement between Walter and her mother, their banter and broken conversation in French peppered with phrases like '*tu sais*' and '*si tu veux*' and '*mon chéri*'. Trying to ignore the bloodied lumps of cherries on her plate, limp and sullied. Concentrating instead on the yielding sweetness in her mouth.

The bathwater is freezing and Celia shudders involuntarily. She has been chewing on air and there's a bitter taste on her tongue. Her eyes ache from having stared at the red candle so long.

Red.

Like anger and cruelty.

Like misunderstandings that grow and fester. And erupt.

Blood red.

Then her right leg tears free of the seaweed, out of the bath: NO! and splashes back in. NO, DAMMIT! SHE DOESN'T NEED THOSE MEMORIES! She couldn't care less where the water goes just now. She'll mop it up later. The candles gutter. They hiss at each other. Wax slops over, runs down into mingled roots and shoots, red, black and white. A few drops have fallen into the tub, tiny free-floating islands jostled by waves and seaweed.

Only the black candle survives – due to being bigger, perhaps.

10

IT'S NEARLY DARK when Celia gets back from the ice rink next day. Another first. She had to hire skates. To begin with, she'd felt like a toddler trying to walk. Then, once she dared let go of the handrail, like an ice-pick on legs, steel blades hacking into the slippery surface for extra balance. In the end she'd managed to do figures again, even some slow-spun pirouettes, and hardly knocked into people. Not bad after almost twenty years. It was the cold that drove her home eventually. Too much like being in a deep freeze. The cold and, perhaps, the music too, treacle-dripping from the speakers through a maze of Valentine-Day fairy lights and heart-shaped balloons on to the heads and shoulders of couples gliding round, glove in glove.

The phone starts to ring just as she is savouring the thick salty dregs of the minestrone she'd cooked to get the chill out of her bones. Celia sighs. She is sitting slumped on the floor-level mattress in her bedroom, the now empty soup bowl in her lap, on the night table a glass of Féchy and a plate that holds her Valentine treats from Bänninger's – slices of Tipo di Milano salami laid out around a small mound of purple grapes, a pile of white asparagus topped with a swirl of mayonnaise. The portable TV in a corner of the bookshelf is giving the news round-up.

With another sigh she unslumps herself to fetch in the phone on its extension cord.

'Hello,' she says, a little breathlessly, flicking the 'mute' button on the remote control. The weatherman gulps like a fish out of water, nods and twitches his head at the map with its pig outline. (Sun symbols in the south, clouds with cartoon snowfalls for the rest of the country.)

'Celia?' The old man's voice is hesitant.

'Uncle Godfrey! How are you?' (Night temperatures around freezing in the Mittelland, up to minus ten in exposed areas.)

'I phoned earlier but there was no reply,' he whines. What's the matter with him? He doesn't normally talk to her like this, petulant like a jealous old woman.

'I spent the afternoon at the ice rink, that's all. I was going to call you myself, later.' (Danger of avalanches in the Alps.)

While he inquires, rather nervously, about the details of the Thirtieth Day, the memorial service he had requested for his sister, Celia takes a sip of the Féchy. The weatherman has vanished and it's the local news now, with a frozen-looking reporter in a suede jacket and flowery skirt at the Carnival Parade.

'A week on Tuesday, Uncle. Seven thirty in the evening. I'll speak to you beforehand, don't worry.' She reaches for the plate with her Valentine treats, selects a piece of asparagus and licks off the mayonnaise, 'You don't mind me eating, do you?' The asparagus is short and fat and succulent. It oozes apart deliciously when she squelches her tongue along its length, leaving the head, smooth, taut with the faintest trace of roughness, for last.

'No, no, of course not. *Bon appétit*! It's good to hear you're well and . . . and . . . how is the flat doing, the decorating? Everything all right with you, Celia?' Followed by a grunt.

For a moment the slice of salami wadded between her thumb and forefinger reminds her of liver-spotted skin. Whyonearth is her uncle so uncharacteristically concerned about her?

'Sure I'm fine. Or shouldn't I be?' She closes her eyes, then shoves the salami into her mouth and chews with determined savagery. It suddenly dawns on her what's wrong with the old man. He sounds guilty. Guilty? What about?

She watches the TV camera panning across the riot of colours: the costumes and bunting, the snow glittering in the watery sunlight against the red roof tiles of the *Bürgerhäuser*, the verdigris dome of St Nikolaus's. Hundreds if not thousands of people are lining the main street and surging around the Sämannsbrunnen like a new crop that's wildly propagating. Some of them grimace, a few smile and wave, craning their necks, others throw confetti. The floats start off with the Lady leading the Lion on his gold chain – as if the two of them had stepped straight out of the town's coat of arms.

Celia leans her head against the wall. Quite composed now, she states: 'So, I suppose you've heard from Walter. Complaining about me, was he?' Her tongue squishes an asparagus against the roof of her mouth. Then another.

Finally he stammers, 'Well, yes. Yes, Walter did get in touch. He phoned me after your row. Terrible, terrible thing to have a row like that, Celia.'

He pauses and Celia slowly counts to ten, fighting to contain her anger. The TV camera has skimmed across the crowd again, capturing someone in a carmine robe beside a chic older woman with red hair – Margaret, Lily's mother! – before it zooms in on a muffled-up man in a wheelchair who is peering at a float of rappers and breakdancers and clapping his thin parchment hands to the silent beat.

Just as quietly, Celia munches a few grapes, having decided to bide her time.

'If only poor dear Gabrielle, God bless her soul, had been a little more . . . forgiving,' her uncle says in a shaky tone. Then he clears his throat. 'I think it's up to you now, Celia. You'll need to show your brother that you don't intend to . . . perpetuate things.'

A gigantic poison-green crocodile on three sets of legs is clacking its long plastic teeth at the TV camera.

'Walter's obviously not told you everything, Uncle. Because I did offer him a fairer share of the money, but he wouldn't bloody listen!'

Forgodsake, why's the man defending Walter? She's done her best to be accommodating, dammit – pretty generous of her, too.

'I am sorry, Celia dear. I ought to have talked about this sooner. Sorry. I just didn't feel –' There's the crash of a door and his voice drops to a whisper: 'That's my Housekeeper from Hell back from the Carnival Parade. I'd better hang up. Bye.'

Why is he so anxious to get off the phone? The new home-help must have overheard dozens of his conversations by now. Unless – here Celia's frown turns into a smile and she bursts out laughing – unless the woman has designs on him and he's retaliating with evasive action, safeguarding his seventy-six years of bachelorhood. Whatever, she'll ring him back some other time.

As for Walter, she has already posted her letter to him and Lily; the ball's in his corner, *et voilà*. She presses the 'mute' button, drains her glass of white and finishes her meal.

The house is old and at night it creaks. It seems to creak at the touch of a moonbeam, the settling of a snowflake, a few scatters of needle-thin rain.

Now, though, a different kind of creaking has started. Celia can't ignore it. Not after she's been roused from her sleep by Rolf and Carmen's homecoming, their laughter as they'd stumbled up the stairs, crooning snatches of songs. The creaking is getting more vigorous by the second. There are no voices, just the breathless straining of wooden slats near breaking point.

Like a child's rocking horse. A rocking horse. Rocking and rocking. This is how Celia tries to stop herself from getting all hot and tangled up in the bedclothes. But it's no use tonight. The horse is clattering out of control. It scrapes and bangs against the wall. Celia's lower legs twitch. They kick instinctively, like in some reflex test. Then she can't bear it any longer. She jumps out of bed and puts on the kingfisher-blue kimono (Franz's last present, brought back from a climbing expedition in the East).

In the lounge the snow light filtering through the window clashes with the purple shadows of the ceiling and the warm yellow glow from the corridor. As she pads past the faintly luminous sheets spread over the furniture, she has a distinct sense of *déjà vu*. And, gazing out at the street and gardens freshly coated in white, at the flounces of ice crystals along tree branches and the curved necks of streetlamps, it's easy for her to picture her mother in that ghostly Carnival dress of long ago, silhouetted against the plum-coloured curtains of the casino. For all Celia knows, her mother never even realised she'd been spied on.

She is about to turn away from the window when her eye falls on the apartment block opposite. Its tenants are a 'strange sort', as her mother used to lament – with what moral right, Celia has no idea – the police and social workers visit freely, removal vans and self-drives clog up the bicycle lane most weeks. Last October they had a sale on in one of the first-floor flats: EVERYTHING MUST GO a notice screamed in red capitals. Deli-Doris, who'd been and got herself a 'virtually new' mattress for her massages, told Celia that the couple had done a moonlight flit after falling into arrears with their rent and credit payments.

Nothing suggests any hurried departures tonight: most of the lights are out or the shutters down, and the balconies look like sad cold swallows' nests vacated for winter. But one of the windows on the top floor, with a close-meshed net curtain, has suddenly become brighter. As if someone had been standing there a minute ago and wasn't now. Celia blinks: beyond the streetlamps' haloes she can feel the presence of veiled stars. When she glances over once more, the window is dark.

11

EARLY MONDAY AFTERNOON, and Celia is aware she'll be going back to work very soon now. Even her food has begun to remind her of the office. That turkey mince she's just thrown out because it tasted like wood shavings – Lapis would have chomped it up in a flash.

But first she needs to make a start on the Beauty Room. The gold letters on the door advertising BEAUTY TREATMENTS are tarnished and Celia greets them with a surreptitious spit, no polish, before she goes in.

The room smells. Not so much of treatments or stale air – it smells of women. All the women ever ministered to by her mother have left traces behind. Bits of themselves. Droplets of sweat, spittle and perfume soaked up by the pale-blond carpet, the natural-finish wooden shelves, the birch veneer of the vanity cabinet, the picture frames and ivorine wall-coverings, giving the place a jaundiced restless look. Hairs, scaly bits of skin, slivers of nail that hooked themselves into the fabrics – cushions, towels, beauty caps, make-up capes, curtains, upholstery and carpet pile – with no intention to let go, like stings or the heads of ticks.

It's a complex smell, slightly sickly, and in its very sickliness reminiscent of beeswax. Or honey. And honey, of course, is 'bee vomit'. As Celia's biology teacher had announced one fine day, his eyes swivelling round the class sharp and black as an insect's, with a sneering satisfaction at their shocked disgusted faces.

Every so often afterwards Celia's grandmother tried tempting her. 'How about a mouthful, my dear?' she'd say, her Cupid bow lips parted in a smile. 'Honeycomb on croissant, sweet and crunchy.' Strewing a few flakes of pastry on a chunk of the thickly dribbling hexagons, she'd hold it out from her knobbled fingers like the hag in her gingerbread house.

Celia crosses the Beauty Room to open the window and the balcony door. Then, for the sheer hell of it, she rips off the lace curtains. A thin cloud of dust rises from her hands towards the tulip cornice, blurring the winter brightness before being driven out by a sudden sweep of wind, like a last exhalation.

It's a snow wind, she can tell, scouring down from the Voralpen to make the timid hills of the Mittelland cringe. It tears and grabs at her long hair, scratches her skin with sandpaper sharpness. Perhaps it'll blunt her features too, just as it's blunted those razorblade edges of rock. She has never liked the cruel slant of her cheekbones, the jut of her chin; has always felt that between the two of them they seem to trap and fold up her face.

When still in primary school, she'd refused to have her shadow profile drawn on the white sheets of paper Frau Wickli had tacked to the classroom wall. While Lily stood motionless, head tilted back to show off her pretty snub nose to best effect, Celia had twisted her own face away from the hot light angled up at her. Twist-twist-twisting so there'd be no charcoal lines, slovenly, inept, exaggerated, to smear her out of existence . . .

Someone's rung her doorbell. First three, then two, then again three separate jabs. The decorators, back from lunch. She really ought to let them have a set of keys. Having shut the window and balcony door, Celia gives her jaw a quick rub-and-pinch – as if that might help improve its shape. Instead, she ends up smudged from chin to earlobes, courtesy of her mother's dusty old lace curtains – and doesn't even notice. The *three–two–three* sequence keeps echoing in her head as she moves down the corridor towards the buzzer, past the sour paint fumes wafting from the lounge, its door ajar because the frame has been done.

Three–two–three. Not the usual bland long ring of workmen.

Then she recognises it: the signal she and her friends had used when they were kids. No one else rings like that, certainly not now. There's a slim chance it's Nita, come down from Albula to apologise for not making it to the funeral. (Well, you know how it is, Cel: high season in the Alps and never enough snowboarding instructors to match tourist demand.) Just as she did that other time, after Franz died.

Celia wipes her suddenly sweaty hands on her jeans. She presses the entry buzzer. 'Hello?' she says. 'Who is it?'

Nobody answers.

For an instant she pauses, fingers curled round the keys in the lock. Could it be Lily? On a surprise mission of round-the-world reconciliation?

Celia all but wrenches the door off its hinges and rushes downstairs. Slips back the latch without bothering to peep through the spyhole – *In case it's a robber, rapist or killer, remember?* – and pulls. Her eyes extra wide to welcome old friends.

There's no one there.

She takes a step outside to review the street. Last night's snow has been churned to slush by hundreds of tyres, only the roofs and gardens are still white. Beyond the ash tree and her neighbours' scruffy beech hedge she can see all the way up to the Co-op, and can't see a soul – except for a big black dog waiting by the entrance. Some birds are twittering and rustling about the hedge, their beady eyes switching from her to the feeder to Schildi, who is sunning herself on a heap of leaves, pretending to be asleep.

Across the side street where the blue-and-gold-striped awning of Bänninger's cuts off the rest of the pavement, Deli-Doris has rolled her mountain bike into the stand and is fumbling for the keys to open up again. It couldn't have been her, could it? Nettled into getting back at her customer for rejecting the massage? Celia hesitates, wondering whether to call out. But the girl is gone.

The traffic has thinned now that the frantic midday rush back to work and school is over. An empty bus is slowing for the stop at the pink housing estate further down and is passed by a convoy of military jeeps rumbling in the other direction, back to base. Helmets lolling above grey inert faces, the soldiers sit zonked in their seats – too tired even for a whistle or a shout today.

The windows of the apartment block seem to stare at her, blank and lidless, from their frozen recessed depths. Suddenly, like the blink of an eye, a curtain moves. Is someone watching her? They might have been watching all along. Watching the person who rang her doorbell . . . Celia is about to risk a wave when she thinks better of it. The curtain might have fluttered in a draught or because some bored pet is playing games with the furnishings – there's that dull-witted parrot she'd heard screeching 'naughtygirl, naughtygirl' all summer from one of the balconies; maybe it's testing its wings for a change?

The cold is beginning to bite – and Celia has no desire to catch her death because of some doorbell prankster. She must have misinterpreted those rings, she tells herself, and memory's a funny thing, tricky. Just then, someone stirs behind the fence around the vegetable plot of the farmhouse diagonally opposite . . . But it's only old Frau Müller easing her back before bending down again with what looks like a knife, perhaps to harvest some snowed-over lamb's lettuce.

That's when Celia's foot stumbles against something, right next to the threshold.

A bunch of tulips. *Black* tulips, forgodsake! No wrapping, no note. Whatthehell is going on? First the bouquet at the funeral, and now *this*! If it's meant as a belated Valentine, it's in bloody bad taste. One of the flower heads has been half torn off – trodden on, more like – and several frays of inky petal are mashed into the snow-and-concrete.

As she stoops, there are faint sounds of laughter from the backyard and the scrunch of someone's footsteps. The soft chuckle is getting louder by the second.

'Well, well,' Celia says, 'I'd never have guessed!'

The decorator's assistant is gawking at her, abruptly silenced, his face red and crinkly.

She nods with relief. 'So it was you.'

But he clearly intends to keep on playing the clown. 'Now where did you grow these?' he asks, pointing to the flowers in her hand and chuckling again. 'In the darkroom perhaps?'

'They're from you, aren't they? They have to be,' Celia insists for she wants to believe it, can't afford not to. He has nearly reached her, his fingers pointing at her face now. Damn rude. He'll be stroking her cheek next if she doesn't move or say something, anything: 'From you. To apologise for your inane remarks.'

He's stopped dead, both arms by his side, his hands like shot birds.

Got you, Celia smirks to herself. You and your jokes about tulip cornices and rosettes. Turning away, she hears an almost imperceptible *blip*, a slippery wet sound, as if he's raised his eyelids too quickly. She doesn't glance back.

'Problems, Dominic?' Lehmann has rounded the corner from the backyard. He is hugging a tin of Amethyst acrylic eggshell for the lounge radiators.

Dominic merely shrugs, twitches his mouth into a grin. 'Naw,' he says, his eyes safely hooded once more. He watches Celia mount the short flight of stairs and disappear through her door. 'Stupid cow,' he mutters, and can't quite stifle a guffaw. What on earth's up with her? He'd be the last person to give anyone flowers, let alone black ones! And those charcoal marks on her face – like spiderwebs along lintels needing to be brushed off. A woman expecting anything more at *her* age . . . A sad case.

Moments later the two men are standing in the lounge and shaking their heads at their handiwork so far. The second coat of Deadly Nightshade on the walls is almost dry. The door and window frames glisten, still untouchable. Seriously wicked, Dominic thinks, wrinkling his nose, the whole room's begun to have a seriously wicked atmosphere. Nothing to do with the smell of paint (he's used to that, after all). This is different. No amount of airing will ever get rid of it, not even the icy gusts blowing in through the window, batting the loose sheets of lining paper about.

Alex is gazing at the dull magenta of the ceiling. The way it's punched in the middle and squared at the sides by those rows of purplish tulips reminds him of a patch of flesh that's been cut and bruised, then stitched up – a thoroughly unprofessional thought he suppresses immediately.

But he's never been any good at suppression, or repression, or whatever the hell it's called. Already there's yesterday's scene again with Pascal, his younger son, who is ill with inflamed tonsils. He'd pinned the boy's tongue down with a finger for a quick fatherly inspection, gingerly (because he hates that fat vibrant slug feel, hates it even when he makes love to Jacqueline, which is seldom enough these days). The tongue had rippled and squirmed and flailed under his touch. Then, without warning, the mouth snapped shut – he's still got the bite marks. He'd fought the urge to swear, to hit out, and asked Pascal instead to please be sensible, he wasn't going to hurt him . . . just open up, dammit. In the end he'd been forced to use a wooden spatula, prising the teeth apart like a puppy's.

Dominic sees his boss wince and grimaces back in return. 'Seems those tulips in the cornice and rosette aren't enough for her. She's going for the real thing now. In bunches.' He strides over to the window, closes it, and the flapping paper noises cease; the room calms down.

'What?' Lehmann is rubbing his finger.

'Real tulips. Fucking black ones, man,' Dominic says and, looking sidelong at the finger that's being rubbed as if it's got frostbite, he adds, 'She was at the door with them when I arrived. *Accused* me of giving them to her. ME! Christ! I never –'

'I think I'd better go and speak to her . . . about that radiator paint.' Alex hurriedly picks up the tin he has brought in from the van. There's nothing wrong with the paint of course, but he needs to get out of this room for a while.

'Hey, don't forget to try her for coffee,' Dominic shouts after him. Then he has a rummage through the cassettes in the sports bag. A few spiky-sharp pieces of rap and *he*, for one, won't be in danger of losing his marbles. The jobs left to do for the present are quick and straightforward: the door itself, the fireplace surround, the two radiators, and the skirting. He starts on the inside panels of the door, wishing the tin of Burgundy chosen by the woman was drinkable.

After making her brisk getaway from the assistant, Celia has collapsed on her mother's stool in the Beauty Room. The wind has blown the sky into a gigantic wad of grime-yellow cotton-wool that's pushing up against the bare window and balcony door, but she's turned her back on the outside world and sits facing the cosmetics trolley.

Laid out on the glass top, empty for months now of its glittering flasks, gold-capped tubes and pots, its tray of scissors, tweezers, orange sticks and emery boards, are the tulips. They look as if suspended in mid-air, their black heads splayed slightly, doleful and drooping, their leaves like stunted wings straining upward in vain. The remains of the broken-necked specimen are in the silver pedal bin, leaking darkness into the mass of scrumpled-up lace curtains.

Celia tries to think logically, gathering reason round her like a shawl, drawing it close so nothing irrational can slip through.

First of all: if she really wanted to, it wouldn't be too hard to trace the shop which had sold those flowers. Black tulips are a rarity. Even for a funeral.

God, that funeral reception had been so exhausting; the black-beamed ceilings of the Schlosshotel had felt like burdens on her shoulders and her feet had seemed to drown in the lush carpets as she played the daughter-and-son-and-host's part in the very place where Walter had done his apprenticeship . . . She'd been glad when it was over. When the mourners had had their fill of Dôle Blanche du Valais, *bouillon aux chanterelles*, *vol-au-vent au ris de veau*, saffron rice and French beans, with strawberry mousse and *café au lait* for dessert (venue and menu had been stipulated by her mother, in a handwritten note affixed to the will). When they'd pressed her hand, looked into her tired eyes, kissed her goodbye, saying in low reassuring voices how they were sorry but that it was a release, wasn't it? (Sorry for what? Celia had wondered. For whom? Sorry they could no longer go visiting at the nursing home, no longer linger over her mother's decay? Sorry to find that now *they* were next in line?)

Celia shakes herself, tries to pull the invisible shawl tighter around her shoulders. She mustn't let her mind wander again.

So, point two: the assistant, or Lehmann himself for that matter, can't have anything to do with this. They were engaged *after* the funeral, which means the paint job on the plaster tulips is quite unrelated. Celia smiles up at the cornice opposite; for an instant the flower figures seem to unfurl their leaves and wave at her, nodding their faceless heads. And anyway, how could the men possibly have known about the *three–two–three* doorbell signal? No, no, it's all a lot closer to home, this much she has to admit. And despite the shawl – yes, she can almost feel the wool fibres scratch the nape of her neck – Celia shivers.

A sudden burst of rap music followed by outrageous work noises brings her back to the present. Her rare flowers need tended to. Not that she'll tear out their petals again, not this time. She slides open the drawers of the vanity cabinet which complements the wall-length mirror, and starts searching for a pin. Because the best way to preserve tulips, her mother had taught her, is to prick the base of their heads. Was this maybe what her mother had been hoping to achieve during those hateful (and short-lived) violin practice sessions in the lounge – pin-pricking little Celia's fingers back into position to make the notes sound more pure?

Instead of pins Celia finds half a dozen metal nailfiles, a couple of them with tips so scalpel sharp they draw blood when she tests them. One by one she sets to pricking the flower heads. Pain in exchange for a new lease of life, for new life full stop. Like giving birth. Not that she can speak from experience, of course – and never will, sohelphergod. No need to repeat her mother's mistakes, even if middle-aged motherhood has become fashionable.

For a moment she stares at the flower pictures on the walls: only orchids, roses and edelweiss had been deemed exclusive enough for her mother's beauty clients.

Most people around her have kids, and every time she dares to confess that yes, she quite likes children, but no, she doesn't really want them herself, she prefers to remain childfree (and carefree), thank you, she gets either lashed with good advice and stories of oh-so-happy families and oh-so-lonely childlessness, or tarred and feathered with snide remarks and sideways glances (just like when she showed her new red nightdress to Carmen).

Celia replaces the last of the tulips on the trolley. Pierced and prostrate, the flowers remind her that refusing to join the club of harassed parenthood is still regarded as a major offence: a betrayal of the human race. All the feminism in the world (or post-feminism, she's lost track of the terminology) hasn't changed *that*.

For a second she sees her boss, the master of gems, holding court in his king-size swivel chair, his slack thighs resting on the leather seat like two worn-out cushions. She giggles, then breaks off, shamefaced. No, Eric would never do. But how about some toyboy eager to be taken under her jewel-studded wing, dazzled into affection by a fairy godmother? Celia smiles to herself. Handsome Henry would be the perfect candidate. And he's got a kid already. A kid that might need a weekend mother, if those continual quarrels with his wife are anything to go by. She could always try him. Play at motherhood with him.

Celia's hand squeezes and squeezes the tulip leaves – until they give a crisp sappy creak.

'Frau Roth, could I have a word, please?' Alex wishes his voice was firmer and curses the queasiness in his stomach. Tugging some stray blond strands of hair from under the straps of his overalls, he strolls across to the large oval mirror. Frowns self-critically at his reflection: plenty of life in the old dog yet. He's proud of his pale-blue eyes and strong teeth (all his own), the thick natural curls (dyed, but so bloody what?), the jet-black eyebrows and neatly trimmed beard. Only the skin could be a trifle less freckled perhaps and certainly less blotchy along the hairline where the allergy has struck again. He runs a hand through his hair. 'Strawhead' is what Dominic calls him some-times when he's riled. Dominic with his round-the-clock cap 'to protect myself against the vagaries of the job, man' – well, Alex suspects it's more a case of a thinning crown. From the lounge comes a loud surge of drums, then monotonous talking, more drums, then both.

'Frau Roth?' This time he shouts. He knows the woman's around. Impatiently he bounces the tin of radiator paint against the wall beside the mirror. *Knock-knock*, *knock-knock* it goes, but no one appears. The old wall-covering is as rubbery tough as a devil and gives a nasty retch when he claws a strip off. Bastard'll need a proper hedgehogging all right. That'll be his task – an ideal opportunity to check out the woman's movements at closer quarters . . .

Then he notices the keys. They're poking from under a jumble of bills and letters on the telephone table. The hook nearby is empty and he can see another set stuck in the front door. Acting quite without thought, Alex removes the keys from the table, slips them into his pocket. Just like that.

Five hours later, at home having supper, he hardly listens to his older son's recent football exploits and his wife's tale of how she'd clinched a deal for wood finishes 'thanks to my skill and charm!' Frankly, he couldn't care less.

He chews away at some *Bündnerfleisch* and hopes to Christ the Roth woman won't miss her keys. She didn't give him a ghost of a chance, did she, opening that door so abruptly? Of course he would have put them back. He is an honest man. Has never done anything like this before. Bloody stupid. Never taken anything. What the hell got into him? If the woman hadn't distracted him, he would have put them back. It'll have to be tomorrow now, soon as he gets there. End of story.

Still, Alex feels vaguely excited, and guilty at feeling that way.

On waking the following morning Celia resolves to go back to the office. When the two men arrive, she is all dressed up and in the middle of towel-drying her hair – making it swirl and swish about her head, more than ever reminding Alex of a mermaid – not really paying any attention to them.

Before she leaves, she unlocks the store room so they can get the shutters.

'That's me off,' she calls out from the lounge door. 'There's a spare set of keys on the telephone table for you. Bye.'

Alex nods. 'Have a nice day,' he says and smiles over at her from the radiator he is giving its second coat of Amethyst – the picture of innocence.

12

BY THE TIME Eric has removed his reading glasses and heaved himself out of his king-size swivel chair, Lapis is already running in and out of Celia's legs, panting with pleasure at having his ears flapped, his tail like a brush that furs her shiny grey tights black and white.

Lapis is allowed to do pretty much anything, Celia knows. One of his predecessors, also a spaniel, had been an incurable thief apparently, with an appetite for sweet rolls and soft-boiled eggs. One day he'd snatched away Eric's T-bone steak. Eric had yelled at him to let go, but the dog had bolted it down whole. Then died of a heart attack. Ever since, Eric has been a lenient master. When Lapis, as a puppy, mistook a cat's-eye cabochon for a choc drop, he merely gave a shrug. 'It'll re-emerge, Celia, don't worry,' he said, helping himself to a butter biscuit. 'A proper rinse-and-polish and no one will ever be any the wiser.' They'd sold the cabochon soon afterwards.

Thank God little Celia is beginning to grow up at last, Eric thinks; he has noted the shorter tighter skirt, the high-heeled boots and the deep red of her lips. But of course that's not what he says as he holds out both arms for a clumsy welcome-back-to-the-office hug: 'Celia, how well you're looking! So much better than I'd –'

Lapis has started up a jealous bark and Eric retreats a step. He is an old fat single man, after all, and the art of butterfly flirting is not for him. He is glad to have Celia back. Angelina, his new apprentice, can't be depended on except to write letters from dictation, package gemstones – provided they're laid out and labelled, foolproof, beforehand – and deal with clients whose requests aren't too specific, or well informed. A few days ago he'd actually caught the girl wrapping up one of his costly Kashmir sapphires instead of the cheaper Australian variety the client had ordered because she 'assumed' the cornflower blue was less valuable than the inky dark one. He'd given her quite a talking-to on how never ever to 'assume' anything again if she was at all keen to stay on.

'ASK when you're not sure. ASK! Okay?' he'd thundered in his loudest tones.

The girl had started weeping then, her lovely brown hair sticking limply to her wet cheeks, and he'd felt bad at making her cry yet angry too at her damn stupidity. He'd put his white silk handkerchief on the desk in front of her and returned to his office, mindful not to slam the door overmuch.

The thick wings of Eric's eyebrows tremble. His hand is at the breast pocket of his jasper-brown suit, tucking and untucking today's cotton cloth, fumbling at the soft folds while he wonders whether he'll get the silk one back from Angelina or should he perhaps ask for it. He bends down awkwardly to pat Lapis on the head – 'Off to your bed, that's a good boy' – and straightens right into Celia's smile. She must have greeted him because she is now indicating the long narrow box which lies open on his desk. Lined up in its velvet groove are the pearls from an old necklace he has been trying to re-string (mainly transferring it from safe to desk to safe) on and off for the past week.

'Just leave that to me, Eric,' she says. 'Angelina will have to be shown anyway. Unless there's more urgent business.'

'All yours,' he replies with a grin of relief and a sweeping generous gesture. Dear little Celia, quite a gem in her own right. He knows she'll string those pearls up in no time, perfectly and precisely, including the blasted tiny in-between knots his fingers can't be bothered with any more, and the delicate gold-and-diamond catch at either end. *And* she'll manage to keep up a running commentary for Angelina.

Celia's eyes have followed the sweep of Eric's arm, but now she forces herself to look away before the room is completely dismantled.

Already, the glass-display cabinet opposite has been stripped of its chunks of rock crystal, malachite, onyx, agate, lapis lazuli and all kinds of carved-stone *objets d'art*. To the left of the door, the monstrous old safe like a walk-in fridge has stopped looming – painted or papered out of sight, no doubt. The ceiling-high bookcase in beween has wedged itself deeper into its corner, as if to escape the blankness encroaching it on both sides, and the instrument counter along the right-hand wall has been precision-balanced, proportion-and-microscopied out of existence.

Only over by the window, and furthest from Celia, are things still more or less intact. At least half the heavy mahogany desk with Lapis on his blanket underneath and most of the filing cabinets – though their steeliness appears rather blunted by the razor glints of the Black Star of Africa and the yellow spitfire of the Tiffany Diamond framed above.

The moment passes like a bad dream or the prick of a pin, and Celia crosses over to where the desk rests quite whole and solid on its four legs and Lapis's tail is beating a frantic tattoo on the floor. It's having those decorators around that does this, she thinks. Every room, every house, every shop she enters these days becomes a mere potential for instability, full of movables, rip-outables, pull-down-ables, steam-ables, chisel-and-scrape-ables. She leans over the open box on Eric's desk. How beautiful those pearls are. How calm.

'Cultured?' she asks, picking one up and letting it roll round her palm in small appreciative circles. She knows Eric has a thing about pearls, loves exploring them with his endoscope, shining light through their drill holes endlessly.

'Natural ones, in fact. Fascinating reflections, absolutely fascinating.' He comes to stand beside her and together they stare at the pearl in her hand.

There's an awkward silence made worse by the sadness she suddenly feels layering itself on her like invisible nacre.

Eric, meanwhile, has edged away towards the front of the desk, his furtive progress carefully monitored by Lapis, and is now crouching down, wheezing a little. He isn't sure what to do and so is going to offer Celia a chocolate from the Fémina box-selection – turquoise lid with moonstone-white-and-gold writing, nothing less would do – he keeps in the bottom drawer.

'My favourite exercise,' he jests with a final wheeze as he tugs the box free.

Lapis's head jerks up the same instant. He inches forward on his belly, snuffling, his serrated black lips wet with drool.

Celia replaces the pearl and tells herself to smile, please.

In the outer office Angelina is sorting through the fax messages received overnight (the boss, as she prefers to call Eric, hates e-mail): a short inquiry from their lapidary in Germany; an assessment report from a private gem expert in Zurich; two offers of Rare White brilliants from Antwerp and one of Cognac Fancies from New York, the latter sent at 1.16 a.m. local time – diamond dealers, she's learnt, work at all hours, just like those poor charlies down the mines; several ads for the ultimate in synthetic stones; and a rambling note from Martin, their travelling salesman, who never goes anywhere without his portable fax machine.

She has started on the e-mail, changing the format so the boss won't have any reason to complain about the printouts, when she remembers the silk handkerchief. Damn, damn, damn. He is sure to miss it by now and expect it back. Just her luck. No way can she return *that*. Not after Saturday evening in Kurt's car. Celia might understand, though. She's nice. Cool in an oldie fashion.

Angelina's eyes slide past the bullet-proof glass partition between the office and the reception area, whose door Celia forgot to close when she arrived. Past the four maroon leather seats they slide, past the ceiling-high Swiss cheese plant, the framed photographs of gems and gems and more gems, right up to the heavy security entrance. Celia did look changed this morning. Not drawn and shapeless like Mamma after Nonna died. Here Angelina quickly touches the crucifix with the three diamonds she's wearing on a silver chain round her neck. But sort of eager and excited, dressed younger too – bet she got those lace-up ankle boots and the velvet Lycra number from H & M.

The phone rings. It's one of the jewellers in Lausanne Martin has visited with the New Year price list, bleating into her ears in French. First something about the recession. Then the Russian mafia, their control of mining in the Urals. Then nationalism and its effects on the world's stock markets. Then gem trading. On and on and on in a whiny voice till she's had it up to the eyeballs and puts him through to the boss in mid-sentence. At least that'll get Celia out of there. She's been in for ages. Angelina's index finger jabs at the return key, again and again, emptying out the screen, as she waits for the inner door to open.

The doorbell's been rung downstairs; Celia, snaring yet another pearl with yet another knot, glances up at Angelina to switch on the video entry-system.

'Hi there, it's me,' someone croaks, hardly audible above the explosive rattle of a jumping jack going off nearby – celebrating the last day of Carnival. Then they recognise the face; whatever's happened to Handsome Henry?

Angelina grins: 'Like a crow knocked about in a storm.'

'Mmm, must have had a pretty rough night,' Celia says. Thinking: The trials and tribulations of family life. Doubtless they'll hear about it, again.

Angelina, grinning now like the cat that got the cream, pulls an extra-languid hand through her chocolate-brown hair, head tilted to show off the thick dark curve of her eyelashes. Having pressed the buzzer, she brings out a little round pink-and-gold plastic mirror from behind the video screen – she's got twenty seconds.

Celia's seen it all before, and smiles. Angelina has at least half a dozen of these palm-snug vanities hidden about the office (a different colour for each location), ready to flash back reflections like quicksilver. Martin, who adores any kind of gadget and is rather vain himself, fixed a special clasp to the *Gemmologists' Compendium* to hold the blue mirror in position after it kept dropping from the pages every time he wanted to read up on something. And she herself has had the red one wink at her from the in-tray with wicked regularity.

She is fond of Angelina. The girl's so wilful and self-assured, a bit like Lily used to be. So fleshily handsome with her Italian looks – as sleepy-eyed as a cat in the sun, her cheekbones beginning to push through the puppy fat, her nose just aquiline enough to suggest sensuality. Yet so vulnerable too. Celia wishes she could have been more like her when she was that age. Eric has told her about the sapphire mix-up and Angelina's tears, mentioning in greatly embroidered detail a certain white silk handkerchief (which meant as much as: *Would you please ask Angelina for it back, Celia? I couldn't possibly myself . . .*).

Feet can be heard slogging along the corridor. There's a *rat-a-tat-tat*, one more video security check, then Angelina (mirror-free now and with her eyebrows moistened into shape) punches in the access code . . . and here comes Handsome Henry.

Only today he doesn't do his name much credit. His black hair sticks up in unstylish tufts, his stubble straggles across sallow skin, and his eyes, normally the vivid greenish gold of sphene, are bruised and dark, flatly opaque like cheap pebbles. Celia feels for him, whatever's wrong. Pure motherliness. Angelina is irritated. She can't stand Henry making such an exhibition of himself, so seriously uncool. Because in the secrecy of her bedroom she fancies him, even though he's already 'past it' as her friends would say – past thirty, that is. What the hell's wrong with him?

'Christ,' he sighs and dumps himself down on a chair next to the still-empty dispatch counter over by the window, as far from the two women as he can.

He must be feeling bad all right, Celia concludes, the way he avoids looking at either of them and lets his head sink deeper into the foliage of the big umbrella plant behind him. As if he hopes its leafy fingers will smooth his hair, give his face a quick brush-over.

'How about some coffee to freshen up the week?' Angelina asks in a scratchy voice.

Celia motions for her to sit down again, leave him be. And sure enough, as they carry on with the re-stringing, Henry launches into another tale from the home front. This one culminates in his wife throwing 'her worst ever tantrum' because he'd taken their young son up to Plättli Zoo to see the lions at feeding time.

Dio mio! Angelina has stiffened in her seat and is watching Henry's heart-shaped lips resentfully. Why is he always droning on about his wife and kid? It makes him sound so bloody ancient. Bloody boring: a man in bondage.

Celia, who'd been staring past him, out of the window at the quadrangle of sky between the shingled roof of the castle and the tiers of red tile, verdigris and gold of the Town Hall spire, glances over at Angelina, nods and smiles as if she could read her thoughts, and agreed with every word.

13

THE PEARL NECKLACE is finished at last, nestling in its box between cushions of black taffeta, ready to be returned to the owner.

Angelina's long filed nails are clattering across the keyboard. She is typing some letters via Dictaphone, and tossing her head. Every other toss whips out the wired earpiece so she has to keep rewinding the tape, but to her mind that's a small price to pay. Because Handsome Henry is still around. Over by the dispatch counter. In full view of her gloss-sprayed hair floating like the silkiest scarf. If he cares to look, that is. He's helping Celia wrap and label some parcels that need delivered. Only it seems to Angelina that Celia is standing rather close to him. Standing and bending down. Letting her clingy skirt ride up against his thigh. Too bloody close for comfort, or Celia's own good. Henry will get a real eyeful of all those wrinkles and blemishes, the crêpey skin of her throat. The thought cheers Angelina. A few flecks of Galactica polish gleam faintly along the curve of her nails where she hasn't removed it properly after the Carnival Ball.

She clicks PAUSE and taps out a fantasy letter to pretend she's busy.

Loads of men (and women, though she'd actively discouraged them) had wanted a feel that night. The soldiers were the worst, drunk and sex-starved, with hard-ons even before they'd touched her, or her crystal ball. Three or four of the costumed men must have been older, they kissed her with such sloppy greed. Especially that *arlecchino* outside the Métropole – him and his pink women's glasses which made her giggle when he held her pinned to the wall. He never said a word, just panted like he'd been jogging – randy as anything, of course. Afterwards the beetroot-red paint of his mouth was all over her face.

For a moment Angelina rubs at the star shimmer on her nails, utterly self-absorbed.

The boss has a no-perfume-no-nail-polish-no-hand-cream policy, to protect his merchandise from what he calls 'aggressive attacks'. Lucky his list of no-no's doesn't include Coke. Angelina couldn't do without it, she loves the way it fizzes on her tongue, and always has a can or two stashed at the bottom of her pouchy leather handbag. Better the boss doesn't know. Celia had lectured her on the subject when she'd spilt some drops on her desk shortly after starting her apprenticeship.

'Please don't drink that in here, Angelina,' she'd said. 'Have a seat over in Reception. Coke's something of a hazard in our line of business. To pearls particularly.'

One word about tooth enamel or stomach linings, and Angelina would have told her quite sweetly to cut it out, she doesn't need *two* mothers, thanks very much. And anyway, hadn't Celia registered yet that Coke was harmless nowadays?

Celia had flipped a hand towards the glass door, half-smiling and almost apologetic, it seemed to Angelina, then calibrated the Mettler scales and pincered up a diamond for weighing.

'Well, what about the pearls?' Angelina had asked, wiping at the spillage on her desk with her fingers and sucking them as nonchalantly as she could. Drawing Celia out a little, for the fun of it.

Celia had kept her waiting. Finished writing down the carat value on the stone paper in front of her and folded the diamond back into it before lifting her head: 'Put one in a glass of Coke and you'll soon find out. There won't be much left in a while. Usually a nucleus. A piece of grit or the like if it's a naturally grown pearl; if cultured, probably a small bead of mother-of-pearl, spherical in most cases – though all sorts of shapes and materials have been tried down the ages, in China even tiny metal Buddhas. So, you see . . .' On and on and on.

To stop her, Angelina had slipped off one of her own earrings, silver with a rose-coloured freshwater pearl, and placed it in a small leftover puddle of Coke. It worked like a dream: Celia cried out and snatched the piece away, then dabbed it dry on a clean cloth.

'Silly girl!'

'Only joking.' Angelina had tittered uneasily. 'That earring's from an ex-boyfriend.'

'Doesn't matter *who* it's from! Don't ever do such a thing again . . .' The tone had been ominous.

She hasn't had any more run-ins with Celia since then, *grazie a Dio.* Angelina continues typing: '*Per favore, signore, un poco d'amo–*' At this point she tosses her hair extra-violently because she's just observed Handsome Henry touch Celia on the shoulder. When she glances back at her computer screen, the fantasy letter she'd been writing to a Signor Spaghetti in Carbonara has vanished. All that remains is an infinity of pale grey dots, as if the space bar had gone into spasm.

'Sorry about your mother, Celia.' Henry had paused and, after squeezing her shoulder very gently (affectionately, she realises now, only it's too late), passed a forearm over his face, perhaps to make himself look more respectable. 'I meant to come to the funeral, with Eric. But then my wife and I . . . well, things went completely haywire.' His eyes, suddenly bright and golden again, had rested on hers for just that split second too long, and something turned over inside her.

'That's okay,' she'd replied with a shrug, unable to smile, and to her horror had heard herself add, 'A card would have been nice though.'

Goodgodwhywhywhy had she said that? She didn't mean to. She likes Henry. Likes him a lot (more than she's prepared to admit to herself) and wouldn't mind getting to know him a bit better. She must be cracking up. And now he's ignoring her, has even taken a step away and is gazing over at Angelina, fixedly. Longingly.

The girl is conscious of his interest, Celia can tell: already she's started playing to the gallery, putting on her 'diligent apprentice' act and clearly surpassing herself. Her silver crucifix swings wildly, flashing fire; and as she leans forward, her wide-necked red Benetton sweatshirt frames rather than conceals her breasts.

'No bra,' whispers someone. Who? Celia wonders. Then, all at once, everything bends and buckles and blurs around her and she is off, staggering through the glass door, past the maroon leather seats to the washroom in the corner.

Angelina has shot bolt upright, her cheeks mottled chalk and scarlet. Henry's eyes have swerved down and away to study the carpet fluff along the skirting. There's a patter from the umbrella plant as a whorl of dead leaves falls to the floor.

Celia is hunched up on the toilet seat, face in hands, knees cuffed together by the metal-grey fabric of her tights. She hasn't pulled down her knickers. Her elbows are pressing into the flesh of her thighs.

Of course she's had other boyfriends besides Franz. Several with whom she slept, a few with whom she laughed but didn't sleep, and two or three she laughed and cried and slept with. Franz has outlasted them all. A prerogative of the dead, perhaps their only one: they never leave you. Even if she hadn't moved back to her mother's, even if she had chucked in her job and gone abroad like Walter and Lily, the memory of Franz's death would have followed her like a shadow.

But she doesn't want to be celibate, goddammit. Or jealous. She knows there's no chance in hell she could ever compete with a smooth-complexioned olive-skinned soft-bodied girl like Angelina. No chance she could ever claim Henry's sexual favours. Damn right she knows.

It's warm in the cubicle. The radiator on the wall next to her gives out puffs of hot dopey air.

Celia doesn't stir.

She's not really the jealous type, is she? Temporarily a little more distrustful perhaps, a little more emotional – which is hardly surprising. And those blasted tulips yesterday didn't help. As if her mother had employed some kind of spirit messenger to taunt her now that she herself is no longer around.

Celia pictures her kitchen table with the vase of tulips dead centre: the stems are in contortions and the waxy black heads have split open towards the pale light seeping through the unwashed net curtains. (She'll buy new ones when the paint job's done, when her kitchen is sunny day and night – 'Yellow and orange, with the merest hint of red,' she'd told the decorator on their tour of the flat. 'The warmest tones you can get.' By that stage he had no longer put up a fight, just sighed and beamed his electronic measuring tape round the room, then scribbled in his notebook.)

The two men will be having their mid-morning break about now, complete with meat-filled rolls from Bänninger's and Nescafé from the jar out on the worktop, prominently displayed next to two old mugs and spoons, some sachets of sugar, cream in portions, and the pink post-it with her office phone number. They might be going into the kitchen this very moment. Celia can almost see the arm reaching out to push the vase roughly up against the wall so the tulip heads bob and shake, raining pollen on the shiny wood inlay. Easy to guess who the arm belongs to. No one but Lehmann's assistant would behave in that carefree manner.

'Cheers to the lady of the house,' she imagines him saying, his mug of coffee lifted grandiose-style, the way he'd raised his brush yesterday to wave her out of the lounge after his boss had test-painted a radiator panel for her, 'and thanks for leaving us alone.' Then he'll take a bite out of his roll, his mouth stretched wide.

Lehmann, who is no doubt munching away already, may just give a noncommittal nod while squinting at a lock of hair he's holding pinched between the fingers of his free hand, scrutinising it for paint stains. He'll be glad she isn't there. No danger of her bursting from the Beauty Room like yesterday afternoon when she'd made him jump nearly out of his skin. All she'd wanted was to fetch the agate vase (a birthday present to her mother, hence its tasteful interbanding of light greys and reddish browns) for the tulips.

At first she assumed he'd jumped like that because she'd surprised him hanging around the corridor mirror checking on his haircut or the Vandyke, and she smiled in spite of herself. In spite of her still-angry feelings towards whoever had left those flowers on her doorstep like a threat.

'Oh, hello again,' she said, trying to avoid the blue eyes. 'Anything you need?' Swiftly, after a glance at her reflection, she rubbed some dust off her chin.

He seemed slightly awkward. 'The music in there's a bit loud, no wonder you couldn't hear me.'

That's when she spotted the peeled-off wallpaper, the scratches and scrape marks on the wall beside the mirror. So it wasn't mere vanity, he must have been busy and genuinely startled.

He held up a tin. 'The radiator paint. Just checking this is the shade you asked for: Amethyst. I had it made up specially.' He'd paused until she looked at him, losing herself in those electric blue eyes. 'Perhaps I could show you –'

Someone has opened the washroom door. 'Celia? I'm sorry . . .' Angelina. Come to apologise for that silly incident before. Sexy Angelina, the victim of her own desires. Like Lily.

'Don't worry, I'm okay.' Celia has taken her elbows off her thighs and is examining the reddened flesh. 'Branded all right,' she mutters to herself.

'Pardon?' Then a flurry of words: 'There's a phone call for you. They wouldn't give their name. Said you'd know. It's a man, I think. Or a woman with a smoker's voice.'

It can't be a woman; none of her female friends or acquaintances smoke that much. Most likely it's Lehmann. Hoping to discuss paints and colours over the phone now, godforbid.

'Guess who?' The voice is deep all right, with a faint foreign-sounding twang. It reminds Celia of someone she can't quite place. Definitely not the decorator.

'Hello?' she shouts into the mouthpiece, pretending not to understand, '*Who* did you say?' She is sitting with her legs folded, her left hand tracing the red patch under her tights, just below the hemline of her skirt.

'You didn't step on them, did you?'

'What?'

'Would have been a shame, such beautiful flowers . . .' A delicate cough, then the line goes silent.

'Bloodycrank,' Celia says, replacing the receiver.

Angelina and Henry are looking at her from the dispatch counter. Angelina's screen saver is on: a sea-floor scene of acid-green weeds, crabs and multicoloured fish glug-glugging away. 'What do you mean? Of course it's a real aquarium,' Celia had overheard Angelina say into the phone on various occasions. 'Here at Eric Krüger's everything is real. We don't go in for imitation and fake, *you* should know.' Angelina's a cheeky little flirt the way Celia has never, never been.

'Bloodycrankbloodystupidcrank,' Celia whispers down into her *décolleté*. She'd taken off her bra before leaving the cubicle and now she can see her nipples. They're hard and unashamed, and the sight of them makes her feel strangely invincible all of a sudden.

She's not afraid. No, no, not really. She is safe here at Eric's. Couldn't, indeed, be safer. She almost laughs out loud as she sits contemplating the video surveillance system, the steel-enforced entrance to the office premises, the bullet-proof glass partition and windows.

14

RETURNING FROM THE Co-op after work, Celia finds the door to her flat unlocked. Lehmann and Co. must have left in a blind rush to catch the last few hours of Carnival action in the local bars and restaurants, no doubt hoping for a final good ogle-and-grab at the waitresses in their skimpy sex-goddess outfits before they're transformed back into Anders housewives once more, cleaning and washing and cooking in their no-nonsense family homes. She'll have to speak to the men tomorrow.

She's just set down her shopping bags to put on the corridor light when she hears a faint sound from inside the flat. Then it comes again. Her finger bends away from the plastic switch. She breathes in quietly, listens. Nothing. Not Schildi.

It's after six. With the wallpaper steamed off, gargoyle figures have begun to lurk in the shallow indentations of the corridor walls. Shadows have crawled in among the coats and jackets on the hangers near her, hulking them into dummies which are swaying a little in the draught she's caused on entering, swaying without noise, slyly alive.

The door of the Beauty Room is shut, but she now notices a streak of light from underneath. Someone's in there – with or without black tulips. She'll show them. She's had enough. Leave me ALONE, she wants to scream, you STUPIDSTUPID-CRANK!

Her heart is thudding against her ribs as she slips into the shifting shadows of the coat rack, reaches for the old torch – nice and heavy, the perfect truncheon to fight off intruders – which her mother had always kept on the slatted top in case of unexpected power cuts. Then she glides towards the thin line of light and shoves open the door.

He is in plain view, down on his knees at the far end of the room. Still in his dirty white overalls, his hands and forearms inside the built-in vanity cabinet with her mother's jumble of beauty products. His head has swivelled round in slow-motion embarrassment, making his wavy blond-bleached hair fan out like a woman's.

'Oh, it's you!' Celia exclaims, lowering the torch she's held at shoulder height, ready to strike.

'I was just leaving. Thought I'd give the back of the cupboard a quick check to see whether it'll need painted too.'

Lehmann's mouth tries to smile at her, but his lips have got stuck to his teeth and only lift at the corners.

'The back of the cupboard?' she repeats lamely, wondering what he is talking about.

She takes a few paces into the room, stops. She feels weak, bereft somehow. They're alone in the flat, just the two of them. She clutches the torch in despair; she must avoid his eyes, mustmustmust avoid his eyes.

He has withdrawn his hands and, straightening up, wipes them surreptitiously on the paint-splashed camouflage of his overalls.

No stains will show on there any more, not even her mother's fluffy Magic-Pink cream.

'Well . . .' Celia struggles to say something. 'Maybe I forgot to mention it to you last Tuesday, but I'd decided this room was to be my new bedroom and –' Dumbfounded, she breaks off; whenthehell *had* she decided if not right now, put on the spot, as it were?

The man's lips are frozen in the same silent grimace as before.

'So, you see, the vanity cabinet and the wall shelving will have to go – once I've cleared her out . . . pardon me, cleared out my mother's things.' Celia laughs nervously. 'Except for the wash-basin. And the mirror. I'll keep them.' She shrugs. 'Call me sentimental.'

Lehmann has managed to unstick his lips and is passing and repassing his tongue over his teeth. He is looking at the picture of the spider orchid behind her. Eventually he says, 'So sorry,' and Celia realises her little joke has fallen rather flat.

She ought to be angry with him, she tells herself, for desecrating her mother's shrine. Surely she ought to be angry. Raging like one of those furies with snakes for hair. How dare he touch her mother's possessions? All the exquisitely presented lotions, creams and oils? The jarfuls of gleamy-capped kohl pencils, mascaras and make-up brushes she remembers flanking the mirror above, multiplied in reflection? The trays studded with rainbow selections of eye shadows and nail varnish, with sleekly glistening lipsticks, bottles of foundation, concealer sticks, flasks of perfume? Instead of anger, though, she is aware only of gratitude – and relief. A little-girl relief at not having to be the first to tamper with those relics.

'Don't worry,' she says towards his flickering gaze, doing her best not to sound too exuberant, 'as I said, that stuff's going to be thrown out. Help yourself to whatever you fancy.'

Yes, this *will* be her new bedroom. Spacious and bright – bright pink in fact, apart from the leaf-green and pure white tulip cornice and rosette – with a balcony that gets the sun all afternoon. Triumphantly she smiles beyond the decorator, into the mirror. But as she crosses over to him, her fingers loosen and tighten, loosen and tighten on the torch.

Lehmann mutters, 'Dominic might be interested, thank you. For his girlfriend. I'd better head off. Bye.' He swerves away, sidling past the window, the balcony door, past the plinth and the two padded chairs pushed up against the back wall, his face averted.

Then Celia's fingers unclench. She is in complete control now. She has seen what he's trying to hide, seen the feathery grey smudges on his lids, the glitter trail along his hairline, the trace of garnet-red lipstick. He hasn't merely investigated the contents of the vanity cabinet, he has actually used them, forcing and prising open, unscrewing, twisting off lids! Doing himself up for the Carnival bars probably. Celia can't imagine any other reason; in her opinion, the only males to get away with wearing make-up as a matter of course are pop stars.

Beyond the snow glimmer of the balcony floor, the darkness seems to be growing thicker, more impenetrable. She shivers. All of a sudden she is desperate to keep the man in the room with her, just a bit longer.

He has almost reached the door.

'One more thing, Herr Lehmann.' She beckons to him. 'Would you mind?'

She has no idea what to say next. Could she offer him a cup of coffee perhaps? Or compliment him on the work in progress? Ask how they're getting on with the steaming? The torch handle feels slippery. She grips it harder as he comes strolling back, and watches him wipe his mouth and eyelids in a clumsy pretence at tiredness.

'Yes?' he yawns.

What will she say, forpitysake, what?

The torch in her hand flashes on as if of its own accord. Its beam arcs across the mirror, settles on the colour-speckled Reeboks which have stopped dead in their tracks, two steps away still. She must be quick now, and playful. The light flits up his shins, past his knees and over the bulge of his thighs, resting on his crotch rather longer than necessary – until he looks down in alarm and she changes the angle to pick out his face. His eyes are staring. They're so blue. Much more brilliant than she remembers. Magnetic.

'That glitter suits you,' she says hurriedly. 'It really does. Let me . . .'

Now her coat has slid off and she's touching his hair, the torch somewhere on the floor.

Alex stands immobile, guilty and confused. 'I'm sorry. I couldn't resist,' he says. He has no excuse. The woman could ruin him and his business if she chose to. He's never before committed an indiscretion like this (sneaking those keys was a brief aberration, he swears), and never will again (unless you count the occasional private note or letter left lying around, simply begging to be read).

He lowers his eyes. And then can't tear them away from what he can't help seeing – either it's freezing out in the streets or her blouse is too flimsy. Nothing else. Nothing.

NO. NO. NO.

Jacqueline and the boys will be waiting for him, their supper on the table: tubs of tepid chocolate yoghurt, in the bread basket *Bürli* rolls and slices of *Zopf*, the butter with its trademark imprint of a grinning fox melting at the edges, on the cheeseboard sallow wedges of Tilsiter, Gruyère and Appenzeller covered in droplets of saltwater – like sweat on a girl's skin . . . One day, he has vowed to himself, he'll grab a wedge when no one's looking. Grab it and lick it clean. But not just yet.

He jerks his eyes free. Moves away.

Celia follows him praying inwardly, Pleasegodlethimstayafew-moreminutes onlyafewmoreminutes pleasepleaseplease. It's unbearably dark outside; the glass panes have turned into mirrors and the room seems suddenly flustered with couples. A moment later, the heel of her right boot gets tangled in the coat on the floor and she's losing her balance.

When she comes round, Lehmann is squatting at her shoulder. He is holding one of her mother's flasks of perfume to her nostrils and pressing a wet cloth to the back of her head where it hurts most. On her chest she senses a former weight, as if he'd been feeling for her heartbeat.

'Frau Roth? You all right?' His voice trembles a little. 'You tripped and hit yourself on the stool here.'

Celia blinks, heaves a sigh. 'Thanks,' she says. She gropes for his hand, clasps it. Then, taking one–two–three deep breaths, she quickly draws it towards her, and on to her left breast.

Alex tries to pull away. This is insane. The woman's head must have got muddled in the fall and she doesn't know what she's doing. Pretty unexpected after her little shows of coyness – he hasn't forgotten how she brandished the stripping knife to hustle Dominic and him out of the house before dark that first afternoon; nor the ancient monogrammed bedsheets spread over her furniture like she wanted to protect it from contamination. He tries to block out the memory of the other time. The time when she seemed to go into that trance.

Her fingers have locked round his wrist now and, keeping it steady, start guiding it up and down and over her breasts. Up and down and across like it's a gear lever. And he a bloody engine. But already he can feel himself warming up.

'A good seeing-to is what this one needs,' Dominic had said only yesterday.

What about Jacqueline, though? He mustn't do this to her, he mustn't cheat on her. Poor Jacqueline with her familiar floppy thighs and buttocks that won't strain or push any more, merely flounder at his thrusts. Jacqueline with her big lazy mouth reserved strictly for kissing. His wife. The mother of his two sons. Doesn't he remember how they were born? Each of them ripping her open with pain, and love for him?

Alex's eyes have begun to sting; his face is damp. It's the heat, he tells himself; he's feeling so very, very hot. The body next to him is gasping and quivering, invading his thoughts.

His fingers have nearly undone her blouse. She isn't wearing anything underneath.

'Lovely,' he says. 'Lovely!' He squeezes, bites a little and sucks to taste her skin, rubbing her long mermaid's hair all over her. All over, till she is panting and grinding her hips against him. He recognises the look of wildness that's come into her eyes.

She moans as he runs his tongue along her earlobe and round the shimmering shell inside.

She's slid up her skirt, her moans more urgent now. His overalls are unbuttoned easily enough, his jeans have a zip. And her hands are already unbuckling his belt.

Gently he moves closer. He kisses her eyes, her nose, nuzzles the softness of her lips, careful to avoid her tongue.

15

THE PHONE SHRILLS Celia awake. Alex, she whispers and reaches out a hand. The space on the carpet beside her is empty. He's gone, having left her wrapped in the winter coat, sleeves tied loosely across her chest. Swaddled like a newborn babe. Which is just how she feels. Chuckling to herself, she blunders out into the corridor. The light is on, thankgod, and there's no sign of him.

'Hello,' she mumbles, trying to wrestle herself into the coat without dropping the receiver. A strand of saliva-wet hair slaps her shoulder. She smiles as she catches sight of her breasts, hard and pert, in the oval mirror and for an instant her image is eclipsed by those sensations again – like flowers bursting and bursting fiery petals into a black sky.

'Cel! How are you? Boys just went off to school so I thought I'd give you a buzz.' Lily of all people. Prurient Lily hot on the scent, tracking her down from the other side of the globe.

'Lily, hi. I'm okay . . .' If Lily knew, she'd never stop asking questions; she loves private gossip, the more juicy the better. Celia remembers her account of the twins' birth in graphic detail, including various recipes for cooking placentas. She grins, glances down at her bare feet, 'Yeah, pretty much okay. And yourself?'

She wiggles her toes as she hears Lily's usual, 'Fine, fine.'

'So, did you get my letter?'

'Letter? No. When did you post it?'

'Last week some time. Everything's kind of topsy-turvy right now. I'm having the house revamped and –' Celia sucks her teeth.

'Don't worry, Walter's calmed down. Tell you though, he was bloody mad after that call!' Lily laughs her breathless giggly laugh which Celia will always associate with winter bedrooms and rose gardens.

'Not with you, Cel, honestly. Probably more with himself even than your mum. He must have realised he can't expect to be rewarded for legging it. And she did set up that trust fund for the boys. But you know, what with him being the only son and having his own business *and* a family . . . Anyway, he specifically asked me to say hello because he's still away. An extended business trip to Australia actually, some wine-growers' seminar. He said to make sure and ring you, see you were doing okay.'

Why can't he find out for himself? Celia kicks the wall, rasping her toes on the grit-rough plaster. He's got the number, hasn't he? The back of her head has begun to throb; the swelling's the size of a five-franc coin.

'Listen, Lily, I'd be happy to make more of that money over to you, I told Walter.' If the decorators hadn't removed the upholstered chair for the steaming, she'd have given it a good shove down the corridor. 'Instead he got more furious. Ranted and raved about Mother and what a bitch she was. How he'd always done what she wanted.'

There's a pause at the other end of the line. Celia feels dribbles starting on the insides of her thighs, a feeling whose sleaziness she finds she adores and intends to prolong. No more kicking now. The throbbing in her head has subsided into a tingling – nothing a cold pack won't cure. Idly she rubs her legs together.

'Hey, Cel, you're not crying, are you? Walter didn't mean it, you know.'

Didn't he just! Then Celia says, 'No, no. I'm fine.' She smirks, wet to her knees now. 'A little knackered that's all. It was my first day back at work today.' (And my first lay in years – a workman, in fact – but of course she won't say *this.*)

Better get in touch with Dr Caveng tomorrow for an emergency prescription, she thinks, and blurts out hastily, 'Thanks for the photos, Lily. The twins have certainly shot up – young men almost. Are the girls double-queuing at your door yet?'

Alex isn't likely to have AIDS, is he? That's her only worry now. Dr Caveng can deal with the rest.

'Oh Cel, it's good to hear you joking again. They're gorgeous boys, aren't they? Quite innocent to all appearances.'

Celia decides to bring up the subject next time she meets Alex. Lily is still talking about her kids. Something about Lyell pouncing on the phone at first ring and the frequency of Peter's underwear change forgodsake. Now she's giggling. Celia laughs, dutifully.

And laughs a bit more. 'I do look forward to seeing you all in the autumn, as you promised – it's three years since your last visit. By then the flat should be in perfect nick: rich glorious colours, different ones for each room, to imitate the gemstones I work with.' Barely hesitating, she adds, 'No ruby red, I'm afraid. That's too much like blood. Too unsettling.' There. It's said. A dare between friends.

'Mm, yes. I'd go for something more muted myself.' Lily is obviously playing dumb to avoid getting caught in the past, or has she forgotten their childhood games? 'It must be so exciting to be your own mistress, Cel – total freedom, and no questions asked.'

That's one way of putting it. One way of reminding her that when all's said and done, she is alone. By herself. Partnerfree is also partnerless. Her legs too have a near-dry feel to them. But then Celia recalls the caresses of Alex's lips on her skin, his hands rippling through her hair, and all along his squat hardness slowly twisting, stretching her insides into an ache.

She pulls herself together and replies, 'Such a shame you didn't get to fly over for the funeral. I missed you, Lily. It would have been great to have had you around. Like in the old days. Before Walter –' She swallows. Lily has never regarded Walter as a wrecker of friendships. 'Your mother was there, though. Funny thing is I saw her on the telly the other evening; they were showing the Carnival Parade.'

'Cel?' Lily coughs. 'Cel, I've been thinking. About that extra money you offered . . . Were you really serious? Because, well, I'd love to try my hand at oil painting. Evening classes. Walter would doubtless see it as another of my "doomed hobbies", so I'm hoping to surprise him when he gets back. You *were* serious, weren't you?'

Celia shivers inside her coat. 'Oh yes,' she says. 'I was serious all right. Sounds like a good idea. Just give me your bank details and I'll transfer a few thousand. As long as one of the pictures is for me!' She forces a laugh. Her legs are perfectly dry now, and for a moment she wonders whether she has hallucinated the whole thing.

They hang up soon after. Everything's been said.

By the time the phone rings again, an hour later, Celia has finished clearing the shelves in the Beauty Room, inside the vanity cabinet and along the walls. She'd started by unstoppering and unscrewing a number of the dusty old bottles, pots and tubes to have a sniff, but eventually gave up. Some of the stuff had gone rancid, some cloyingly sweet, some brick hard. Much of it had separated. With one arm she'd swept the lot into two empty banana boxes from the cellar, not even bothering to check which of the sprays, lotions, powders, creams and oils might still be of use, which wax mixtures and face masks, which mascaras, eye shadows, kohl pencils, lipsticks, nail varnish. Then the plastic clips and curlers, the scissors, files, tweezers. Balls of fusty cottonwool, powder puffs, brushes, lumpy tissues, lint strips, greyish face towels. No wavering, Cel, she'd told herself, if you want a clean break. And the four custard-yellow nylon make-up capes had glided on top obligingly enough. The only thing she'd saved (and put straight into the washing machine) was a stack of almost new fluffy towels.

The caller is probably Lily, ready to apologise. It's what used to happen when they were kids and had some sort of argument: the one with the guiltier conscience would invariably get back in touch to patch matters up.

Celia lifts the receiver. 'Hello,' she says in a bright friendly tone to indicate she doesn't bear a grudge.

'Celia? Celia Roth?'

'Yes.'

'Just checking you received those flowers for the funeral.' The same voice as on the office phone. At least Celia thinks so. For an instant the corridor shudders around her, naked without its customary padding of wallpaper.

'The flowers?' she asks flatly. 'We did have quite a few, as you might –'

'Tulips. Black ones.'

The receiver in her hand is trembling ever so slightly. She does her best to stay calm, but she can feel a runnel of sweat between her breasts. This has to stop. Stop now. If *she* doesn't do something, no one else will. She's been trained in client management dammit, under Eric's personal supervision.

Speaking with crisp deliberation she says, 'It was nice of you to remember my mother.' And pauses. She's heard Rolf's footsteps upstairs. Moments later a window opens, shutters clatter, the window bangs closed, and she continues. 'I'd have sent you a card, only there was no name or address. If you prefer to remain anonymous . . . ?'

She waits.

There is no response.

'Well, do you mind telling me who you are and what's going on?' She can't quite help a note of fear and anger muddling up her question. 'It was you, wasn't it, that called me at Eric Krüger's today.' Accusing now.

Still no response.

'Nothing to say for yourself?'

She waits again.

'No? Then fine, and thank you.' As she replaces the phone, she is shaking all over from the sustained effort to appear firm, and polite.

In the kitchen she makes herself a double espresso, no milk, one sugar. Does her mother still have secret admirers? Lovers even? Leaning against the worktop, Celia stirs and stirs. Until the clinking of the spoon gets so loud it begins to reverberate inside her head. Turning into the rhythms of Johnny's Carnival Band all those years ago. Now the saxophone's joined in and lurches into the kind of gut-wrenching solo that sends people swooning into each other's arms. Soon the casino's old plum-coloured curtains will start to swing in time to the beat, and it isn't hard to picture the dim figures of the ghost woman and her partner in one of the window recesses.

Celia still hasn't a clue who that partner was. Indeed, whether it was a man; a man with exceptionally graceful ankles and plump round calves. She adds another sugar to her espresso and keeps stirring. Her mother had also liked women – Margaret, of course, but she was a friend and naturally beautiful, just required the weekly facials and manicures. No, her mother had definitely seemed more keen on the less attractive women, the ones that needed her and her expertise. Those with lank hair and bat ears, with beak-shaped noses, small round mouths and eyes like dead fish. She loved fluffing them up. She'd spray and highlight their hair, drape it so intricately that large ears would lose their prominence. She'd blend different shades of foundation, apply a dash of powder here, some pearl blusher and rouge there, making even the worst profiles look stylish. Or she'd use various kohl pencils and liners to give more sparkle and fuller lips. She was, Celia has to concede, quite an illusionist.

She raises her cup, takes a sip. On reflection, though, it was after Walter had left home that her mother really applied herself to the beauty business. Threw herself into it. As if determined to drown in the scents and lotions and colours of appearance. And disappearance.

Celia had been eavesdropping the afternoon her brother made his big announcement.

'Sorry, Gabrielle, but I can't go on like this. I need more space.'

No wonder, she'd thought to herself, with you being number-one son and nephew, and always in demand. Her ear was pressed to the keyhole of her bedroom door. The others were where she is now, right here in the kitchen.

Earlier, Walter had given her a brand-new Astérix book, warding off her thanks like blows, his palms pushing up and outward in that splayed ambivalent gesture of his. '*Voilà*, sis. To keep you out of mischief for the next half-hour.' His tone had been gruff, more like a command.

Not a sound from their mother, not a word.

He plodded on: 'My own space. I'm old enough, *you* should know.'

Another silence, then, 'You of all people. Gabrielle? Say something.'

Not a word. Nothing.

'The Schlosshotel has offered me board and lodging now that my trial period's over. GABRIELLE? You hear ME?'

Nothing.

Suddenly, the thump of chair legs hitting the kitchen floor.

'Listen, I'll never tell. How could I?'

Coughs and gurgles, then crying noises and Walter's voice, low and cooing now and quite unintelligible.

Later he said their mother had been sitting with her chair tilted up against the wall, 'gulping black coffee by the gallon and staring into space like I wasn't there, never mind talking to her – till she swallowed the wrong way.'

Celia wasn't that stupid. So she'd punched him in the face, squarely, but not too hard – he was her brother, after all. He had laughed and pulled her hair, coming away with a thin fistful of her rat's tails.

16

'HOW ABOUT LUNCH in Casino Mall for a change, Angelina?' Celia suggests after the church bells have finished their traditional eleven-o'clock ringing. With deliberate casualness she adds, 'My treat. To apologise for yesterday. I wasn't quite myself.'

Angelina is quick to accept and Celia envies her don't-look-a-gift-horse-in-the-mouth attitude; she wonders whether the girl would have taken that bunch of tulips on her threshold for granted too . . .

At five to twelve they're out and away. The Carnival decorations have been removed and most of the confetti and streamers swept off the cobbles; Anders is a clean town once more. Eric's jade-green Jaguar with its white leather upholstery scuffed by dog paws is parked on the corner of the pedestrian precinct. Celia smiles to herself, the old man is a dab hand at networking with the police.

As they cut through the short arcade near the Old Town Steps, Angelina mocks the shoe displays, 'Real provincial, don't you think? No class, no style. They could learn a thing or two from us Italians.'

Celia merely clears her throat and swishes her hair into a curtain to blinker-walk past; she's had it with shoes *en masse.* A little further along, though, she prods the girl in the side of her faux leopard-skin coat and points at the male dummies modelling the new spring fashion – headless torsos with sturdy wooden poles for legs. 'All brawn and no brains: the perfect men,' she says.

They're still giggling when they start down the Steps. A few desultory snowflakes are swirling round them in the milkiness of another cold sunless day.

They pass some students from the local grammar school who're wolfing hamburgers and pastries, and slurping from cans. Then there's a man in a white lab coat mounting the steps towards them two at a time, presumably to keep warm. Celia recognises him: it's her impatient bottle-squirting optician. Just as he draws level and she is about to greet him, he calls out, 'Oh, hello, Frau Roth. How's the blinking?'

'Fuck you,' Celia mutters, glaring after him.

Angelina stares at her in astonishment and, two flights later, stops abruptly. 'Celia, can I ask you something?'

'Yes?' Celia hopes it's nothing personal. She doesn't know the girl well enough for that.

St Nikolaus's on their right and the Protestant church over by the castle have begun to strike noon in a straggle of peals that makes it sound more like sixteen or seventeen had either of them bothered to count.

'It's about the boss . . .' Angelina is looking away and Celia's eyes follow hers terrace by rose-garden terrace, down, down and across to the small turret in the far corner where she and Lily used to play at Rose Red and Snow White. For a moment she imagines the earth in the flowerbeds, underneath their mantle of snow, warm and brown and pulsating like a bear's fur. Then she notices the ripped streamers caught in the thorns, red, pink, green, purple, blue, yellow – the rags of a rainbow.

Angelina has embarked on a garbled story about Eric's handkerchief. Kurt, her boyfriend, had run out of Kleenex in the car and she'd realised about the hankie too late. 'I mean, that it belonged to the boss. It's ruined now. Time of the month, you see.' She hesitates, bites her lip. 'So, what should I do, Celia?'

Celia gazes into the face turned towards her. The sensuousness oozing from its every pore, from the shimmering forehead down to the small mole on the chin, is almost insulting. Godknows, if

Angelina had talked to her with such frankness only yesterday, she'd have blushed and fled, all the way home probably. But now she can allow herself to stay and smile indulgently. 'Don't worry,' she says and pats the girl on the shoulder, half-stroking the luscious thick hair, while her left hand fingers the envelope in her pocket with the emergency pills she'd picked up earlier from Dr Caveng's practice. 'Just don't worry.'

Celia likes the Casino Mall Restaurant. Perhaps because it reminds her of a cave; the civilised version of a cave, that is. Not what her father and Walter used to slither about in. More a sort of rococo grotto, with soft indirect lighting, satiny curving walls, a ceiling wreathed in ivy and other climbing plants like a hanging garden, and miniature trees in ornamental glazed pots between the tables. A grotto humming with voices and the clatter of eating.

Angelina is putting on a little luncheon performance for the two men smoking at the table to their right, behind a tall yucca. Her head inclined, she seems to meditate over every forkload of polenta-and-broccoli-cheese before guiding it into her mouth with a delicate curl of her tongue.

Celia sees the men glance over and comment to each other as they flick ash, their tanned jaws creased with amusement. They're in their early thirties, Brylcreemed and dressed in bright shirts, orange and sulphur yellow. Their leather jackets are wadded over the backs of their seats, inside out, like designer-labelled cushions. A couple of wet show poodles, Celia thinks. Instants later she chokes on a piece of curried chicken, begins coughing and spluttering helplessly. Angelina holds out a glass of Coke to her, but she rolls her watering eyes and grabs at a paper napkin.

'I'll be fine,' she croaks, flushed redhot. She'll keep her face down for a while. Judging by the intermittent slow scrape of cutlery from opposite her, the girl must have resumed her pantomime, quite happy with herself now that the handkerchief problem has been delegated.

Celia muffles another coughing fit. Angelina's voice out on the Old Town Steps had sounded so much like Lily's, a long-lost echo from more than twenty years ago. And just as she hadn't advised Lily to get herself a new boyfriend, preferably one *with* a brother, she hadn't advised Angelina to buy a new handkerchief.

'Tell you what, Angelina,' she'd heard herself say instead, 'give me till tomorrow and I'll see what I can do. My mother's left a lot of stuff behind.'

Whythehell had she promised that? The clothes are gone, aren't they? She got rid of them herself. Nothing more to find now. Nothing – Celia lowers the napkin from her mouth – except what's inside the locked drawer of her mother's bedside table. Perhaps it's time she started looking for the key; the curved gold-plated handle has been leering at her long enough.

Picking up her knife and fork again, she suddenly becomes aware of the yucca's extraordinary trunk shape. Just below table level it thickens into a bulge twice its normal size, with a cleft down the middle like builders' cleavage. Celia can't help a grin.

'Pardon me . . .'

Angelina nudges her on the arm, 'Hey, he means you.' Her fork is angled to the right, beyond the yucca.

It's the man in the orange shirt. He is leaning towards her, a cigarette between his fingers. His friend's seat is empty apart from the leather jacket. 'Pardon me,' he repeats, 'but weren't you at the Métropole Friday night?'

Celia's heart misses a beat; the Métropole . . . She swallows. Why is he asking her that? Surely Granite Mask couldn't have been him? She'll act dumb, she decides, it's safest, usually.

'Yeah, I kind of went astray,' she admits with a shrug. 'My ordinary clothes must have stuck out a mile.' He's got nice eyes. Violet, almost black. Sultry southern eyes, her mother would have said, and men with such eyes weren't to be trusted: *Better to keep your distance, Celia.*

Celia shifts closer. Until the edge of the seat cuts into her buttocks and she can breathe in his aftershave. Men Only. Franz's favourite. She asks hurriedly, 'So, what did you go as? A pirate? Or were you that Apache swinging his tomahawk?'

Angelina's staring at her sulkily; she has pushed her plate to one side and is winding a coil of hair round and round the fingers of her left hand, pouting a little and in between pouts slowly sipping her Coke.

The man laughs, darts a glance at Angelina before he replies. 'Actually, my pal and I were a couple of devils. Remember us? I thought you were watching . . .' He draws on the cigarette, inhales deeply, his sultry eyes studying her.

The gypsy girl, Celia thinks. For a few breathless seconds it's like she herself had been that girl – *her* flesh spilling over the stocking tops, *her* nipples on display, red and tight as berries, *her* tongue glistening. The image leaves her feeling oddly disjointed. And excited. She frowns at the man and lets her eyes go blank, then plucks at her skirt, pretends to smooth it over her thighs so she can touch herself there unobserved, picturing Alex.

'I was a clairvoyant that night,' Angelina chimes in. 'Never had any peace because everybody wanted their fortunes told. The soldiers were the worst – *mamma mia*! They kept pawing my crystal ball so much it went all cloudy.' She giggles. 'And I'm sure there was a devil in that crowd.' Blinking her lashes in the man's direction, she says, 'Was it you, by any chance?'

'You'd better ask Sergio here.' With a wink to Angelina he blows some smoke rings at his yellow-shirted companion, who's just tossed a packet of Camels on the table.

Celia drinks some of her Rivella. She can feel the heat building up between her legs. Alex, she murmurs to herself, AlexAlexAlex. If she isn't careful, if she doesn't ease those muscles –

'Hey, what's this?' Sergio exclaims. 'A human plant or a planted human?'

Celia relaxes; saved, thanks to a stupid joke.

'Anatomically challenged!' Angelina is never lost for words. Already her hands are on the yucca to feel and fondle the swelling.

The man in the orange shirt is leaning over again: 'Well, Friday night at the Métropole . . . I was watching you too, you see. Especially after that red-caped guy turned up. A bit of advice: tear off the mask next time.' He grins, stubs out his cigarette. 'No offence, okay?'

His remark has jolted Celia. She wasn't aware the incident had attracted attention and is annoyed with him for reminding her. For dragging her fear out into the open so it grows like the yucca, big and knotted and spiky. She hunches her shoulders and looks away into the jungle of ivy and climbers.

'Anyway,' he adds, somewhat doubtful now, his gaze weaving restlessly across her face, from cheekbone to cheekbone, up and down from chin to forehead, forehead to chin. Celia rubs the side of her nose to break the spell. 'Anyway, we'd better head back to the grind. Nice meeting you. The name's Paolo, by the by.' He gets to his feet.

'I'm Celia,' she says, trying a smile. 'And . . . thanks.'

'Pleasure.' Paolo's violet eyes are smouldering down into hers.

As the men pull on their leather jackets, Celia glimpses Angelina's hand squash a fluttery piece of napkin into Sergio's cigarette packet.

17

THE AFTERNOON AT the office passes enjoyably enough. Several jewellers phone to verify items on the new price list, and Celia completes a tricky matching job for a brooch designed by Herr Q, as he is called behind his back. Q for Queen.

Herr Q is in his late fifties and one of Zurich's best-known goldsmiths. Hearsay has it there's a lift at the back of his plush business premises which goes straight up to his bedroom. A bedroom that beggars belief, if rumour can be trusted. With goldleaf mouldings on furniture and ceiling, solid gold handles on doors and drawers in the athletic shapes of his former lovers, gemstones adorning the edges of the mirror-fronted wardrobe, and a headboard that in moonlight provides enough sparkle to read by, courtesy of the clusters of small diamonds, each of them individually wired to an alarm. Wild rumours, but Celia likes them.

For this particular *création* Herr Q has requested green, red and pink tourmalines, all in mixed cut, and she carefully puts together a selection, though not without slipping him three parti-coloured stones, including a large watermelon type in trap cut – for a bit of extra flavour, as it were.

Angelina is all smiles, a bright young looking-forward-to-life-after-work smile. Her hair tied back so it crackles like a bundle of brushwood about to catch fire, she hums snatches of Madonna songs while weighing a consignment of cat's-eye cabochons quickly and accurately. Sergio, the ex-devil from the Casino Mall

Restaurant, had phoned her immediately she got back to the office after lunch, and they've arranged to meet at seven. It's the night of her boyfriend's evening classes, which means he won't be free till after ten. Normally, this pisses Angelina off no end, but today it suits her just *perfetto*.

At break time Angelina operates their new Comtesse de Luxe in the reception area like an old hand. Tipping coffee into the filter, she startles Celia, who'd been thinking of Alex again, almost feeling him inside, by suddenly talking about her own mother and how devastated *she*'d been at the death, two years earlier, of *her* mother. The old lady had apparently shared the house with them ever since Angelina was little. The girl is trying to be friendly, and Celia humours her.

'Now Mamma has taken to visiting Nonna's grave once a week like clockwork – same day, same time as when she died,' Angelina is saying. 'But for quite a while before that we weren't even allowed to use Nonna's name. If we did, Mamma would burst into tears and rush off. One night she left a pot of spaghetti on the hob and it boiled dry. Like a burnt-out bird's nest it looked afterwards. And the pan was wrecked.'

She pauses, fiddling with her crucifix, obviously hoping for a reply. Celia hazards a rather mechanical, 'Yes, that's to be expected,' without turning her head. She isn't really referring to anything specific. Unless she has the blackened dried-out pasta in mind. She is staring at a dichroic pink-and-red tourmaline, holding it up to the light till her eyes begin to hurt.

'Sometimes, though, death brings relief too.'

The voice sounds disembodied, far away, and carries on of its own accord:

'Imagine you yourself are that pot. Simmering away. Steaming. Never allowed off the heat. Things getting scorched inside. Then *pouf*! goes the switch. And you find you're half-cracked by now. All in a tingle. Cooling down very, very slowly. At long last.'

Only when the voice stops does Celia realise it's her own.

In the silence that follows, the air around them seems to quiver as if it, too, was cooling down, until the Comtesse erupts in a sharp series of hisses, spurting hot milk.

Drawn by the noise, Eric is making his way through from the inner office, with Lapis dashing past him, tail going like a windmill in a gale.

Eric doesn't walk, Celia reflects, he waddles. His expensively cut trousers balloon about his belly, then flap deceptively over his old man's stick legs. An eternal bachelor who's got nothing better to do than read up on stones and more stones, with the odd Fémina chocolate melting on his tongue. Or sit glued to one of his microscopes, ogling at the cleavage of some gemstone or the drillhole of a pearl. Poor sad man. If it wasn't for Lapis, he'd probably have fossilised ages ago, right there in his king-size swivel chair. Just like 'Eric the Opalised Pliosaur' from Australia, dead for the last hundred million years at least, whose skeleton picture she's got pinned up above her desk.

At the moment, however, Eric the man is very much alive and brandishing a recent edition of the *Journal of Gemmology*.

'You should have a look at these abstracts, ladies,' he says. 'Very entertaining, very. Some of it old hat of course, but still. Ever heard of cat's-eye rutilated quartz? Or the Sweet Home Mine in Colorado? The ancient supercontinent of Gondwana-land? Well, it's all in here.' He taps his reading glasses on the cover of the journal and chuckles, 'Here for the taking.'

Celia nods and smiles, thinking, *ladies*, mygod!

Lapis, meanwhile, has leapt on to his favourite leather seat by the window and stands grinning his tongue off, trembling with excitement at the biscuits to come.

Quarter past four and Celia can't wait any longer. She must catch Alex before he leaves. They have to talk. Work something out. She'd like to do it again with him, soon, preferably on the bed for warmth and bounce. Or, even better, in the bath . . . Not that she intends to stir up trouble for him on the home front. She considers their affair more a kind of interim arrangement. For a split second the man in the fluorescent orange shirt flashes through her mind, Paolo he said his name was. Perhaps she could ask Angelina to suss his friend, and get the phone number off him. The mere idea makes her go weak at the knees.

Earlier than usual she steps off the bus at the pink housing estate, thanks to Eric's gratitude at having her back and partly to his – pardonable – misconception that she was really asking for time off to grieve in the privacy of her own four walls, at length and at her leisure. It's freezing cold and Celia half-runs, half-slips along the ice-and-confetti-flecked pavement. She can hear Dr Caveng's pills rattle about the envelope in her coat pocket. Behind Bänninger's plate-glass window Deli-Doris is see-sawing at a chunk of cheese with a big square blade.

Alex – she simply *must* see him.

No sign of the van round the back, but the lights are on in the flat, thankgod. There are dark silhouettes on the walls where the shutters used to be. She breaks with her ritual of smelling the winter jasmine by the gatepost, whips open her letter box, grabs the paper, two letters and a postcard. Her breath comes quick and jagged now as she hurries towards the house, and Alex.

The assistant has just finished locking up when she throws open the street door. He grins down at her, reinserts the key and says, 'Hello and goodbye. Boss left at noon, with the rest of the shutters. Felt ill he said.' He ushers her in, tipping his baseball cap like a second-rate hotel porter. 'See you tomorrow.'

'Yes, thanks,' is all Celia manages to croak as she pushes past him into the freshly crimson-papered mouth of the corridor. So that's that. ILL, for chrissake! Trying to avoid her, more like. For an instant she is tempted to dial the Lehmanns' home number. Instead she pours herself a large vodka, squeezes a blood orange into it because she hates tomato juice, and begins to sip. The coward.

The postcard is from Nita and shows a female snowboarder in mid-jump, with the sun star-splintered behind her head in a kitschy gentian-blue sky. 'Dear Cel,' it says. 'In case you fancy a change and some bracing Alpine air after all you've been through, you're very welcome up here at Albula. Hope you're okay. Love and kisses.'

If things continue the way they're going, she might very well take Nita up on this. Celia props the card against the vase with the black tulips.

The heftier of the two letters, a recycled grey envelope with the imprint of the town council's logo, contains the cantonal and federal vote proposals for the first quarter; maybe she will vote, maybe she won't. Celia drops it on the pile of correspondence yet to be dealt with, on the worktop above the rubbish bin. The other letter looks nice and private. The address rather scrawly, the postmark illegible. A *message* now from the black-tulip man? Or from Alex?

Dream on, she ridicules herself as she unfolds the Opium-scented thick cream-coloured paper. A small photocopy flutters to the floor, speckled black and white, and full of whorls, with a shape like a newt outlined in red. Jasmin writing to say, hey, it was great talking to you on Saturday and she's got a little secret to reveal: she's PREGNANT! Thirteen weeks into her term so it's safe to announce to the world (at least as safe as can be). Tests and scans fine so far. Lovely ultrasound picture (enlargement enclosed), a bit grainy, though quite recognisably a thumbsucking little girl, beautiful – no? Name under wraps of course – have a guess! Birthday date all set: 15 August (Caesarean after that ordeal with Igor Junior). Baptism fixed for the second Sunday in October. Please keep that day free and your fingers crossed!

Christ, so well ordered; Celia drains her vodka in one long gulp, then giggles until she gets the hiccups and, still hiccupping, prepares herself another, no orange juice this time but a thimbleful of tonic, for maximum effect.

She won't be in the mood for reading tonight, she can tell, and dear old Eric's Christmas present, *Gemstone-Smuggling in the Twentieth Century*, will have to remain shelved beside the jar of colourful Pasta Festa *fatto a mano* from Angelina and the New Zealand wine-making kit. A quick glance at the paper, a blast of MTV while she's having a bite to eat, that's as far as *she* can plan right now. Alex, damnhim!

The phone starts ringing and the echo swoops along the corridor, *brrr . . . brrr . . . brrr,* penetrating doorways and rooms with a crimson insistence that angers and frightens her. She huddles up so tight to the old-fashioned kitchen radiator she can feel the heat from its metal ribs scoring her back. *Brrr . . . brrr . . .*

Once the flat has fallen silent again, she detaches herself and her singed cashmere sweater almost proudly, as if she's won a reprieve. Jasmin's letter lying open on the table reminds her of Dr Caveng's pills and, having fetched the envelope from her coat, she shakes two on to her palm, washes them down with vodka. Pop one and stop one, she can't help thinking, with more giggles. Then, glass in hand, she wanders over into her bedroom. Takes off her skirt and sweater for the hell of it, and switches on the nephrite lamp. She might as well inspect her gemstone collection.

Over an hour later she wakes up, her nose buried in the velour of the inlay tray. Her forehead is throbbing, the skin puckered from the beads of rock crystal and the Australian boulder-opal cabochon (its shifting ripples of colour are the closest she'll ever get to a Klimt original). There's a faint tickly dustiness in her nostrils, strangely familiar . . .

That's when the memory ambushes her: a blazing summer's day with the promise of cool lake water and smooth hot shingle, the dim shuttered lounge, carpet-musty – and terror. That old upside-down feeling coming back to haunt her, with a vengeance.

the top of her head searing hot, grazing the floor –

sweat and tears on her face and the blood pumping and pounding within –

SMACK HER! –

her mother's hands on her ankles like leg-irons –

the room juddering around her –

no air –

watery shadows slashed by sunlight –

my fault –

her grandmother's feet tiny, out of reach –

then her gnarled fingers, much too close –

and, cloying and choking everything else, the hard unswallowable soreness in her throat –

The memory still makes her flinch. After a pause she wipes some specks of dust off the sardonyx, the first gemstone she'd ever bought herself, banded a delicate red, brown and white.

Next to it, the ruby sits in its corner compartment with what appears like a smug glow.

As she leans forward to have a closer look, some flyaway strands of her hair frizzle out and cling to the small tourmaline figurine stowed at the back of the inlay tray. Celia laughs out loud – the stone has become electrically charged through the heat and pressure of her head. It's carved in the shape of a woman. A naked woman with voluptuous curves, her minuscule nipples erect.

Then Celia suddenly becomes serious. Yes, she realises, with a shiver that flits all over her body, yes, she is no longer a child. No longer that little girl at the mercy of her mother's grip, and her grandmother's excuses. YES!

18

THURSDAY COMES. Celia is lying in wait for Alex by the kitchen balcony door when the van pulls up below. That's how desperate she is. Split right down the middle; pain on one side, longing on the other. She'd been skimming over yesterday's paper to distract herself, but the reports and pictures of ferocious avalanches in the mountains – the worst in decades – don't help: homes and trees razed to the ground like so many doll's houses and papier-mâché woods, covered under masses of bilious-looking snow; people buried alive, freezing and suffocating slowly to death. Outside it's snowing again, flakes upon dirt-yellow flakes falling straight as bead curtains through the fading glow of the streetlamps. And Alex hasn't come.

'Turns out the boss has a stomach bug,' Dominc tells her. 'He'll be doing the shutters though. On and off, anyway.' He laughs, then gives himself a good scratch behind the ear and saunters off, to do whatever. Celia doesn't care.

It's driving her crazy, this silence and the subterfuges on Alex's part. She decides to take the bus again today, doesn't trust herself with the car. Her foot might slip on the accelerator, or get trapped under the brake pedal. It's happened before when she was upset.

She is still shaking the snowflakes off her coat and stamping her boots on the doormat just inside Reception when Angelina pounces on her with the words, 'A fucking fiasco, Celia, pardon the language.' Referring, it would seem, to her evening out with Sergio.

Celia smiles, waves a hand sharply as if to say, now don't you worry, but really wielding an imaginary dagger: why hasn't bloodybloodybloody Alex sent her at least a note? Then her attention is caught by Angelina saying 'Bluebeard Club'. All Celia can think of is the villain who tricked and murdered his wives, and she stabs him with an extra-hard thrust.

'Nice place,' Angelina continues. 'I'd never been before. But I didn't fancy the show much, with those girls gyrating all over the stage. "I can do better than that," I told Sergio, "just you watch me." Got up from my chair and peeled off my blouse, real slow.' She giggles, scowls, sneers, like an actress practising facial expressions. 'I'd a crop-top on underneath, so no harm done. But then one of the waitresses comes rushing across, almost trips over her tongue stud, says they don't allow this kind of behaviour and would I sit down again. Or go. So I did: sat down, drank up, and went. Sergio never knew what hit him.' She laughs. 'And I was in time for the end of Kurt's evening classes. Lucky, no?' Her laughter sounds brittle, and she lets her hair flop over her forehead. It occurs to Celia that now she won't be able to obtain Paolo's number, won't be able to console herself with the violet promise of his eyes.

No mention is made of the silk handkerchief, and frankly, Celia isn't in the mood. Nothing exciting happens all morning, hardly any phone calls. Handsome Henry won't be back until tomorrow, and Eric waddles off at the first chimes of the eleven-o'clock bells to meet a new supplier for lunch and 'subsequent negotiations', leaving Lapis behind as an office responsibility. Eric will be away all afternoon, 'liaising' between sips of the best local *Beerliwy*, Celia knows, because he'd taken pains to soften her and Angelina up beforehand with several of his Fémina chocolates.

Walking the dog is the apprentice's job, strictly speaking. But Celia decides to take a chance; it's the perfect excuse for her to pay a certain someone a visit. She has checked the address in the electronic phone book.

At quarter to three, their usual coffee break, she whistles for Lapis and puts on her coat. 'Back soon,' she calls to Angelina, over the racket Lapis has started up, barking like a creaky old door. 'You could do a bit of dusting afterwards; listen to some music if you want.' She smiles generously, feeling mean and selfish when the heavy security door shudders locked behind her.

Madame conferring a favour, Angelina thinks, with a grimace at the pomegranate red she'd watched fissuring out from Celia's lips as she smiled. Her espresso is ready now and she sinks into the softness of the nearest leather seat.

With Lapis firmly on his lead, Celia catches a southbound bus and gets off near the ghastly towerblock of Anders Cantonal Hospital, on a hillside built over with the big villas and estates of the wealthy. It has stopped snowing and gone bone-chillingly cold. A grey day that blots out the panorama of the Swabian Mountains behind Seerücken Hill, the long low hump that conceals Lake Constance.

Celia puts up the collar of her coat, presses her elbows against the loose folds of fabric to hold in the warmth. Lapis seems happy enough snuffling along by her side, marking their steps with yellow trickles every so often. But then, halfway up the mostly residential street, just as she's laid eyes on the sign *Painters & Decorators* in the same curlicued writing as on the van, he embarks on a fierce tug of war.

'No!' Celia yells, panicking. Pulling and jerking desperately in the direction of the sign. 'Bad dog!'

Next thing she's slipping and grasping at the slats of a wooden garden fence, steadying herself in time to see him charge down a lane some metres back, his lead whiffling up fine clouds of powder snow.

She runs after him. Alternately swearing under her breath and shouting cajolingly, 'Lapis, come here! Lapis!' Slithering past a girl and a placid black labrador. Then two boys who're pulling up their bobsleighs. 'Chop-chop!' they yell and their laughter pelts her with the force of gritty snowballs, follows her all the way to where Lapis is standing panting and slavering and being patted, his lead looped round the wrist of a sturdy old woman.

'I thought there'd be someone looking for him,' she says regretfully. She has guarded eyes. 'Such a nice dog.'

'Thank you,' Celia gasps.

'Oh, no bother. I love dogs. We used to have them all the time on the farm before the son took over. Dogs are so much nicer than humans, don't you think?'

Taken aback by the old woman's frankness, Celia only manages a nod. Then she reaches for the lead and gently unwinds it from the broad blue-veined wrist, repeating, 'Thank you.'

To Lapis she hisses, once they're out of earshot, 'No more biscuits for you!' At the word 'biscuits' he pricks up his ears and starts to grin. 'No,' Celia says. 'No. Stupid dog.'

They carry on walking down the hill to the bus stop by the grammar school – what else is there to do?

Eric's 'negotiations' with his new supplier had lasted well into the evening and it's twenty to seven when Celia finally unlatches her garden gate. Snow falls off the wrought-iron bars, icy cold. She stoops over the jasmine for a moment, but the scent seems to have frozen within the yellow hearts of its flowers. Then she notices that the little door of her letter box is ajar: inside there's something flat and silvery on top of her daily paper, like a slice of the moon.

A box of chocolates – Lindt Swiss thins, her favourites!

Alex wouldn't know that though, would he? Anyway, the box is too light for chocolates – it feels empty.

She begins to joggle off the lid.

'Haven't seen you in a while!' Rolf, her neighbour, is striding towards her from the house, dressed in the smoke-grey overalls of the sugar factory with the inevitable black biker's jacket on top, and heavy-duty boots that make the thin layer of snow on the path spurt up before him.

Celia hastily shoves the lid back down.

'How're you doing?' he asks. His eyes dance and pierce. They've always reminded Celia of polished iridescent obsidian, like those American Indian arrowheads she'd seen in one of Eric's books.

'All right, thanks.' She indicates the box in her hand to deflect the keenness of his gaze: 'It's a present, I hope!' She smiles.

'Well, I won't tell anyone.'

The next instant he's bent so close she can smell the machine oil off his overalls. She isn't too sure what he means and prays to goodness he didn't hear anything the other evening, with Alex.

'What happened to your beauty spot?' she asks, more bluntly than she'd intended, and points to the space between his nose and upper lip where his toothbrush moustache has shrunk to near-invisibility.

'Ah, *that*,' he says, unfazed by her abrupt change of subject. 'A new party game we played: I shave you, you shave me. You should try. It's good fun.' He winks, laughs. 'I'd better get my skates on. Night shift. Car doing okay?'

'Yes, fine, I just took the bus this morning. Too snowy. Sugar doing okay?'

Now they're both laughing. But as Rolf scrunches off along the street, the phrase he used earlier starts skittering round Celia's skull like a curse: goodfun-goodfun-goodfun. A blackbird is hopping about the feeder in the ash tree, chirping feebly at the heaps of yesterday's husks. Celia seizes the newspaper and clamps the Lindt box under her arm with sudden irritation. She doesn't want to see what's in it; Alex has kept her waiting and now his present will have to wait for her.

A microwaved lasagne and half a bottle of Bardolino later, Celia is ready to survey her lounge. Passing the corridor mirror she sticks her tongue out like a saucy girl, then scoops up the chocolate box from the telephone table.

She won't open it yet, though; she'll tease herself a bit longer.

When she flicks on the light, the room springs alive; its deep purple hues vibrate around her as if in physical embrace. The furniture, too, seems to be affected by the unaccustomed intensity of colour. Without its protective sheets now and pushed more or less back into place, it appears smaller and duller, almost cowering. Celia smiles to herself. Given time, it will no doubt adapt to its altered surroundings; the rosewood bureau will once again glow softly in its corner, the sofa and armchairs uncramp themselves and the standard lamp straighten up. That she might end up having to buy new furniture never even crosses her mind.

Slowly she wanders around the room, the Lindt box half-forgotten in her hand; she tinkles her fingernails on the amethyst radiator panels, tests the firmness of the painted lining paper with her thumb, runs her palm over the window frame's gloss, slippery as topaz. She has just rested her flushed face against the pane when a bus comes swooshing along. It's empty except for the New-Age student couple from the apartment block opposite, whom she's observed on various early-morning occasions scuttling off towards the station with bulging shoulder bags, having missed the bus. Now, arms interlinked, they're standing by the double exit doors, eager to jump off, and for a moment it seems to Celia that they're looking directly at her.

Their stare acts like an unspoken command and she flings herself down into the sofa cushions, tears the lid off the box before that stubborn inner voice can stop her.

Inside is a passionflower, rather dusty, made of pale-purple silk.

Thankgod it isn't a tulip! How sweet of Alex! Celia laughs, delighted. A flower to commemorate their half-hour of passion! Then she laughs a little more, disillusionment kicking in fast. How absolutely touchingly mind-bogglingly naive of the man!

Because she knows better, of course. Not passion, but suffering.

It was the summer Walter started his apprenticeship and went to live at the Schlosshotel that her mother had explained to her the plant's symbolism. 'Christ's Passion,' she said one day as she and Celia were walking past the flowers growing rampant on their neighbour's fence, 'Look,' and taking Celia's index finger, she made her touch one.

They'd counted ten petals, one for each faithful apostle. The corona felt tickly, not at all as she'd imagined a crown of thorns. The five stamens left golden-brown streaks on her skin, like ancient dried-up blood. But she'd baulked at the hammer and the three nails, and snatched her hand away. 'Silly Cel, they can't hurt you!' Her mother had giggled and poked the ovary herself before sliding her fingers up the three round-headed styles. There'd been a triumphant gleam in her eyes.

The following day Celia had mustered up courage; and for weeks afterwards she would dawdle by that fence, select a flower and rub her fingers up and down inside it, from ovary to stigma, stigma to ovary.

She became intrigued by tales of plants thriving on pain. The white lily springing from Eve's tears when, driven out of Paradise, she found herself pregnant. The violet created from the tears of the nymph who'd been transformed into a heifer and couldn't bear to eat the coarse grass. The hyacinth blossoming from the blood of Apollo's beloved Hyacinthus, killed in a game of quoits. The fruit of the mulberry tree turning red from Pyramus and Thisbe's mingled blood. The tulip – symbol of the Perfect Lover – growing from the tear drops of a spurned Persian youth who cried his heart out in the desert (*red* tulips, *not* black ones, Celia is quick to reassure herself now). And, most awesome of all, the mandrake – part man, part drake – also called the gallow plant because it was said to sprout from the semen of hanged men.

The idea of semen had repelled and attracted Celia; in conjunction with hangings, it proved simply irresistible.

The librarian in town, a small thin man with flitting eyes behind wire-rimmed glasses, grinned and tapped the side of his nose when Celia and Lily asked him about gallows and executions in the area. 'Is that what they're teaching you in school these days?' he asked. Then, just as they were about to slink off, he beckoned to them. Lowered his voice: 'I'll see what I can do. Mind you put a volume of Grimm's or Andersen's on top in the reading room, all right?' He gave his nose another tap, and they smiled their most alluring schoolgirl smiles.

With the help of a photocopy the librarian had made for them of an old map from 1825, they located the precise place later that afternoon, trudging through the noise and dust of the construction work going on for the new motorway along the common. But they couldn't find a single mandrake, let alone any telltale stumps of wood or special atmosphere. Just a few picnic benches and some soot-blackened stones round a grate. The only thing that dripped on the ground here now was the grease from sausages fried on hot summer days.

Celia pinches the silk passionflower between her thumb and forefinger to lift it free of the box, then blows off the dust, realising at the same instant that it isn't dust at all: bloody Alex has given her an artificial passionflower covered in ashes!

19

THE ALARM CLOCK goes off much too soon. Celia is still looking for Alex-the-coward who's been eluding her all night. The man of her dreams: taking cover behind the arsenal of jars, tubes, pots and bottles in the Beauty Room vanity cabinet, lurking inside her mother's shiny walnut wardrobe where he's held in check momentarily by snakes and the advancing-and-retreating-and-advancing armies of hemlines, then again barricaded behind piles of suede shoes at the bottom of an antique oak cupboard, holed up in the sloppy roll of the white lounge carpet, or camouflaged with old lace curtains, like a ghost. But when the alarm comes on a second time, more strident now and louder, Alex simply vanishes into thin air. Nothing remains, neither curtains nor carpet nor shoes nor dresses, not even a single eyeliner in its jar.

Only a solitary passionflower, ashy pale.

Quarter to seven already. Celia forces the image from her mind and gets out of bed, showers, dresses, prepares breakfast. On the local radio station the announcer predicts 'a crisp glorious day so don't forget your gloves and sunglasses and, if you're lucky enough, your skis, because snow conditions are *ab*so*lu*tely *fa*bulous. But remember: never beyond the demarcated areas. Flumserberge and the Toggenburg report record levels . . .'

As she bites into her *Weggli* roll, a blob of raspberry jam lands on her napkin, bright red. That's when she remembers her promise to Angelina. Damn that stupid handkerchief! Stuffing the rest of the *Weggli* into her mouth, she pads over into the spare room. The drawer handle on her mother's bedside table gives her a crooked grin. Of course: she needs to find the key first. Back in the kitchen she gulps down more coffee. Closes her eyes, trying to picture her mother's perfectly manicured fingers feeling for that key. Somewhere soft, she thinks, soft, innocuous and within easy reach, unlikely to have ever aroused her own interest or curiosity.

She pauses, hovering. Then, like a sleepwalker, she is being steered out into the corridor. The cleaning cupboard next to the bathroom door seems to spring open all by itself, the lid to lift from the old wicker sewing basket with the gallantry of a gentleman's hat.

And there it is, buried under reels of white and pastel-coloured threads, glittering, gold-plated, its bow like a wedding ring, its bit resembling a neatly trimmed beard.

She doesn't hear the van getting parked in the backyard, the slam of the street door out front, the heavy tread on the wooden stairs, made by one pair of feet. Doesn't hear the key inserted into the lock of her front door, the steps approaching along the corridor, halting briefly at the threshold to the kitchen where muted radio voices are discussing the refugee crisis in the former Yugoslavia. Doesn't hear the steps turning sharply right, continuing towards her.

She is on her knees, the bedside drawer with its honeycomb of cards and jewellery boxes on the floor beside her. She's crouched over a large piece of water-and-dirt-stained paper which had been folded up like a map. Except that there are no agglomerations of black dots suggesting homes and people, no green swathes of woods. Merely a tangle of lines shaped like a bat in flight, and printed names such as Devil's Wall, Nirvana, Witch's Cauldron, Styx, Nile Valley, Titans' Tunnel, *Galerie des 1001 nuits*, Angels' Fort, Lake Pagoda, Tunnel of Hope, Coral Gallery. Though that's not everything. The margins are crammed with smudgy large-scale plans and scribbles in pencil, most of them quite indecipherable, and arrows pointing at the bat shape (*found two large specimens of niphargus, lost glove, perfect for radio reception, fifth handhold missing, replace rope, slipped here ~~twice~~ three times, dammit* are some of the entries she can make out).

Celia's fingers are brushing along the edges of the paper. She has recognised the handwriting; it's identical with the inscriptions in her Schellenursli picture books. So *this* used to belong to her father. *This* was his personal map of the Hölloch. Then she goes rigid, her fingers poised in mid-air. Why did he leave the map behind? Surely, he'd have taken it with him on that last expedition? So whyonearth didn't he?

All at once she becomes aware of a presence in the room. Someone is here with her. Someone . . . The map falls to the floor as she swings her body round sharply, jerking upright, hair flying, her right hand balled into a fist.

'Alex!' Her hand uncrumples slowly, like the bud of a flower. 'How –? What –? You must be early.' She has sunk down on the mattress of the bed, her stomach in a sudden flutter. She tries not to gaze at him. Forheavensake, woman, she admonishes herself, he is the bastard that gave you an imitation flower, and a grubby one at that! Don't let him put one over on you again!

'Or you late,' he says with a smile that would have appeared easy from several metres away. But he is standing in front of her now, close enough to touch her if he wanted to. He'd been spying on her for a good couple of minutes, fascinated by her total absorption, debating with himself what to do. Whether to clear his throat or cough, rap on the door or sneak back down the corridor, then make one hell of a noisy entrance. They need to talk. At least, he does.

Celia has decided to ignore him and glances down at her watch. Shit, nearly twenty to eight!

'I won't delay you, Frau Roth – I mean, Celia,' Alex falters, his eyes straying to the sheet of paper she's dropped and which is lying tented half on the carpet, half on the drawer. 'I just wanted to apologise for the other night. I haven't told anyone, don't worry, and Dominic's away at the workshop, finishing the shutters.' The paper tent is slipping, collapsing under the weight of his stare. 'Celia, I'm really sorry. I shouldn't have taken advantage of you. I promise it won't happen again. I must have been mad . . .'

Celia's mouth twitches, but she can't get a word out. Her tongue feels bloated and heavy, dead.

He fiddles with his curls, then finally looks at her, noticing a crumb stuck to her cheek like an untidy birthmark. 'If you prefer to employ another firm, I can understand. In that case, your advance payment will be refunded in full. Compliments of –'

She's slapped him across the face without warning. His hand's been knocked aside and there are a few blond hairs caught between his fingers. He can taste a trickle of blood and the soft sponginess of flesh.

'Paying me off, are you?' Celia is shaking with anger and hurt. 'Ashes to ashes, dust to dust, that kind of thing?' The breakfast crumb's gone, and she has begun to tear off the embroidered black blouse she's wearing. The bra is pretty much see-through but she slings it after the blouse just the same.

'Well?' she demands, swanking up to him, her breasts out. Feeling powerful now. Fuck him and his pin-prick pupils, his ashy passionflower. Tohell with shame. For the moment everything's been swept away by this flash flood of power.

Alex wipes his lips with deliberate slowness. Mad, he keeps thinking, mad, mad, mad, and moves towards the door. He doesn't want to blow a fuse, never struck a woman before, and he won't start now.

The phone is ringing. 'I'll get it,' he shouts, on his way already. 'Probably your boss. What shall I say?'

She doesn't answer.

He picks up the receiver. 'Hello, Lehmann speaking. I'm –'

'Could I have a word with Frau Roth, please?'

'Oh yes, I'll –'

'Wait a minute, no need to call her. Tell you what. Ask her whether she liked my little present. Thanks.' A click, followed by the dialling tone.

Bloody odd, but none of his business; Alex replaces the handset quietly, to buy a little more time. His initial rage has evaporated and instead he's feeling stunned. Certainly not intimidated, not in the slightest. No woman ever intimidates *him*. In the oval mirror he scrutinises his lips, satisfying himself that the cuts can hardly be seen and that the faintly numb puffiness isn't unattractive, on the contrary . . . He grins at himself and pictures Celia's full breasts.

Afterwards he examines the new crimson wallpaper, running the flats of his hands over it with professional pride. Dominic's done a damn fine job; the join's practically invisible. The overall effect, though, is rather grim, like being inside a body. It reminds him of how his mother used to threaten him with the Jonah story whenever he'd done something wrong, and how the whale's terrible stomach-red would pursue him into his dreams.

When Alex returns to the spare room, Celia is lying on the bed, her face buried in her arms.

'On the phone just now they –'

'I'm sorry,' she mumbles, remaining quite motionless. 'I didn't mean to hit you. Or insult you. But that bloody flower was the last thing I needed . . . Sorry, Alex.'

As if on cue the room is suddenly swamped with winter sunlight from the two corner windows, bringing a gleam to her bare skin, pearly and fragile.

'What flower?' Alex fingers his swollen lips and admires the seahorse curve of her spine from a safe distance.

In reply she states simply: 'This was my mother's bed,' and her arms lunge out to hug the mattress. Like a swimmer in danger of drowning, he thinks. Hasn't she heard him? No, not a swimmer, he corrects himself: a mermaid. Naked to the waist, dark damp tresses, legs twined together into a fish's tail by the longish skirt.

She's raised her body a little to pull something from underneath. 'And this,' she says, 'is my father's old map.' She waves it in the air like a sail and the water image is complete. Alex smiles in spite of himself; that fall the other night must have cracked her head all right. Then he tells her about the phone call.

'Damn, I ought to have known.' Celia sits up abruptly and stares at the empty wall where the waxplant has left smears of sticky nectar and dust. 'How stupidstupidstupid of me!'

Alex is about to shrug dubiously when he sees her glance down at her breasts.

'Of course I won't change decorators,' she says as if to herself. 'Why should I do that?' A small pause, then her eyes are on him, seaweed-green: 'Unless you want me to? Actually, I loved being with you, loved every second of it. No question of you taking advantage.' She blushes, laughs. 'I guess I'd better get dressed.'

There's an intimacy between them, tangibly awkward.

Eventually Alex reaches for the piece of paper she's put back on the bed. 'Map?' he asks, 'Map of what?' and makes a show of studying it to screen her from his view.

The radio noises from the kitchen seem to crackle with static and fill the room.

Her blouse safely buttoned up, Celia inches over to him and says, 'He was crazy about caves, my father. Went down into the Hölloch one day and never came back . . .' Tears are in her voice all at once and she sniffles, uses her sleeve, then both sleeves, hiding her face in her hair. 'I'm sorry, I'm just being silly. No use crying now, after all these years. I hardly knew him anyway . . .' And to herself she adds, hardly knew my mother either.

Alex's hand is on her arm, warm and strong and stroking her gently. 'Easy now. Easy,' she hears him whisper. So he hasn't given up on her altogether, thankgodforthat. He's produced a packet of tissues from his overalls and started dabbing at her wet cheeks, murmuring, 'I can understand. I lost my mother seven years ago and it's still painful.' He doesn't elaborate and for a moment they're silent, and very close.

Finally Celia asks, 'Do you mind?' With her fingertips she traces his sore-looking lips, then quickly kisses him. 'I do like you,' she says, 'a lot.'

By the time she arrives at the office, having taken the Golf to save at least a few minutes, it's after ten and they're all there, enjoying the Friday patisseries. She had rung earlier to explain how she'd been held up because of a misunderstanding with the decorators painting her flat.

Salesman Martin's eternal-boy crew cut seems to have got even shorter since she last saw him, on the day before her mother died. 'My heartfelt condolences, Celia dear,' he says between dainty bites from a tartlet *aux vermicelles*. She thanks him, trying in vain to ignore the wriggles of chestnut purée on the pastry, greyish-brown, like earth intermixed with snow . . .

When Angelina offers her the plate of cakes, she waves it away with a smile that feels all lopsided and trembling. *Don't cry, silly Cel*, someone says inside her head, in her mother's inflection. Angelina is still looking at her and Celia hastily pretend-pats her stomach and nods towards Lapis, whose salivating mouth has already slid into position on the arm of his leather seat.

Yes, her mother had wanted a burial; now Celia almost wishes she'd been cremated. Ash is so much less real, so much less *corporeal.* One breath of wind and it ceases to exist.

'Got the colours for your rooms sorted then, have you, Celia?' Eric asks, startling her back into the world of life, and work.

The rest of the day is encrusted with gemstones – an order of diamonds (Piqué II and III) and another of turquoise cabochons for a manufacturer of exclusive fashion jewellery, some weighing and cross-checking to get the annual stocktaking under way, and a request from Herr Q for a couple more tourmalines, 1 ct. each, mixed cut, dark *green*, please (the two blue-and-green specimens had been promptly returned by courier, but not the watermelon type, much to Celia's surprise, and satisfaction).

Encrusted with gemstones set in thick layers of gossip or, in Celia's case, fuzzy dreams of Alex. Alex with a dribble of blood on his mouth; Alex holding her father's map to hide behind; Alex smiling back at her, saying, 'I like you too,' and the tip of his tongue touching hers, very lightly; Alex sucking at her lips, his Vandyke rubbing up against her chin; Alex lying on her mother's old bed, fully clothed except for the overalls on the floor and the unzipped jeans she's leaning over (no time for belt buckles now), teasing his hard-on first with her hair, then with a lick, then another and another, swift and darting and making him groan, grab her head . . .

Things had veered wildly out of control after this. It was only once she'd cleaned her teeth, washed her face and was bent over the bath, sluicing off the shampoo, that she began to regain a sense of herself. The first clear image was an upside-down one of Alex – standing barefoot in the doorway in just his Levi's, his chest and round thin-nosed face tinged crimson by the sunlight slanting in through the narrow arched window at the end of the corridor.

While he stood there waiting for her to finish rinsing her hair, he kept brandishing something she couldn't quite see, and shouted, 'Found this in the lounge. How about one before you're off, Celia?'

That's when she recognised the silvery chocolate box, and gasped. After that business with the ash, she'd stuffed the silk flower back in, squashed down the lid and thrown the lot on to the coffee table – sick at heart. But now that she knew Alex had nothing to do with it, she couldn't very well go on playing her game. Or could she? Carefully draping one of the freshly laundered Beauty Room towels round her head, she coaxed, 'Mm, yes, open it.'

And he did. Started to exclaim, 'What the hell –?' as a few wispy-grey flakes drifted to the floor, then concluded in a much calmer tone: 'So *this* is it, the "little present" your caller was talking about. Your "flower". Want to tell me?'

Alex is looking at her even now, though his eyes seem a lot darker suddenly and not needle-sharp either.

'Celia?' a voice says, but it isn't his.

And again, a bit louder, 'Celia, are you okay?'

Martin's voice. His head craned forward, he grins at her from the other side of her desk. She notices the *Gemmologists' Compendium* in his left hand and a flicker of reflections coming from his right. He must have tried flashing one of Angelina's little mirrors, counting on her vanity to spring to attention.

She blinks. 'Fine, yes.'

'God, you were miles away!' Chortling, he slips the blue mirror back under the clasp inside the book. Then he says, 'Eric's asked me to do a spot of research for him, but this editon here is years out of date. Maybe you could show me some websites?' With a wink he adds, 'Angelina is busy – strictly professional, of course.' He points to the reception area where the girl's brown hair is cascading over two pairs of shoulders, hers and Handsome Henry's, as they pore over what appears to be a very tiny magazine indeed.

Celia smiles at him: 'No problem.' She logs on, banishing Alex and the passionflower from her thoughts – for the moment, at any rate.

20

UNCLE GODFREY'S HOME-HELP stares, mouse-faced: 'Goodness, Frau Roth, what are *you* doing here? Some warning and I'd have bought more food . . .'

Her tone is too shrill and she seems nervous without reason, guilty almost. But perhaps Celia only imagines it. A classic example of projection, as her friend Jasmin would have said, going into therapy mode, and she'd probably be right because, yes, Celia hasn't been to see the old man in months.

Managing to fake a smile, she says, 'Well, hello, Frau Keller. Is Uncle in?' A superfluous question; of course her uncle's in. He can't go anywhere much on his own any more. 'Don't worry, I won't be staying for supper.'

Briskly, she tries brushing past and inside, but Mouse Face proves astonishingly strong. Her thin arms shoot out, wiry as a climber's rope, and bar the way. 'Now, just a moment, please.' The 'please' flips into a near-squeak. Then, with a thud, the door is pulled to.

Bloody insolence, she is the man's niece after all, not some prowling stranger; Celia can feel herself getting hot despite the dusky winter cold that's begun to creep up on her, frosting the house walls and shrubs and her rapidly cooling Golf in the drive.

Shreds of mist are rising from the disused fish ponds and the river at the bottom of the garden; like tattered white ghosts they're encroaching on the former hatchery at the edge of the lawn. The snow lies deeper out here in the country, though not quite deep enough to cover the longest of the grass blades, which are sheathed in ice like diminutive frozen swords.

What's keeping the woman, forgodsake?

A light breeze is scraping over the glitter-hard ground. The forsythia bunched around the drain pipe by the entrance swishes very faintly, and every so often its stiff bare twigs scratch against Celia's head. Their touch reminds her of the Carnival night when she and Lily had squatted in the dark outside the casino; there's the same sense of forbiddenness, and of foreboding.

The door opens as abruptly as it had been shut. 'You can come in now. He's in the living room.' The home-help's voice has dropped an octave, in a futile attempt to regain some dignity. But her eyes are as keen and beady as before, and her smile, which succeeds only in sharpening the points of her chin and nose, exposes the small jagged overbite. Then Celia notices that Mouse Face has put on lipstick. LIPSTICK! A livid shade of mauve.

She hurries into the house with a thank-you flung over her shoulder to avoid any further discoveries.

The lounge door is open and she slips inside with a cheerful, 'Hello, Uncle Godfrey.'

He is seated in the familiar wing chair she remembers from way back. Originally upholstered in red, it went through a green, then a yellow period. By now it's well into the blue one, and he is running out of primary colours.

'What an unexpected pleasure, Celia dear. How *are* you?' Is she imagining things yet again, projecting her own emotions, or does he really sound a little furtive? Her impression isn't helped by his quick glance round the room before he holds out an arm; the other is cradling Mitzi, the tabby cat, who lies curled into a silent ball on his lap.

For a moment it's as if she is gazing into her mother's eyes: deep-set moss-green eyes with unusually large pupils. His face is still handsome, big-boned and generous, with a certain aristocratic elegance that's enhanced by the pouchy crinkly skin and the flesh sagging on his cheeks. But his body sprawls heavy now and aimless.

As they kiss, Celia wonders why he looked around like that, like he wanted to check on the three doors, see whether they were all closed. Two of them are. She had swung hers shut on entering; and the double doors of amber-stained glass connecting with the dining room appear firmly wedged and locked, judging by the key. Only door number three, concealed under the wallpaper opposite, between the antique pitch-pine sideboard and the window, is ajar. She wouldn't have thought it in much demand these days, for it merely leads to the small bedroom where Walter used to sleep as a boy when spending the weekend. Has the home-help made it her boudoir, maybe? The idea of Frau Keller scurrying into there to daub her lips with that mauve, then rushing out again to smile her mouse smile, has something ominous about it, and Celia quickly draws up a chair. Her uncle's hand is gliding over Mitzi, stroking and stroking.

'There's something wrong with her,' he says. 'Old age, no doubt. Like me.' He ignores Celia's clucking noises, then finally rallies himself: 'Anyway, what brings you here, my dear? I've been thinking of you.'

With a jolt Celia realises she forgot to ring him back after his odd rushed call on Sunday. What with those damn black tulips and work, and Alex – bad-boy Alex and his fantasies, and hers . . .

Not waiting for an answer, her uncle carries on talking, getting into his stride, 'Frau Keller was pretty upset just now. No decent food in the house, she complained. What's new, eh, Celia?' He frowns mockingly. 'Though I'm sure she'd be happy enough to feed you some of her Chicken Chew. Or a fossil-boiled egg, haha –'

A door has crashed shut somewhere at the back of the house and he flinches, his eyes black, as if swallowed by pupil. The cat lets out a pitiful miaou.

'What's the matter, Uncle?' Celia has half-risen out of her chair and pats his arm. Mitzi stares at her for an instant, her triangular face gaunt and reproachful, before rearranging her body in a series of furry ripplings.

'Turning a bit jittery, I'm afraid,' he says, fidgeting. 'Can't abide loud noises any more, bangs and shots, you know.' He giggles. The moss-green colour has trembled back into place and his gaze shifts from her over to the framed photographs on the sideboard.

There are at least a dozen of them. Several sepia-tinted ones of her uncle and mother as children, posing in front of their parents – Celia's grandmother kindly and wrinkled even then, her grandfather younger, almost like a boy with that big moonface of his. Two of the pictures show herself, both in colour. One is a studio shot of her and Walter shortly before his move to the Schlosshotel – the photographer had asked her to stand on one of his Greek-style plinths so she'd be the same height as her brother, with the result that more than ever she resembles a piece of badly done sculpture, all angles and rough chipped corners; Walter, dashing in his new suit, is smirking past the camera towards where she remembers their mother hovering on the sidelines, smoking a Muratti Ambassador, a habit she'd started and kept up for a time after he'd announced he was leaving home. The other picture, with herself flanked by her mother and uncle at table, had been taken a few years later, during one of their summer Sunday lunches on the patio here. Her face is out of focus; her eyes, nostrils and mouth are dark wavy blurs because she'd caught sight of two dragonflies skittering across the lawn just as the old housekeeper clicked the camera; like opalescent darts they'd been swooping and leaping, nearly colliding, away towards the river. Her mother, perfectly made-up, is smiling with photogenic charm over at Uncle, who is grinning at a large trout he is holding up by the gills.

The most tantalising picture, to Celia's mind, is the black-and-white wedding photo of her parents. Her father's shining eyes are almost hidden behind his high cheekbones and old-fashioned horn-rimmed glasses as he stands tall and rather wide-hipped in his dark suit. Her mother is leaning away from him, displaying her narrow sashed waist and the tightness of her small breasts under the lacy bodice; her hands are clasped around a bouquet of roses and lilies she's raised to just below her lips which are parted slightly, as if in secret amusement.

But these aren't the pictures her uncle is looking at now. He has chosen a happy family slice of southern hemisphere life: Walter, Lily, and the twins – perhaps ten years old – in their vineyard in Hawke's Bay, mouths smeared red, a luscious ridiculous clown red.

Celia has got up and strolled over to inspect the Happy Family portrait. 'Lily phoned the other night,' she says casually. 'We'd quite a nice chat. Walter's away in Australia. Seems to do a lot of travelling these days. All for the family business, I suppose.'

She half-faces round, flicking her hair out of the way, over her shoulder. 'You should have visited them, Uncle, when they invited you. Why didn't you?'

He nods abstractedly and sits up more straight, easing the bulk of his body gently, so as not to upset Mitzi.

'Uncle?' she repeats.

He doesn't reply and she suspects that, quite possibly, he wouldn't know why either. Just a mixture of laziness and a dislike of long-distance flights, strange beds, the kiwi fruit that gives him an itchy red rash, and the noise and wild games of two boys he hasn't seen in years.

Celia turns towards the sideboard again. Behind the clutter of silver frames, blending in with their shadows and the thick reflections of antique pitch pine, she's glimpsed a huddle of something, a greasy-looking piece of brown cloth, crumpled over a tin of furniture wax. Has her uncle taken up wood-polishing as a hobby, following, belatedly, in his father's footsteps? She picks up the cloth by a corner and, for a dizzy moment, smells the sweet pungency of turpentine tempered with lavender.

'How this reminds me of Walter,' she murmurs with her back to the old man, unaware of his silent watchfulness. 'Funny, I'd forgotten about this. But he really got into polishing things, didn't he, after Father went missing. Used to shine the floor tiles in the kitchen and the bathroom till they were deathtraps.' She laughs. 'Didn't you tell us he once tried wiping gutted fish and their scales came off?'

Celia recalls being jealous of Walter. He'd shined his way into their mother's heart, it had seemed to her, lavishing his affection on the Beauty Room and the challenge of its surfaces. In lieu of payment he'd get special care and attention. Which invariably meant a closed door, conspiratorial whispers, bouts of stifled laughter and nails buffed to a sheen. It was only when he started his apprenticeship that his home efforts flagged. Then stopped altogether. As did their mother's fondness of him. Strange, Celia muses, how she could have forgotten. A blatant case of suppression, that's what, she can hear Jasmin comment.

It suddenly occurs to her that her uncle hasn't joined in her memories, let alone chuckled along with her. His head bent over Mitzi, he is combing his fingers through her fur as if checking for fleas. Good old Uncle, all slumped and humped and so palpably uneasy. Obviously Walter isn't deemed a suitable topic of conversation. She'll have to try a different tack.

'I found something this morning, Uncle. In Mum's bedside drawer.'

At this he winces, lifts blank eyes. 'Yes?'

'Father's map. Of the Hölloch.' She pauses, waiting for his response. When none comes, she continues, 'But there's something I don't understand: how could she have got hold of it?'

Her uncle breathes out slowly. 'Oh, didn't Gabrielle tell you? It was recovered by the search party. The only thing they ever did find of him, poor dear Peter. He must have lost it and decided to go on without it . . .'

As Celia contemplates the idea of her father burrowing further into the dark unknown, there's a knock and Mouse Face pushes the door open with a tray of coffee and crunchy Migros Carnival pancakes salvaged from the depths of her kitchen cupboards – yawning depths, in Celia's imagination, which stretch into the infinite blackness of underground galleries, lakes and rivers and tunnels without end.

Later, licking the papery crumbs and icing sugar from her lips, she does her best to forget about that sad memento in her mother's drawer and, with exaggerated enthusiasm, describes the newly decorated lounge and corridor. The name Lehmann crops up a few times, perhaps more often than necessary. Still, that's the least of her uncle's worries; he is glad they have steered clear of subjects too distressing and, yes, why not admit it, too distasteful to him. Visibly perked up now, he asks some questions about the overall colour scheme, quite unperturbed by the bewildering details she gives him, of hues and gradations and types of paint. His cheeks look firmer, his eyes glimmer with specks of gold, like sunlight caught in moss.

Then, after some office gossip to pave the way, Celia relates the story of the silk handkerchief, severely edited and with a deliberate sad shrug at poor Angelina's mishap. She feels a little devious but he is eager to be of help, and instead of ending up with *one* of his spares, she drives off with a small boxful on the seat beside her.

Coasting along the base of Cemetery Hill on the eastern outskirts of Anders, she is suddenly overwhelmed by its looming mass and has to pull over on to the verge for a short rest. She sits with her head bowed and her hands clenching the wheel. *Your mother's up there*, says a voice inside her, *dead and buried. And you haven't visited her grave once since the funeral.*

As she swings the car into her backyard, the headlights play over some frozen tyre marks and compressed scatterings of snow – all that's left of Alex and his van, and no doubt gone by tomorrow if the most recent forecast is to be believed: a major thaw in the Mittelland, with temperatures soaring to well above ten degrees Celsius. Celia switches off the radio, then the engine, the lights.

A moment passes. And another.

She remains where she is, muffled in silence and darkness. Staring over at the fruit trees. Noting their pathetically thin limbs silhouetted against the sodium glow of the sky and the chalky walls of the house next door. Dwarf trees they are, stunted, cultivated for the average-size family garden so as not to occupy too much space. Or pose any dangers. No child would want to climb *them*.

Not that Celia had been much of a tree climber in her days. The cherry tree at Lily's parents', still standing proud, higher than the two-storey house, had put an end to that ambition early on.

She remembers as if it was yesterday stretching her hand towards the cluster of sunburnt cherries dangling just out of reach, like tiny swollen mouths bright with laughter. Then . . . blackness. She hadn't felt a thing. Not the fall, nor the cuts and sprained ankle, the voices brushing over her. Not until that prayer-request-cry, her mother's, pierced her to the heart. Like a breath it's stirring above her now, floating in the stale dust-heated air of the car:

Dear God, even if I didn't want her then, *don't take her from me* now. *Dear God, not after all these years.*

Dimly she had become aware of her mother kneeling at her side and caressing her face, weeping and whispering. Margaret seemed to be there too, her arms round her mother in an embrace, while Lily stood in tears.

Celia releases the door handle as though to let the voice escape. Or perhaps in the vain hope of getting rid of it. She'd never asked her mother why she hadn't wanted to have her. At first out of sheer cowardice. Later because she believed she knew the answer. The kinship she felt with her mother had nothing to do with flesh and blood, she'd realised, and everything with independence.

She won't see Alex now till Monday. Three long nights fraught with creakings, silences, and the threat of bad dreams. Two long days of more clearing-out. And more of that sadness she could sense seeping into her at Uncle's. All of a sudden she feels nauseous, coils of barbed wire are twisting inside her belly, and she struggles to get out of the car. The lock on the garage is iced over. She scrapes and jabs at it with the key, then keeps jiggling. Two days and three nights of holding everything in, holding everything together.

Before going upstairs Celia steps into the boiler room for a bit of instant warmth. It wraps round her like a blanket, soothing the spiky pain that has spread all through her body. The evening of her fall from the cherry tree her mother had baked a chocolate cake for her, decorated with swirls of whipped cream, jelly diamonds, Hundreds and Thousands and the words GET WELL SOON! in pink marzipan. Celia can almost taste the cake now, moist and sweet like heaven in her mouth, then melting into an oddly thin salty flavour while the oil-fired heating blasts away more and more tunelessly. The silk handkerchiefs are still in the car but she is too tired to fetch them.

She's about to put off the light when the pivot window, which is partly open as usual, draws her attention. In its right-hand corner, trapped by spiderwebs, are two fluttery objects. Like big watchful eyes. MORE PASSIONFLOWERS, GODDAMMIT! Celia slams the door behind her, shivering as the cooler air of the stairwell smacks her in the face.

After his initial what-the-hell-ing this morning Alex had

laughed at her. 'Why are you so upset?' he'd asked. 'A passion-flower's quite a compliment, no? Plus a follow-up call? Well, well, still waters –'

'You shut up! You don't understand a fucking thing!' In her fury she'd pummelled her towel turban as she shouted it all out, starting with the funeral tulips . . .

Alex had sobered up instantly and dropped the silk flower back into the box. Then he began fingering his Vandyke and shaking his head. 'If you need help, don't forget I'm here too,' he repeated with a sheepish out-of-my-depth expression every time she paused for breath. Gone was the entrancing needle-sharpness of his eyes, the flippant half-jealous tone, and in an obscure way she'd felt rather sorry.

NO! Celia has reached the door to her flat and there, tied to the handle, are two more passionflowers. BASTARD! This is going too far!

Inside the house now! The street door is kept locked and that bastard must have . . . Trust Carmen upstairs to press her entry buzzer.

Inside the flat soon! If the night curtain hadn't been pulled across her landing window, those eyes would have snooped through the garland of roses cut in the frosted glass, straight into her corridor . . . She can't go on staying here, it isn't safe any more. Has he – whoever he is – been watching her and Alex, perhaps? Celia's nerves are jangling. They're scraping and twitching under her skin, ready to tear loose. She ought to leave. Or call the police. But they won't do a thing. Nothing stolen, they'll say, no damage done, and what's wrong with flowers now? At best they might suggest monitoring her phone, then let her be.

The corridor is a shadowless black gullet and she scrabbles for the light switch, clutching the key ring so the house and office keys protrude from her knuckles like vicious metal blades – just in case. Even with the light on, every step she takes seems to ricochet around the house. The floorboards groan under her feet. All the doors are ajar: the lounge door, the store-room door . . . And there's a smell of locked-in-ness, much stronger than ever before.

Then Celia laughs and claps her hands; the shutters have been restored, that's why. Throughout the flat they've been fastened together with not so much as a hairline crack in between. Driving past the house earlier, she'd been too preoccupied to notice. Dear Alex, for all his doubts and disbelief, has made sure she feels sheltered and secure. Celia is grateful to him. Fortressed up like this she'll be able to spend the night here at least.

In the Beauty Room, the peacock-blue shutters behind the window and the balcony door give the illusion of a rich tropical sky – a perfect non-pale non-blotting-paper-blue sky. The room itself has grown more bleached and lacklustre, dominated now by the insipid expanse of the blond carpet and the dull ivory of the walls from which the shelving and flower pictures have been removed. A heap of veneered boards and panels have replaced the vanity cabinet. Celia grimaces at them and mechanically rinses some dust from the rim of the washbasin, then she splashes her face with cold water. Running her wet hands through her hair, she turns towards the wall-length mirror: just like Mitzi she looks, gaunt and exhausted, with wrinkles thick as cat's whiskers at the corners of her eyes.

She isn't old yet, is she? Not that old? Not too old to have children if she wanted to? She could still have a family. She could afford it. If she wanted to. But she's never felt the urge. Never felt the gooey drooliness she's observed in other women when they peek into a pram. It's nice, of course, to gaze into the clear round baby eyes that bounce everything back unsullied and innocent for that one split second: the sun-dappled shade, clouds, the toys hanging from a string, the beholder's face. Nice, oh yes. Humbling. And yet, she's always felt a fraud pretending to admire tiny fingernails and thin marbled veins, limp slicks of hair; pretending to enjoy the gurgles, screams and milky sick slobbering out of those red holes.

Alex has two kids. Boys. 'A bit of a handful at times,' he'd told her and pointed to his discoloured knuckle. 'But I wouldn't *not* have them for anything. The older one's a football aficionado, which keeps me fit too.' His laughter, and his eyes, had been soft and pleased. No mention of his wife, though, and she hadn't asked.

Celia stands staring at the tulip cornice thinking, Two sons, just like Walter. *Three–four–five* she has started to count the plaster flowers as if compelled. Walter. Is this what he used to do *eleven–twelve–next–one's–broken* while he was getting his nails manicured? Counting the tulips up there *nineteen–twenty* and telling himself this was nothing out of the ordinary *twenty-four* this filing *twenty-five* this softening and shaping of cuticles *twenty-eight–twenty-nine–thirty* this nipping and clipping *thirty-three* this buffing, *et voilà*?

All of a sudden her mother's voice seems to echo around the Beauty Room for real: *Irresponsibility, carelessness, lust – that's the evil trinity, Celia . . . You don't want to learn the hard way, now do you?*

Celia doesn't want to hear more. Yanking the door shut, she hurries down the corridor to the spare room. It's been dust-sheeted because of the steaming and lining Alex started today. Beside the bed she hesitates for a moment. Then, lifting a corner of the sheeting, she grasps the gold-plated drawer handle. Pulls. And grabs her father's map like a trophy snatched from the jaws of death – that's how it feels, now that she *knows*.

Her hand has knocked over some jewellery boxes and a stack of old letters and postcards. Tucked underneath, held together by a thick green rubber band, is a bundle of cards. Face down – no, front to front. Godknows what more surprises she's going to find here.

Celia's breath hisses a little as she slips out the first card. The rubber band, brittle with age, snaps. And so does her breath, for a second.

The picture shows a black tulip. A single black tulip, its head tilted slightly to expose stamens and stigma.

The next card's the same, and the next: eleven cards in all – eleven black tulips. A vague memory stirs at the back of her mind. Years ago she'd seen a card like this propped against some towels on a shelf in the Beauty Room.

Now, one by one, she folds the cards open.

Nothing except the printed words: **A Declaration of Love!**

Valentine cards.

Her head's swimming. So, *black* tulips too are tokens of love . . . and her mother did have a secret admirer . . . someone who's still alive . . . and stalking the daughter now, it would appear.

Before Celia has time to ponder this, the phone begins to ring. Impetuous. Insistent. Ringing and ringing. Making her feel like a spinning top prematurely jolted to a halt. That bastard with his imitation passionflowers, no doubt. Will she answer it or won't she? The shutters are in place, the door is double-locked – and she's already lost her peace of mind. Tohellwithit! She tosses the cards and map back into the drawer. But she won't hang up afterwards; she'll contact the police from upstairs to have the call traced.

'Yes.'

'Hello there, Frau Roth. Surprise, surprise: it's Rita! Could I make an appointment, please?'

A woman's oldish voice. Celia is tempted to put the phone down.

'Well, actually, I'm her daughter. I'm afraid my mother –'

'Oh, just tell her it's Rita Stettler. Back from South Africa at long last. She'll remember me. The loveliest skin ever, she used to say.'

Celia laughs hysterically. 'I'm really sorry, Frau Stettler, but my mother died four weeks ago tomorrow. She's dead.'

She lets the line go silent and, rather unnerved, tugs a tissue from the box on the telephone table. Dabbing her eyes, she glances towards the front door and the curtained landing window, then at the coat rack with its swaying dummy-like figures and finally at the oval mirror, which reflects no gnome's grin, thankgod, nor any ghosts, only one of Alex's business cards stuck in its frame.

'*Celia* –' it says in a sexy angular handwriting. '*Don't forget you can reach me on the mobile any time! Take care. Alex.*'

Behind her back, beyond the rooms and their shutters, she imagines she can hear snow clouds puffing and swelling above the matchstick fruit trees and the roofs of the neighbouring houses.

Goddammit, she isn't afraid. Just shaken, dammit. But already she has lifted the receiver and pressed the memo button for Nita up in the Alps.

She swallows hard.

21

CELIA'S DOG-TIRED, hardly slept after phoning Nita, then packing. She'd lain dozing amid the night noises, trying not to think about tulips and passionflowers, about Alex. Getting startled into wakefulness by the merest hum and drone of a passing car, by the street door banging shut and Carmen's work-weary feet on the stairs. Every sound seemed magnified by the darkness. Every sound like a warning. Telling of some stone-faced monster that had crawled from the bowels of the earth, its horny paws clobbering the frozen roads towards her. She'd got up just after six. Had left the new peacock-blue shutters firmly closed until the last minute. To make sure she wasn't followed to the station.

As Celia steps off the train at Albula four hours later, the snow-wind lashes out at her like hands. She staggers, almost drops her travelling bag. The old brown rucksack she's slung over one shoulder lurches heavily, a dead weight, against her side. The air feels icy after the overheated carriage, it pinches her nostrils and stabs right through her poncho, making her shiver. Her eyes have started to water from the unrelieved whiteness all round: the plateau with its twin sets of tracks and the station behind her, the fir trees, power lines, the village below and the mountains above – everything is hooded and cloaked and shod in white. It's a narrow valley and the peaks lean into the sky far overhead, cutting out a jagged circle of deep Alpine blue.

'Let me help you,' a voice says at her elbow, in a soft mixed-up accent.

Not a voice she recognises. Not Nita's.

She turns round slowly, ready to shout at whoever – half-expecting to be confronted by Granite Mask again.

Then she relaxes. The voice belongs to a wholesome-looking woman in her thirties, small and bouncy, with big dangling cloisonné earrings.

'Oh, it's only you. Thankgod!'

For a moment the woman stares at her, puzzled. 'I don't think we've met before,' she says stiffly, putting up the collar of her sheepskin coat. 'I'm Christine. Nita said you'd made her promise to pick you up but –'

'Nothing wrong, I hope?' Celia asks, suddenly weak to the pit of her stomach.

Christine has begun to say something about Nita's duties as a snowboarding instructor – when the wind gusts up again. Celia can't help glancing back at the people who've got off the train after her. Just some families with skis in transparent plastic, sledges of all sizes, and suitcases – tourists obviously – and a group of teenagers in extra-wadded neon-bright jackets moving off along the tracks, shouting to each other in Romansch. They're throwing around schoolbags and holdalls like crazy jugglers. Nothing to worry about.

Christine's eyes have followed hers. 'Home from school for the weekend. They always go wild, especially on the pass-road sledge run at night.' She pauses, laughs. 'Anyway, Nita said to give you her love and a welcome-to-the-Alps hug.'

They smile, brush cheeks three times the way friends do who want to feel safe, and noncommittal.

Meanwhile, like a red-gleaming snake, another train has slid down the bends in the mountainside from the opposite direction, the keening of metal on metal dulled by snow and trees. It's a single-track railway and Albula Station one of several passing points. The bells whirr into action, then the loudspeakers. At the sound of the guard's whistle Celia whirls round. She needs to scan the faces before her train continues its journey. But her view is blocked by the new arrival and its stream of passengers. She can't see a thing – let alone identify an unknown person, if there is one – only a dozen or so carriages with two panorama cars like glasshouses on wheels, and a blur of faces and windows behind more windows, more faces, as the train gathers speed.

'Coming, Celia? You're not a trainspotter, are you?'

Celia tears herself away, forcing a laugh while thinking, Keep your cool, girl, he isn't here. This is the mountains – safety!

She can see Christine standing by the entrance to the roofed-over waiting area, chatting with the *Glühwein und Bratwürste* vendor. The man can't be more than thirty, his dark good looks half-hidden under a purple headband, Raybans and a thin moustache. Close to, though, his tan has a wooden quality and his teeth seem to glisten a little too much, a little too white, when he smiles goodbye and starts to slice a crusty loaf for the lunchtime hordes of sledgers.

Christine, it turns out, is joint owner of the Crusch Alva, the White Cross, a former barn converted into an ethnic restaurant with small funnel-shaped windows, black-painted rafters, cowbells hanging from metal-embossed leather collars, burnished brass *Engadinersonnen* with big grins and flames for hair, a couple of dull-eyed ibex heads mounted next to the bar as if for company, and – Celia flinches at the sight of them – masks. Large soot-stained masks carved from wood and trimmed with bits of fleece or fur into gargoyle faces. They'd have scared the hell out of anyone, even the mountain spirits that cut climbers' ropes, chase animals over precipices and set off avalanches.

'Museum pieces by now. I inherited them from an aunt who collected curios.' Christine hands Celia a glass of grappa. 'Cheers! It's on the house.' Then she checks herself. 'How very thoughtless of me. Nita's told me about your mother, I'm so sorry . . .'

Celia takes a long soothing sip before nodding a curt thank-you, her eyes glazed over to preclude any more offers and advances of commiseration.

Afterwards they talk about her plans for the weekend. She has none – apart from trying to enjoy herself without fear. 'Certainly not skiing. Or snowboarding.' She can feel the grappa sear her throat, fire up her body. 'I broke a leg skiing when I was eleven, an arm at thirteen. After that, my mother refused to let me go, and I'd had enough myself. Something of a heresy in this country, being a non-skier!' She laughs, has two quick sips. 'Wouldn't you say so, Christine?'

But had she really had enough? It was her mother who'd hated winter, hated frost and cold with a ferocity Celia had never understood. If friends invited them for trips into the snowy mountains, to the Toggenburg or up the Säntis, say, her mother would sneeze-and-grimace in a politely restrained manner. 'As if we didn't have enough snow down here,' she'd whisper, then spin a graceful excuse in public.

Christine is smiling, telling her there aren't actually any heresies unless you let others dictate to you, and she, by goddess, has always fought authority. Her cheeks have flushed a fervent apple-red and the heavy cloisonné earrings swing emphatically. I must have touched a nerve somewhere, Celia muses, pleasantly drowsy now from the grappa.

'I don't believe in marriage, for one,' Christine carries on. 'Nothing to do with faithfulness, I simply don't like its institutionalised status. You aren't married, are you?'

'Married?' The question jerks Celia out of her semi-slumber. 'Oh no. I'm not married.' She tries to look suitably shocked at the notion and thinks of Alex. She can feel the rucksack pressing up against her left calf. Franz's rucksack. It nudges her like a reminder.

Having surveyed the other guests in the restaurant, Christine confides in a low voice, 'You see, when I came to live in this village, seven years ago, I brought two daughters with me from a previous relationship. Tom, my partner, is local. From Preda. But people here didn't exactly make things easy for us. They're pretty conservative – "narrow-valleyed", if you get me. It was only after that soap was filmed in the area some years back that they started regarding themselves as part of the real world!' She laughs, pushes back her chair and says loudly, 'Anyway, I'd better go – time to get my kids some lunch. Ciao for now.'

Celia's thanks are lost in a clatter from the salad buffet near the bar where, with urgent haste, a young blonde waitress is depositing plates and big glass bowls of lettuce, French beans, grated carrot, sliced tomato, pepper and cucumber. Celia rests her head against the whitewashed wall. Thankgod for those motherly duties. A discussion of relationships, love and parenthood is the last thing she needs. Her table is at the back of the room, well away from the men with their pipes and dark old faces, playing cards and chalking up their scores on the slate inlay of the *Stammtisch.* She shuts her eyes, tired to the bones, and lets her whole body slump against the wall.

Something is tickling the side of her cheek: a piece of fleece. Christ, not another mask! Had it been there, so close to her, all along? It's small, oval rather than round, quite unlike the others. Not the least bit grotesque or frightening. The wood feels satin smooth . . .

Next thing she knows, she's lifted the mask off its hook and placed it over her face. It's not at all heavy, perhaps a centimetre thick, with perfect hollows for her jutting chin and cheekbones. As if it had been made to measure, *her* measure. Greedily Celia inhales the sweet-sharp pine smell. When she peers through the eye slits, the interior of the Crusch Alva fragments into / the brassy grin of an *Engadinersonne* / half a man's face and pipe cupped in a leathery hand / an aerial photo of a gorge whose river seems to drain into the folds of a curtain / then nothing. Someone's passed right in front of her. Celia whips the mask away.

Nita has already sat down. 'Well, well,' she chuckles, 'you certainly can't be trusted on your own, Cel. Hiding behind masks now!' Then she leans over for the three-kiss ritual. 'Sorry I couldn't meet you off the train. I had to stand in for one of my colleagues. Poor sod hurt his ankle on the sledge run last night.'

'You look great,' Celia blurts out, noting the vermilion lipstick, the cropped and hennaed hair.

After the blonde waitress has poured Nita some spring water, smiling broadly and exchanging a few words, Nita says how she'd always admired Celia's mother: 'She was the most glamorous mum I ever saw.'

And *amorous*, too, Celia can't help thinking. Forcing the memory of the Carnival Ball and the Valentine cards from her mind, she replies, 'That's very kind of you. I'm sure my mother would have appreciated it. Yes, I guess glamour *was* her problem. She couldn't bear being ill, especially once the lumps began to disfigure her.' Then, aware of how bitter she must sound, she adds hurriedly, 'Don't get me wrong, Nita, I did feel sorry for her. She suffered, and not just physically. All the visitors she had! Quite a few of them former clients come to gloat because even the most professional make-up couldn't save her any more. And the smells . . .'

Nita's brightly painted lips seem to have sighed in sympathy. Celia blinks and rubs her eyes – for a fleeting moment she had glimpsed her mother again, holding the tarnished silver hand-mirror up to her face, sobbing and bleeding from a shapeless nose. 'Just picture it, Nita: the aging beautician plastering her hair over the sides of her nose with gluey gel to conceal the swollen bits before visiting hours. Towards the end she asked *me* to do it for her, but by then nothing and no one could have made any difference. *That* was the saddest of all.'

Nita hasn't seen Celia for more than a year and is surprised at the change in her. She looks lost and uncertain. Looks her age too, nearer forty than herself, with eyes rimmed pink despite the mascara and kohl, and a forehead puckered faintly in distress. Still, she's got those chiselled features that promise beauty in later life. Nita smiles as she pats Celia on the shoulder.

'I'll do my best to get you back on your feet, don't you worry. Even if it means teaching you the basics of snowboarding!' Noticing that Celia's glass is empty, she motions to the waitress, 'Could we have two grappas, please?'

Celia's eyes haven't stopped blinking and now they're wet and she has to keep blinking to stop the wetness, and to wipe away the image of her mother propped up in bed, nostrils flared by wads of gauze, mouth painfully open, a handkerchief in one hand, the silver mirror in the other.

'I'm sorry, Nita, I don't mean to cry. Sorry.'

Nita just squeezes her shoulder.

They sit in silence for nearly a minute.

When the waitress sidles up with their drinks at last, her furtiveness reminds Celia of Angelina and how she'd tiptoed round the office after that anonymous phone call, so obsequiously discreet. They can stuff their bloody concern, she doesn't want it. She seizes the mask still lying on the table beside her, places it over her face once more and –

'Boo! Boo! Boo!' she snarls. The wood vibrates and the sound that escapes through the mouthhole is more like *boohoohoo*, but Celia can't hear.

The waitress has retreated behind one of the tables, with a baffled look towards Nita, who shrugs apologetically.

Already, though, Celia has turned away to put the mask back up on the wall, taking her time to rearrange the bits of fleece. Then she smiles at the two women and sits down, pointedly ignoring the card players staring in her direction.

'Too much grappa on an empty stomach,' she announces. The words slip out quite easily. Perhaps they're even true.

Nita's left front tooth is chipped, Celia observes. They're having *Gerstensuppe* à la Crusch Alva, a belly-warming, thick and slimy broth of barley and vegetables that comes with wheaten rolls and a mixed salad, in Celia's case a modest portion of French beans, red and yellow pepper strips.

Nita says why don't they go sledging tonight. 'Five kilometres in all, down the pass road. It's glorious – as long as you use cushions to keep your bum from getting knocked black and blue!'

Celia laughs and spikes up a length of red pepper. 'Sounds fun. I haven't been on a sledge for years.' But will she be safe out in the dark and cold? Somewhere in a corner of her mind she sees her mother shake her head, *No-no-no*, her mouth pursed in shell-pink disapproval. When Celia lowers her fork, its prongs glint back at her challengingly. Of course she'll be safe. All she needs is a weapon.

‘We could ask Christine along if she’s free. And Silvan. Silvan’s my man of the season.’ Nita giggles. ‘You might have seen him at the station: guy behind the food-and-drink stall, purple head-band –’

‘– moustache, Alpine tan and Raybans,’ Celia interrupts. That chip in Nita’s tooth is pretty bad. The result of one of her snowboarding excesses, no doubt – and the perfect advert for recklessness. Then it hits her: she is jealous! Jealous of little Nita, who used to wear hand-knitted woolly tights that sloughed round her ankles like dead skin!

Pulling herself together, she jokes, ‘Tall, dark and handsome, and no stranger! Young, too.’

She finishes her salad, then starts to shine her fork and knife on a paper napkin. The prongs seem a lot duller suddenly, a lot less pointed – not much of a weapon. But the blade cuts through the soft tissue like butter. If anything, she’ll take the knife.

Nita has launched into an account of what she calls ‘the frissons of seasonal love’, which Celia can’t help associating with fruit and veg, and some of the more daring bedroom games she and Lily used to play when bananas were still a winter treat. Does Nita remember the afternoon she’d joined them, dressed in her sloppy tights, and didn’t have a clue, wouldn’t stop whining, ‘But how? How?’? Does she remember Lily’s soft puppy sounds and the snow shutting them in, a bit like now?

‘Hi there, Nita.’ It’s Christine. ‘Enjoyed your meal?’ And she’s off again, carrying away their plates, soup bowls and cutlery. But not Celia’s knife. At the last moment she’d sneaked that under her place mat. To be borrowed or left behind, at her own discretion.

The restaurant is filling up. Chairs scrape the slate floor and there’s the *ding-dong, ding-dong* of some cowbells swinging away on their beams for the camcorder of a Japanese tourist. The locals seem to have fled, their peaceful card games replaced by children beating tattoos on tables with fingers and spoons and getting shouted at by frantic parents.

Their cappuccinos arrive. Now’s the time, Celia decides. Now she’ll tell Nita about her stalker. Her mother’s death is only the beginning, after all. She isn't sure yet whether she'll mention Alex.

Nita laughs when she hears about Granite Mask. 'It's just fun and games, Cel,' she says. 'You're taking this way too personally. So you got a scare, well, fair enough. But then, you also got a glass of champagne – nothing sinister about that, is there?' She laughs again, blows into the frothy milk in her cup. 'We all need to let off steam once in a while, that's why Carnival is so healthy. It's a safety valve.'

Celia licks some chocolaty foam off her spoon. 'And what about the black tulips sent for the funeral? The bunch left on my doorstep?' she asks. 'What about the phone calls and now the passionflowers? That's more than a hoax, I can feel it in my guts.' For an instant she can almost hear Jasmin's therapy-speak: Too right you're feeling it in your guts, girl. You're in denial, that's what.

Nita is gazing at her with a mixture of pity and compassion, doing her utmost to be considerate, Celia realises.

'There's something else, Nita . . .'

'Oh?'

'Last night I found a whole bundle of anonymous Valentine cards in my mother's bedside table. All with the same design: black tulips.'

Nita's tongue presses up against the chipped tooth and Celia watches as a slither of red appears on the white. Somewhere in the front of the restaurant a child has started wailing for more chips and there's the hiss of a woman's voice: 'Enough, that's enough!'

Moments later Nita has recovered her usual poise. 'Mmm,' she says, sipping her cappuccino, 'sounds rather messy. Though I don't think you're in any real danger.' Then she brings up the police as a last resort. 'Just relax, Cel. You're here now. I'll ask Silvan to be your bodyguard for tonight. Okay?'

Celia is on the verge of declaring she doesn't want a bodyguard, and certainly not Silvan with his face all headbanded, moustached, and Raybanned-up. But she bites back her remark and thanks Nita for being so generous.

* * *

Christine agrees to meet them for the sledgers' train to Preda at quarter past seven, when the pass road is again closed to cars. Avalanches don't seem to be a problem in Albula Valley, Celia notes with relief.

As they get up to go off to Nita's flat, Nita reaches over for the rucksack.

'Would you mind taking the bag instead?' Celia says. 'Pure sentimentality, really. The rucksack was Franz's.'

On hearing the name, Nita glances up and their eyes lock; another funeral missed – is this what she's thinking?

Celia quickly transfers the knife from under the mat to one of her coat pockets. Better safe than sorry. On the way out she keeps fingering the blade, running her thumb along the cutting edge. She isn't quite so vulnerable now.

22

THE TRAIN TO Preda is packed. Sledges are crammed into the compartments, upright, alongside their owners, like strange docile beasts squatting on their haunches, reins hanging down, saddled with quilts, cushions, furs and sheepskins. Celia has counted four carriages, all of them a dirty old red. The seats are thinly disguised wooden benches, their yellow-brown vinyl upholstery full of cracks and holes; the floors never stop creaking, as if straining to hold on to the wheels; the windows rattle like loose mouths, sucking in draughts of icy air and howls from inside tunnels – and all the time there's the sharp blood smell of iron she can taste on her tongue.

Christine has brought her two daughters, Chloe and Diana. They're nine and eleven and give Celia the X-ray treatment, long, hard and unsmiling, staring first at her face, then her jacket (her mother's 'Arctic gear' as she used to call it, and of an indefinable ochre shade Celia wouldn't normally want to be seen dead in, but at least the microfibre will keep her warm). Then at her old rucksack with the extra jersey. Then her bulging right-hand pocket. As though they knew about the knife wrapped in its square of tissue paper and stuck inside her mitten.

Ever since they got on the train and squashed themselves into a corner, Nita and Silvan have been sweethearting in low tones, murmuring and kissing and sliding hands into each other's zip-up suits. Now that she's been introduced to him, Celia likes Silvan even less. Something about the man makes her go hot and cold inside, wave after wave after wave till she feels nearly sick. It's nothing to do with his looks; they *are* strikingly good. Even little Chloe, Celia is sorry to see, isn't impervious to the polished planes of his face, the slate-blue eyes and shiny teeth, and has shot him a series of admiring glances from across the aisle. Catching his attention at last, she nudges her sister and they burst into giggles. Then, with busy self-importance, she adjusts her forget-me-not kirby grip, wriggles off her seat and minces over to him, burying her nose and forehead in his hair. Her lips seem to nuzzle his earlobes.

Celia is about to protest and looks round at Christine – who's already rolling her eyes at Nita, groaning, 'Not *more* Chinese whispers!'

A few seconds later it's Celia's turn: *The humbug was heard and the bitch is paid hearts.* When she repeats the nonsense words out loud, Chloe laughs and laughs. 'I didn't say *that*,' she splutters, as if Celia had made it all up, forgodsake. '*I* said: "The humpback wizard and the witches play darts." '

Wizards and witches – they're the last thing Celia wants to be reminded of. But she joins in the laughter the way she's expected to. Her right hand, meanwhile, has slipped into the mitten in her pocket. The knife blade feels warm through the tissue paper; warm as her body. She is grateful for the thermal tights Nita has lent her and squirms with guilt at her uncharitable thoughts in the restaurant.

After their walk home from the Crusch Alva, Nita had suggested a bath in her heart-shaped tub. Which was what they'd done. Just their feet were touching – Nita's nails were varnished black with speckles of silver – and their arms brushed only if they happened to flick the pages of their magazines at the same moment. Celia had merely pretended to read. She'd seen Nita was shaved smooth between her legs, her flesh swollen like a ripe fruit freshly split. Lying side by side in the hot sleepy water, it was hard not to imagine Silvan in all sorts of positions, bruising those lips to a glazed purple; hard not to fantasise about Alex and herself.

And hard not to remember her fifteenth birthday, when she'd locked herself in the bathroom with a razor blade. Stepping out of her skirt and knickers, she'd placed her mother's magnifying mirror on the rim of the bath. Then she stood astride it, the blade between thumb and forefinger. For an instant she hesitated, fondling her belly button with her free hand as she anticipated the pain, the blood. To be a real woman she had to do this, and do it now. Much easier to endure the pain inflicted by yourself. That way it became part of you, became something you had to accept, perhaps even love a little. She'd bled a good deal that day, and walking or going to the loo was agony for a time. Later, in bed with her first man, she found she'd cut herself in the wrong place and bled again, profusely.

Through the rattling window Celia watches the floodlit pass road weave in and out of the feeble moonlight and the mountain shadows. Sledges are flitting down it, the figures on them curiously small and insubstantial between the walls of snow and safety fencing on either side. Deep in the gorge the icy waters of the River Albula glisten – like the whites of those eyes under the mask, revealing nothing but a coiled red vein. Granite Mask hadn't come up again in her conversation with Nita. Nor the tulips and passionflowers, the phone calls and Valentine cards. Not even during supper, which was a cheese *raclette* and a dry Fendant from the Valais.

And Alex is still a secret. Hers. Celia wonders what he is doing just now. Maybe he's taken his wife out for dinner or to the cinema. Or they're at home together, sitting on the sofa. Touching. Playing with each other. Sucking and licking and . . . Will he spare a thought for *her* at all?

Diana, Christine and Nita have started a discussion about crampon trekking and snowboarding techniques, including jumps over Alpine rooftops, and Silvan is fooling around with his pretty little admirer, trying on her crash helmet, which is a luminous blue and perches on his head like a flashing police light.

A few times, in fact, Celia has felt his eyes on her, reflected in the window. No, she definitely doesn't like the man.

The water in the horse trough next to Preda Station is a humpback mass of ice – 'The humpback wizard,' Celia whispers to herself – crouching like some nightmare creature she can't resist stroking for a moment, placating it with pats from her mittened hands, the knife handle hard against her wrist. An icicle has grown from the pipe opening above the trough. It glitters in the strip lighting from the station wall, long and sharp and crystal clear. Before she knows what she's doing, Celia is running her tongue down it, as slowly as she dares. The cold pierces her flesh. Then there's a rip of pain, the taste of blood.

She swallows and swallows. The others don't seem to have noticed. They're standing at the sledgers' bar no more than a dozen metres away. It's built entirely of ice bricks, like the wall of an igloo. '*Röteli, Grappa, Glühwein*!' she hears the barman shout. His hat is as pointed as a dwarf's. Not far behind him looms the blackest most impenetrable-seeming part of the night: the mouth of the six-kilometre tunnel into the next valley, the Engadin. Celia tries in vain to suppress the memory that's sprung up in her mind, the memory of the Hölloch and her lost father. She gasps at the damp murky clouds of breath she can feel wafting out of the blackness.

Perhaps she ought to have a glass of *Glühwein*, after all.

'Oh, here you are, Cel,' Nita says, pulling Silvan in Celia's direction. 'We'll take care of her, won't we, lover boy?'

The teeth beneath his little moustache gleam whiter and stronger than ever.

Celia swallows a last dribble of blood and tries to smile, but her lips have gone numb. She nods, then puts up the hood of her jacket, tugging at the drawstring.

Christine's in the middle of telling everyone in her vicinity how she adores going sledging with just the moon and stars for guides, forget the floodlights. 'It's magic,' she enthuses. 'A blessing from outer space. No need for religion.' Smirking at her audience from underneath her fringed scarf, she suddenly resembles one of those evil mountain spirits. The impression is so vivid Celia has to look away, only to catch sight of Diana chasing after Chloe, the sledge skittering and leaping and pouncing behind her like a mad dog. Diana, she thinks, goddess of the moon and the hunt.

The frozen slush sparkles diamond bright as they follow the tyre marks of the cars along the flank of the mountain, down the almost imperceptible slope of the pass road before it falls away into the hairpins Celia had seen from the train. With its drifts and hollows and shadows the snowscape around her is like a close-up version of the face of the moon. The wind has died down. People's breath hangs in the air like stardust.

'HELLO! HELLO!' Chloe and Diana yell towards the gorge, listening for an echo that comes much too soon and in too many voices – yodelling, laughing, screeching, howling.

They'd decided to let the other sledgers go first; 'To avoid a traffic jam,' Nita explained smiling. But Celia knows better: this is her friend's way of reassuring her. She is grateful, with a touch of resentment.

There are perhaps a hundred people in front of them. Young children with their parents, gangs of teenagers, couples, singles, even a few old-age pensioners; everything from veterans to first-timers. Some of them have miners' lamps clamped to their foreheads. Some sport caps with leather earflaps like early pilots. Celia recognises several of the students from the morning. Without their bags now, they're doing their damnedest to trip each other's sledges up, parking themselves on the seats or stepping on the runners from behind; two of the girls are wearing face paint.

Then Celia sets eyes on what she has feared all along. A man – or is it a woman? – in a dark balaclava. And then there's another. And another. A whole group of people in balaclavas. Which one is it? Which one? Her breathing is quick and shallow; inside the mitten her right hand has clenched into a fist. And inside the fist is the knife, unwrapped and half-protruding. Easy now, she tells herself, Easy . . .

They've reached the small bridge that spans the beginning of the gorge when Silvan pulls out a piece of black material.

Another balaclava! As if to ridicule her.

He is supposed to be her bodyguard, not her tormentor.

The mere idea of having to cling to him on the sledge makes Celia break into a sweat. The idea of having to cling to anyone just now makes her feel burning hot, despite the cold shrivelling up her body.

'A game of tag!' she cries, snatching up the rein Silvan has dropped. 'See if you can catch me!'

And already she's running, bent double over the sledge, pushing it with both hands towards where the road dips.

'Hey wait, Cel! It's too dangerous, too many sledgers! Don't be silly, Cel!'

She's flung herself on to the cushioned seat at the last moment. Franz's half-empty rucksack bangs into her back like someone clapping encouragement.

She's not afraid any more. She's got the knife.

Pellets of snow and ice spurt up her legs, cold air cuts into her skin, sculpting her face. She shrieks with laughter. She's ready.

She leans into the first hairpin, hacking her heels into the glass-hard ground to steer the runners. Grasping the knife tighter.

Into the next, getting caught for a lurching instant in some rut or other, overtaking here, nearly crashing there. Out again by the skin of her teeth.

Kicking the snow to go faster, whipping off the right-hand mitten, thrusting the blade out, just a little.

Hurtling into the third.

Hurtling and whirling, powerless now, roundandroundand-round into the steely whiteness of ice and snow over rock . . .

. . . And that's when her mother's face smiles into hers, larger than life. Smiles with pain as it becomes more misshapen and gaunt before finally splintering along the cheekbones, the nose and jawline – to re-form itself into Franz's. Into the face of a mountaineer, full of corners and slightly eroded, burnt a scrubby brown. Nowadays Celia hardly dreams of him any more. He's been dead almost six years.

It was too late when she got to the hospital. The doctor was bald with ripples of pink flesh down the back of his head. She followed him into a small windowless room that had a beige carpet and nondescript art on the walls. Classical music was seeping through the ceiling, low and mournful. The doctor was talking to her but she didn't hear what he was saying. He must have started shouting at some point because she remembers glancing up at him and being struck by the turkey-red cheeks, the bulging eyes and the mouth opening and closing.

'A terrible, terrible fall. No one . . . sorry, I am sorry,' she could just about make out. 'You were his . . . ?'

Were. The violins were screaming in her ears. Squealing. Their tautly stretched strings live guts in torture. Franz had gone off at dawn, alone. His rucksack was intact, the nurse had assured her on the phone. As if she cared. When they gave it to her afterwards – after she'd looked at the battered face under the long hair and held the unhurt hand they'd placed on top of the blanket, the hand with which he used to stroke her inside and out – she noticed that the pockets were still zipped up, the lengths of nylon cord still looped through the clasps and the holes in the tabs.

The first time she'd seen Franz secure his rucksack so fastidiously she'd giggled out loud and said, 'Poor old thing getting trussed up like that, worse than a chicken! And not much use in an emergency, I'd have thought.'

'For safety,' he'd replied, quite earnestly, his fingers busy with a fresh knot. She'd stopped giggling and from then on called it the Rucksack Ritual. She realised soon enough that most of his friends and fellow climbers also had their private little mascots or manias (anything from polishing their boots three times instead of just the once to dead Brazilian gold bugs swaddled in cottonwool and carried in the left breastpocket, over the heart).

And in the event Franz's rucksack was the only thing to survive. So incongruously ridiculously safe it usurped her dreams, turned them into nightmares from which she'd wake up crying, her body streaming with sweat:

Always, he's climbing away from her. Up and away. His boots grow gigantic with distance and height, as big as boulders. Always, his back is to her. His rucksack is tied and double-tied, festooned with cord ends that swing from side to side. The rucksack bounces on his back as if there's something alive inside, kicking to get out. Always, just as he is about to climb out of sight, the leather bottom rips open and a bundle falls out, tumbles down towards her, hitting rock overhangs and ledges, down towards her, spraying blood . . .

23

CELIA HAD ONLY closed her eyes for a moment, it seemed. But the moment unfolds like an enormous blanket, stretches and stretches and goes on stretching until it becomes the sheerest see-through silk that floats her into the next morning, then midday.

By now the effects of the painkillers are wearing off. Cel's eyelids are flickering, Nita is glad to notice. She has been sitting at her friend's bedside most of the time, waking her every two hours to check she was still lucid, asking her name and date of birth as she'd been told by the doctor, in between catnapping, reading and sneaking off for the occasional quick snuggle with Silvan on her king-size bed. What on earth got into you last night? she addresses Celia silently. Grabbing that sledge and careering off like a bat out of hell? At least the cuts on Cel's hand aren't too bad. Not as deep as the blood had made it look at first. She'd swabbed them clean, then stuck some gauze and plaster on top, as instructed. Those metal runners can be right bastards if touched by mistake.

Nita wrings out the face cloth in the yellow plastic basin on the floor and places it across her patient's forehead. The eyelids flutter sleepily and there's a contented sigh. Nita almost heaves a sigh herself. She reaches for the cereal-and-apricot bar on the bedside table, bites off a big chewy chunk.

It wasn't that much of a smash really. Considering how crazy Cel had acted, the knock on her head could have been a lot nastier. Lucky she'd had her hood up, though. Nita had found her lying near the snow wall six hairpins down, a little groggy but so what, happens to most of us once in a while. She helped her up no problem, holding her steady the way she does with her snowboarding pupils.

Christine, like some New-Age bouncer, had told the rubber-neckers to get lost, for goddess' sake, and Cel had smiled and tried to brush the snow off her clothes. Which left smears of blood all over. 'Blood from the rucksack, it's torn again mygod,' she'd moaned, staring in horror. Christine, ever practical, slipped off her fringed headscarf and wound it round Cel's injured hand, saying not to worry, we'll sort you out again, and gesturing to Silvan to keep an eye on her girls.

Just then that old hippy-doing-very-nicely-thank-you with his flowing iron-grey mane, curly beard, camelhair coat and Bally boots arrived on a sledge painted a vibrant pink. 'I used to be a doctor in a previous life,' he announced, almost cheerfully. And that's the moment dear old Cel chose to take a tottering step and crumple back down into the snow, her scarf-wrapped hand flying out pathetically, like part of a scarecrow.

'Fainted from shock,' the man commented, the switch from happy hippy to laconic doctor-in-charge apparently effortless. As he knelt down to examine Cel, Chloe broke into sobs and Silvan ended up walking her and Diana away, his arms over their shoulders, whispering into their ears and making them titter – if they'd been a few years older, Nita would have got pretty cross with him.

But her attention was drawn to a group of sledgers who'd braked to a halt and begun circulating tales of how Cel had laughed and cried out and rammed into everyone like she was playing dodgems, at *her* age, just imagine, stoned out of her bloody mind probably! Good for Cel she'd passed out and couldn't hear those unkind remarks.

Nita has eaten her cereal bar. The sun is shining outside and a couple of blackbirds are trilling their melodies into the monotonous whine of the skilift further up. She can feel her legs starting to twitch with impatience. Sexy Silvan left hours ago, off to do some 'blitz skiing' before slaving it behind his stall.

She sighs for real now, then glances over at Celia and renews the cold compress. That stalker story yesterday did sound a little hysterical. At the very least it's a wild exaggeration, Cel's always had a dramatic streak, even as a kid. Is this, maybe, an attempt to distract herself so that her mother's death won't hurt too much, too soon? Some weeks back Nita had read an article about endorphins in a sports magazine and been rather impressed by the fact that certain people's brains produce these substances in vast enough quantities to completely block pain sensation.

Half an hour later Celia is sitting up in bed with a cup of tea balanced on her knees (a 'restorative secret blend of herbs' from Christine's kitchen garden). No one had thought to remove her contact lenses last night, and she'd been relieved to find them safely lodged in her eyes on waking. Celia stares at the framed photos of snowboarders and skiers which adorn the walls of the guest room. But the breakneck stunts and spectacular crashes, the smiling groups of learners practising stem turns in caterpillar formation or reclining on their gear in the snow are lost on her entirely. She is pondering what Nita had told her about the accident. A gently expurgated account, she's sure. Her headache has almost gone by now, but she still can't remember much beyond a sudden feeling of numbness, a bit like when she'd fallen out of the cherry tree as a girl. Her right hand is scabby with gauze and sticking plaster. Thankgod she hadn't harmed anyone else; the knife must have been catapulted out of her grasp just in time. Whatthehell had she thought she was doing?

Drinking Christine's tea, Celia feels a keen flush of embarrassment.

Through the gap in the red-and-gold striped curtains she can make out a few branches of the tall rowan tree she'd admired yesterday afternoon. What she hadn't noticed then is the icicle sparkling from one of its forks, right in front of the window. A drop of water has gathered at the tip and now hangs trembling, barely clinging on. As she watches, Celia feels a strange tingle of empathy. For a moment she seems to become *it*. Perfectly self-contained. Refracting rather than creating light. Held together only by surface tension. No real skin. One nip of frost and the drop freezes, gets reabsorbed by the whole. One gust of wind, one prick of a pin and it bursts, scatters into atoms which will never even affect the general level of humidity.

But that's not the point, is it? There's no need to have some great universal impact, a voice inside her insists. It's enough to *try and do* something. *Create* light rather than refract it, for example.

Celia finishes her tea, then dives back under the duvet, squeezing her eyes shut so she won't have to see that drop. Won't have to see it fall.

When she walks into the kitchen at last, barefoot and still in her nightdress, the Babies? – No Thanks! fluorescent-red number, Nita is perched on one of the slick bar stools at the breakfast counter, gobbling bread and soup while leafing through the fat sports section of the Sunday paper. 'Good to see you've made the vertical again,' she says, looking up with a smile.

Celia slides on to the stool next to her, in front of the powder-blue linen place mat and napkin, the gleaming cutlery. 'Nita,' she mumbles, 'I'm terribly sorry . . . I'll never forget your kindness. And you've even cleaned the blood off my jacket, I saw it hanging up in the bathroom. Thanks so much.'

Nita shrugs, briefly lays a hand on her wrist. 'S'all right. That's what friends are for, no? Here, have some soup – Knorr's de luxe winter veg. Help yourself to bread,' and she fills a white porcelain bowl from the tureen at her elbow, sprinkles some greenery on top that Celia could have done without, but she won't say anything. She'll do her best to be good: nice as pie, her mother would have called it. She tears a slice of bread in half and begins to chew.

'Hey, Cel, you really serious about that?'

'What?' Celia asks, splashing the first spoonful of soup back into her bowl and pushing her hair out of her face.

Nita is nodding towards her red nightdress. 'You know, no kids and all that? Isn't your biological clock ticking overtime by now? Mine certainly is.' She laughs, slurps more soup, then picks at a smear of leek that's got trapped between her front teeth.

Celia doesn't want to offend her, doesn't want to pretend either. 'Well . . .' she prevaricates and hastily bends over her food.

The piece of leek removed, Nita says, 'The difficult bit is finding a man that's big, blond and brainy, and disposable. Who wants to be lumbered with the same guy all her life? What for? To end up unwadding his smelly socks before every wash?' She giggles, pauses dramatically. 'I'd keep the kid, of course.'

Celia raises an eyebrow at her, 'So Silvan isn't going to be a proud father then, is he?' Her spoon clinks against the side of the delicate bowl, far too loud.

'Afraid not, Cel, he's out on two counts at least!' Nita winks, quite unconcerned. 'How about yourself? Wouldn't you like to have a dinky little baby one of these days, very soon?'

Celia takes a deep breath, 'Actually, no.' She hesitates, reminding herself to tread softly, Nita is a friend after all. 'I mean, I don't feel I need a child to be happy.' She gulps down some soup to stop herself; she'd rather scald her lips, preferably even her tongue, but the liquid isn't that hot any more and all she can do is listen, with horrified gratification, to what she's never before voiced in so many words:

'No, I don't need a child to be fulfilled. Or to be in touch with life. Or to be a real woman. Or a good Catholic. Or a deserving member of society. Or to provide for old age – or whateverthefuckelse people are always telling me.'

In the silence that follows she suddenly becomes aware of her knuckles; they've gone as white as the porcelain bowl she is gripping. 'Christ, Nita, I am sorry. I shouldn't take this out on you. It's just that I've been asked the question a lot lately – mother's funeral was a prime occasion – and I'm sick and tired of that Whydontyouhavechildren?Isthereseomethingwrongwithyou? Sick and tired of those suspicious glances, those fingers raised in warning like I'm some kind of renegade or betrayer. Sick and tired of those oily looks of pity which are so hard to wash off afterwards.' She laughs nervously.

Nita doesn't join in. She is cradling her bowl in both hands and sipping from it, her eyes hidden behind the rim.

'It's a matter of choice,' Celia pleads. 'And I choose *not* to.'

Carefully Nita sets down her bowl, then dabs at her mouth with the napkin. No, she is thinking, Not simply a matter of choice, a matter of responsibility too. Is *this* what Cel is shying away from? She crumples up her napkin and says, 'Don't worry. I understand.' But does she? Until now she'd automatically assumed Cel would want to have a family. And after Franz's death it had seemed only natural when she didn't rush into a new relationship, let alone parenthood. Well, so much for trying to gauge other people . . .

'Anyway,' Nita rakes a hand through her short coppery hair, 'if you've had enough soup, how about some coffee?'

The *Hauskaffee*, tasting more of brandy, gin and herbal liqueur than water and cream, has the soothing effect of a peace offering. They don't talk much as they stir and drink, stir and drink, then decide to go for a walk to clear their heads.

The path has been snow-ploughed and zigzags along in the glittering sunshine, past a piste and a drag skilift hauling up children like sacks of flour, before it dips down through the shadows of fir trees and pines to skim the banks of the River Albula. The water has frozen over in parts, with black swirling channels under the ice.

'Do I have to?' Celia can't help asking. They have reached a narrow slatted bridge – there are no railings, not even a rope to hold on to.

The white hillside beyond is etched with the hieroglyphics of bird claws and punctured along its wooded edges by the hoof prints of deer. A train honks, far up-valley.

'It won't collapse under you, Cel, you're quite safe,' Nita smiles from the other side. 'The authorities here are scrupulous about the maintenance of their *Wanderwege*.'

As she taps one foot in front of the other, testing cautiously, Celia chokes back the fear rising in her throat. She resists the urge to close her eyes and focuses instead on an old pine tree a little way off, where the path curves upward again. Beneath its snow-heavy branches the legs of a bench stick up, stumpy and aimless, the seating planks removed until the spring thaw.

Just as they pass the big pine, a muffled shot rings out from the sunless gorge behind them.

Like thunderclaps several mountain crows lift from the depths of the tree, cawing, flapping and scattering snow.

'Hey, watch out!' Nita cries and jumps away.

For a moment Celia stands with her head bowed, wet and blinded, back in the nightmare of stalker and stalked.

'What . . . was that?'

'The police out on a manhunt,' Nita replies nonchalantly. Then, noticing the haunted expression on Celia's face, she laughs. 'Only joking, Cel. Probably a poacher.'

In answer Celia grabs hold of a branch and yanks it hard, viciously almost. More snow comes tumbling down in a silty sibilant rush that strokes her with ice-cold fingers. 'What about avalanches?' she says, letting go of the branch as abruptly. 'Won't the shots start avalanches?'

'Not with all those trees in between. Come on, Cel, race you to the signpost!' Nita points up ahead and spurts off in a cloud of snow.

A metre from the post Celia catches up with her and wrestles her to the ground. They lie laughing and gasping. Later they roll apart to make angel shapes with crooked wings, like they used to when they were small and still believed in the magic of images. They're blissfully unaware of the group of Japanese tourists in moonboots and padded jackets who've emerged from the Stübli Restaurant halfway up the slope and, bemused by the quaintness of local customs, zoom in on them with their Nikons and Minoltas.

24

AND NOW IT'S Monday night, quarter to nine. Celia's just got off the train from the Alps and hailed a taxi to take her up to Anders Cemetery.

Nita had persuaded her to stay an extra day – 'You'll be all the better for it, trust me, Cel!' – and the answering machine at the office hadn't complained when she left her message late on Sunday, after a bottle of Pommard. But she didn't call Alex. Let the man wait a little, let him fret, whet his appetite, her last shred of pride had insisted.

The impromptu holiday had seemed full of promise, like a vast playground with enough snow around her for a thousand snowmen and millions of snowballs. In the end, though, she slept till lunchtime, fixed herself a cheese-and-tomato sandwich, then sat out on the balcony, wrapped in a sheepskin, reading the paper, listening to Nita's transistor radio and dozing, the sun hot on her legs. So hot, she'd felt weak with desire and climaxed right there, without even touching herself. And again, this time with her unhurt hand inside her jeans – a fierce follow-up dedicated to Alex. Mid-afternoon, Nita returned from the snowboarding school and they went for a snack at the Station Restaurant.

The graveyard spreads like a terraced garden down the flank of Cemetery Hill, made for the living, not the dead. Celia tells the taxi driver to wait and he parks next to the chapel of rest, clicking on the interior light and pulling a crime paperback from under his seat. 'Fine by me,' he grins. 'The meter's running.'

A few steps from the taxi the night closes in on her, frosty and dark with the blackness of a nearly new moon. The chapel of rest is where her mother had been laid out, three and a half weeks ago now. So wraithlike she'd looked, thin and tight-skinned as a girl, as if their roles had been finally reversed. For an instant Celia almost loses her footing on the iced-over gravel path.

'Don't be scared, Cel,' she whispers to herself, clutching the carrier bag with the pine-tree branch she's brought back from Albula. 'Don't be scared.' And to prove she isn't, she makes herself walk down to the front wall of the cemetery. There's still some snow up here, clinging to the earth like a blanket for the dead. Below her the Thur Valley stretches wide and level as a plain, crushed smooth by glaciers ice ages ago. She can only guess at the sleek line of the river halfway across and Seerücken Hill in the black distance beyond. Here and there clusters of brightness illuminate the land like solitary beacons of humanity.

Celia turns away and hurries off towards her mother's grave. The waist-high lamps cast a greasy pallor over the snow, the bushes and headstones. Candles flicker inside red glass containers, left to burn themselves out alone. So quiet it is, so very quiet. There's no one around.

But the peace doesn't last. A roar has erupted further up the hill and is dying away again into a sleepy growl. One of the lions at Plättli Zoo, probably. Handsome Henry had once told her that lions dream just like dogs, only more violently – their claws scrape against the floor of their cage and they snarl, gnash their teeth while they pursue imaginary prey across imaginary savannahs. She shivers, glad the savagery is contained.

A bell tolls the hour from across town, then another, like an answering voice. The cemetery church and the small chapel remain silent – as if the dead *could* be woken, Celia jokes to herself, before becoming suddenly serious. Although she doesn't really believe in resurrection, she is terrified by the prospect of encountering some indefinable sign to the contrary. That's why she'd put off visiting her mother's grave. But now, after her narrow escape on the sledge run, she is determined to do away with irrational fears. From now on she will fight them. Or confront them.

Rounding a clump of shrubbery, she stops short. Someone's lit the candle, the white candle Uncle Godfrey had said was from him. Then she forces herself to go on, right up to the grave. Silly Cel, why be afraid? Confront and fight, remember?

As she tugs the branch out of her plastic bag, the clean scent of resin seems to explode in her face. She wedges the stem through the tracery of snow at the foot of the temporary wooden cross, between a shallow clay pot set with erica and pansies and a plastic cemetery vase holding a bunch of frostbitten roses. No dead black tulips, mercifully. The wreaths have been spread out on the mound in front of her, snow-caked rings of fir twigs and evergreens with glimpses of gold lettering on satin, colour-sprayed cones, dried flowers, and yellow carnations, glass brittle.

She doesn't cross herself. Doesn't even fold her hands. Instead she rubs some heat into them, careful to avoid the taped gauze, then bows her head to conjure up a happy memory of her mother.

That's when she hears the steps. From behind. She spins round, bracing herself for whatever. Whoever.

No one. Nothing. Only the rasp of the night wind in the bare trees. Easy enough, of course, for someone to have ducked behind a bush or a headstone. Surely she isn't so worn out by the events of the past few weeks she is hallucinating? Though that's what Nita seemed to think. Her goodbye had been more like a pep talk: 'Don't worry about things, Cel. Give yourself time, and keep in touch.'

She is about to turn back to the grave when the steps continue. They've begun to stumble and slide, and sudden apprehension knots her stomach.

'Mamma! Mamma!' A voice calls out.

Celia shudders.

'Where are you? MAMMA?' The steps sound much nearer.

No, she *won't* run. *Won't* hide. A rustle, and now the shape of a woman is coming towards her from one of the side paths, partly obscured by a hedge: a young woman with long hair, dressed in a patterned coat that has swung open at the front to reveal a tight top, a glittering necklace and jeans. Not exactly clothes for a cold night. Celia digs her hands into the pockets of her poncho. For a disturbing moment she wonders whether the girl is actual flesh and blood.

Then she realises she knows the voice. Knows the girl.

'Mygod, Angelina, what are *you* doing here? You a ghost or something?' She's pleased with herself for having managed such a humorous tone, in this place of all places.

'Sorry?' Angelina says, moving closer on her slippery-soled Italian boots. 'Is that you, Celia?'

'It is. Unless I'm a ghost too.' Celia musters a laugh and involuntarily glances at Angelina's small diamond-studded crucifix.

'I seem to have lost my mother. She was at Nonna's grave a minute ago, over there.' Angelina jerks her chin towards the eastern corner of the cemetery. 'You haven't seen her by any chance, have you?' She plucks at her necklace, flicks the crucifix between her fingers restlessly.

Celia starts to say, 'Perhaps she's returned to the –' when Angelina opens her mouth again to shout: 'MAMMA! MAMMA!' The corners of her eyes are gleaming with wet.

'Let's walk together,' Celia suggests and reaches for the girl's arm. Looking back at her uncle's white candle, she sees the flame tremble, then steady itself.

They'd had an argument, Angelina explains, and she'd gone off in a huff, leaving her mother to calm down beside the grave.

Celia's head has begun to throb. She'll need another painkiller soon. They pass under the interwoven canopy of some willows and quite unexpectedly find themselves in a small gravelled space with a bench in the centre. Seated on it is a slumped figure. Angelina rushes forward, her arms outstretched.

'MAMMA, I'm so GLAD!' she cries, before turning to Celia and blowing her a kiss.

Celia nods and smiles, mimes a flimsy 'Goodbye' that's swallowed by the nocturnal shadows between them.

'ANGELINA!' she hears a rich dark voice behind her. '*CARISSIMA*!'

All at once she feels terribly sad, much sadder than at her mother's grave, and she retreats as fast as she can, blundering along the frozen paths, the throbbing in her head like a palpable presence.

A lone cyclist is going past as Celia unlocks her street door. She picks up the travelling bag, then sketches a wave towards the taxi idling at the kerb, and it drives off. The street is dry now, with only a few floury patches of white left where the salt has accumulated.

Pushing the stairwell light switch, she feels her skin crawl. Her head hurts. Such a cold empty night; Anders had seemed a ghostly display of shuttered houses, hushed gardens, shops plunged into darkness, deserted restaurants – as if Lent was back in fashion. For a moment she thinks of the angel shapes again, embedded in their sheets of snow tucked into the moonless shadows of the mountains.

Her eyes scan the landing for any unwanted gifts of flowers: none, thankgod.

But next to her door handle is a small yellow post-it sticker . . .

. . . she shrinks away letting her keys clatter to the floor . . .

. . . from Carmen. To say the washing machine they share needs a new rubber seal and would she please leave the street door on the latch so the engineer has access to the cellar. Dated Saturday.

Suddenly Celia hears footsteps ascending from down there. Heavy stamping footsteps.

Her heart misses a beat, then starts to pump like mad. She stoops for the keys, fumbles the right one into the lock, the blood singing in her ears. After closing the door behind her she leans against it in the dark, listens to the steps outside reach the landing and pause. The landing window is tinkling behind the curtains. She holds her breath, feeling trapped in the crimsonness of her corridor. Picturing her blood being rushed around her body's arteries and veins, being rushed more and more urgently. Faster. Until the vessels give and rupture at the weakest point . . .

The footsteps carry on, past her door and up the stairs. Celia exhales slowly. A false alarm.

At least her mother didn't have to bleed to death or choke on her own blood. In the end she had died of starvation. Month by week by day by decaying minute she'd starved a little more. A drifting-away hinted at only by the hollows under her bedclothes.

'There's nothing else to be done, Frau Roth. I'm very sorry,' the doctor had told her in the corridor of the nursing home.

And she had nodded and looked away, not having the heart – or was it the courage perhaps? – to ask, But can't we help? Can't we help her . . . along? She'd looked away as far as she could, past all those closed doors down that corridor bleached bright white . . .

Celia is still standing motionless when there's a rap at her door.

But she hasn't heard a thing. There haven't been any footsteps, have there? No creakings, no squeaky hands on the banister?

'Celia, hello!'

Carmen's voice comes as a relief – even if she does sound a little drunk.

A double-rap follows, loud and jabbing like Celia's headache.

'Are you there?'

Celia snaps on the overhead light, then flings open her door to get it over with. 'Hi, Carmen,' she says breezily. 'Yes, I saw your note. Thanks for arranging things with the repair people. I was away for a long weekend. Have they been yet?' She notices her travelling bag is still sitting out on the landing.

Carmen shakes her head. 'No. They said, "Saturday possibly or Monday definitely." So now it'll be tomorrow, double-definitely.' She giggles for no reason that Celia can see.

'Everything okay?' she inquires and sticks the post-it on the wall inside. There isn't really much else to say, they are neighbours, not friends.

Carmen hiccups. 'Yes, wonderful!' She breaks into a radiant gap-toothed smile, her tongue stud gleaming. 'Actually, I've just become an aunt-and-godmother. My brother phoned from Madrid a short while ago and now Rolf and I are celebrating with some Cava. Rolf's just fetched another bottle from the cellar.' She hiccups again and the stud chinks against the back of her teeth like hidden laughter. 'Care to join us?'

Celia wonders briefly whether the woman is taking her revenge for the boiler-room episode the previous weekend. Carmen isn't the type, though. Much too good-natured, too well-disposed towards her fellow creatures.

'Congratulations! Boy or girl?'

For a minute or so they go through the motions, then, touching the side of her head where the pain has sharpened into nails, Celia says a decided goodnight and thanks anyway but she is too tired right now, and lugs her bag over the threshold.

Her rucksack, or rather Franz's rucksack, she'd sacrificed to the Alps. As the train rattled along the gorge, in and out of tunnels and avalanche galleries, with vistas of frozen waterfalls like silvery rips in the mountainside opposite and the immediacy of sheer rock less than a metre away, it had suddenly occurred to her that this was what she ought to have done years ago. After the vertiginous curve of the Landwasser viaduct she'd transferred her toiletries and the extra jersey and jeans to the travelling bag, then unfastened every single zip in the rucksack, unlooped every single cord. By the time they were approaching the viaduct near Solis she was ready. The elderly couple in the seats facing her had gawked and gasped in unison when she opened the window, but she'd simply smiled at them, saying, 'Don't worry, it won't feel a thing.' Ninety metres below, the River Albula was a winding band of darkening turquoise in the dusk. At the next stop husband-and-wife had moved to a newly vacated compartment.

Home at last. And home *alone*. But this isn't a film. She isn't a kid. Come on now, woman. What had Nita said? *Don't worry about things.*

First of all she needs a couple of aspirins.

She flips on the bathroom light – and stares, amazed:

The room's been painted a slinky pearly emerald with flecks of red and gold, suggestive of reptiles sheltering in crevices or the cool shade of leaves, underwater even . . . Infinitely more evocative than her original request for seagreen. There's a message on the mirror, in clumsy lipstick letters: A MERMAID'S BATHROOM. SORRY YOU WEREN'T AROUND TO ADVISE . . . The dots at the end are smudgy pink kisses. In a tiny PS Alex offers to redo the lot if she isn't happy. And in a PPS he asks, WHERE ARE YOU?

Celia can feel tears pricking beneath her eyelids. 'Alex,' she murmurs, sliding her fingertips over the textured finish. The cool grittiness threatens to graze her skin and sends a chill of pleasure through her. She quickly swallows the two tablets, then gingerly detaches the protective layers of tape and gauze from her palm. The cuts have the look of raw meat. The water as she washes her hands stings and stabs at them with tiny invisible blades. Flexing her fingers is sore, and she dabs on some iodine.

After leaving a message on Nita's answering machine to say thanks again for everything, she goes into the kitchen, lifts the black tulips from their agate vase – and drops them straight into the rubbish bin. A mechanical action that requires no effort, still less thought. It's as if she has become a wind-up toy and someone's tightened the spring inside her. One step. Then another. And another. She can't stop, the spring has been coiled so tightly.

In the spare bedroom she is greeted by a first coat of azure as bright as a summer sky in the Alps. The illusion collapses rudely enough when she trips on the plastic sheeting and lands on her behind. She giggles. A few bruises more can't do any harm – quite the reverse, they might make Alex more interested in her. For an instant she imagines him kneeling by her side, kissing better every lurid inch of her. She'll phone him in a minute. But first she has work to do. The floor covering, stippled blue and crimson and purple and turquoise like some modern art installation, flaps under her feet.

The Valentine cards are strewn higgledy-piggledy over the various jewellery boxes and letters in her mother's bedside drawer, the way she'd left them Friday night. Their declarations of love, Celia has persuaded herself, aren't her business. None of her mother's private correspondence is. She has no right to pry and play the detective. Better to let sleeping dogs lie, my dear, as her grandmother would have said, her lips curved into a smile. For an instant Celia hears the growl again of that barely awake lion in his cage above the cemetery. Then she gets her mother's lace-trimmed wastepaper basket out of the wardrobe and begins to fill it.

The tulip cards go first. If there's anything she needs to know, the past will catch up with her soon enough. Now for the piles of letters. Among them are several pale-violet envelopes addressed to Mademoiselle Gabrielle, c/o Coiffure et Beauté, 1012 Lausanne-Chailly, from someone called Nicole in Montreux – empty envelopes, so why had her mother bothered to save them? Also a handful of aerogrammes from New Zealand, and half a dozen postcards from herself as a schoolgirl. Celia dumps them all without compunction. But she can't bring herself to throw out a manila envelope she's found which contains photos of her parents she had never been shown – photos of their early days together, before Walter disrupted what Celia now sees as a 'meeting of needs': her mother with that holding-back look on her face while her father is standing or sitting or lying gazing at her, his mouth smiling, his eyes squeezed up with delight, his hand grasping her shoulder, her arm, her waist. And the other thing Celia can't bear to part with is her father's messed-up map of the Hölloch – surely she has the right, if not the duty, to treasure *that*?

The drawer is almost empty. Fluff has got wadded in its corners and along the edges. Although she could describe every single piece of her mother's jewellery from memory, Celia opens box after box. Everything's there: the antique bracelet fashioned from silver coins which her grandfather had given to her mother on her return from Lausanne; her grandmother's small round gold watch; the Akoya-pearl necklace she herself had bought as a sixtieth birthday present; the 24-carat gold curb chain with the three pendants in the shape of a gentian, a rose and a stylised cat, allegedly from her father; the brooch and matching clip-on earrings in filigree silver 'inherited' from an old friend (Nicole of the violet notepaper, maybe?); the solid-silver torque – 'just a gift, don't be so nosy'. And that's it. No rings. Not even a wedding ring. And certainly no stone-set jewellery – or 'dwarfs' treasure', to use her mother's phrase.

The last of the boxes is trailing the frayed end of a black satin ribbon. Hadn't her mother always said she disliked 'fancy trims'? A tug and the box falls open.

Inside is a lock of red hair, tied up in a bow.

Celia's own hair is dark brown like Walter's; her father's was the colour of sun-bleached molehills and her mother's a glossy black, with a little help.

She can't believe what she's thinking: Margaret, Lily's mother! She is the only person with that tint of red, not strawberry red like Lily, but red-hot gold. Titian red.

Margaret. Whyonearth would her mother keep a lock of her hair? Celia repeats the name out loud, questioningly, tentatively, with long pauses in between: 'Margaret? . . . Margaret? . . . Margaret? . . .' More forcefully now: 'MARGARET! MARGARET! MARGARET!' Until it becomes a painful boom in her head.

'FORGODSAKEIDONTBELIEVEIT!' she shouts, over and over again.

Details begin to slot into the blanks of a puzzle she's never wanted to solve. The many beauty visits Lily's mother had been able to afford. The weekly afternoon teas. The small legacy in her mother's will which she'd put down to mere whimsicalness towards a good friend and client. The way the two women had embraced under the cherry tree while they waited for the doctor. That ominous Carnival Ball when not even Lily knew Margaret's outfit.

Margaret. Margaret the person under her mother's skirts? Was it possible?

Celia staggers dizzily to her feet. She is pressing her father's map to her heart like a mascot, perhaps to fend off another round of questions. Questions she couldn't face just yet.

As the letters and Valentine cards settle on the black tulips in the kitchen bin, it's like another eerie *déjà vu*. Margaret the bestower of tulips? But the voice on the phone hadn't been that of an old woman, she's positive. And she definitely would have recognised Margaret. Celia slams down the bin lid, lifts it up again, slams it, lifts it, slams it a third time, extra hard. Who says only mountaineers are allowed their rituals? WHO BLOODY SAYS?

It's late, half past eleven, when she dials Alex's number. She needs to talk with him to touch base again, as it were. If his wife answers, she'll find an excuse, some disaster involving a paint tin and herself maybe, to allay suspicion.

But it's Alex who says (on the seventh ring, she counted), 'Yes, Jacqueline?' He sounds drowsy, and irritated. 'What is it now?'

'Hi there, Alex. This isn't Jacqueline – whoever *she* is.'

'Celia!' At once he seems warm and alert. 'Jacqueline's my wife. Went on a skiing holiday with the boys yesterday. She almost didn't leave because Pascal, our . . .'

The receiver clamped under her chin, Celia begins fingering the three silk passionflowers – from the door and the chocolate box – she'd laid out earlier on the telephone table, in an act of defiance.

'. . . his tonsils. And now Jacqueline keeps calling me. Anyway, how are you?'

'All right. Just got back. Thanks a million for my Mermaid's Bathroom! It's wonderful, Alex! Here's a kiss for you!' Purringly she adds, 'I'm happy to pay you double – cash, and in kind. If you want.' She giggles at his indrawn breath.

'Do I? Christ what a question!' He pauses and there's a soft thudding creak as he turns over in bed. 'By the by, I had some trouble getting into your flat Saturday afternoon. The street door was on the latch so I went in and up. Then this leather-clad biker appeared out of nowhere. Acted like a bouncer when he saw me with your keys.'

Celia laughs, 'Rolf's a nice guy and a good neighbour. More bluff than anything. He must have thought you were an intruder or a secret admirer . . .' She checks herself. Grabs one of the silk flowers and tweaks off a petal, *He loves me*. And another, *He loves me not*. 'I took off at the crack of dawn, so he wouldn't have known I was away.'

'A bit sudden,' Alex comments and goes silent.

'A trip to the mountains to visit an old girlfriend. I stayed longer than intended.' *He loves me.* Celia hopes he'll say, Why didn't you tell me?

But he blurts out, 'According to this Rolf guy I was "the third male to come knocking on that bleeding door" in the space of an hour.'

'What? More men wanting to see me? You're kidding!' Ten petals, she observes to herself, that's bound to end sadly. Better start with *He loves me not* next time. Carefully she puts the ragged-looking remains of the passionflower down on the table, beside the others. *Three* men after her and she'd managed to miss them all. Trying to fight phantoms on a sledge run instead, forgodsake!

Alex has begun mumbling and panting. She is about to ask if there's something wrong when she hears him whisper, quite distinctly now, 'So what are you wearing, Celia? Or are you naked already, like a true mermaid?'

Lying in bed freshly showered and scented after her fun-and-games phone call, her injured hand covered with new gauze, Celia remembers the letter box out front. She's forgotten to empty it. Yes, forgotten, *et voilà*. Forgottenforgottenforgotten, she tries to convince herself, in a vague sleepy sort of way, while a voice deep down keeps butting in: not forgotten, *ignored*. You ignored it *deliberately*. Coward.

Barely awake, Celia finds herself back in the cemetery. The memory of the cold makes her flinch and curl up inside her nightdress as if it's a shell, or a second skin; her knees nestle against her stomach and huddle tightly in her arms.

My mother visits Nonna's grave every week – same day, same time, like clockwork, she hears Angelina say.

Envy, jagged and glittering as crushed glass, cuts into Celia. She hugs herself even harder, so hard her knees start to dig into her breasts, and she has to let go.

Her last thought is indistinguishable already from what might be the beginnings of her first dream: Thirty days – tomorrow my mother will have been dead . . .

25

When the decorators enter after a short knock, Celia trembles a little, doing her best not to betray her emotions. Tonight at six is the memorial service Uncle Godfrey had insisted on.

She addresses Alex as Herr Lehmann and he smiles, then fleetingly places a finger on his lips to say they're sealed. His gaze seems to draw her towards him, into the here and now, and she has to grip the doorjamb of the store room for support.

Out of the corner of her eye she sees that Dominic has picked up the mangled passionflower from the telephone table. 'You don't like flowers, do you?' he states with a snort that conveys his distrust of her so openly her whole body winces. 'Not even bloody real. Might as well finish the job,' he mutters and, like an insolent kid, starts to pull out the rest of the petals.

'Help yourself,' Celia says, grateful for the distraction. The trembling is all but gone now and she risks a glance at Alex.

He is pretending to scowl at Dominic and patting down a few wisps of his Vandyke in a cagey silence – after all, he knows how much she hates those flowers.

The fuzzy silk petals litter the floor like bird feathers after the cat has had its fun, and Dominic stares at them in distaste. Then he grins over at Alex, who's still scowling. Why hasn't the boss tried to stop him, for chrissake? Boldly he waves the two remaining specimens in the air and asks, 'What about these?'

'Chuck them in the bin,' Celia replies, before Alex can clear his throat.

Dominic ignores her and sticks the flowers behind the mirror, between the frame and the wall, in a V-shape. Then he stands admiring them, scratching himself under his baseball cap while the heads on the silk-wrapped wire stems nod at him stiffly.

'Well, we'd better get going,' Alex announces, but he doesn't move.

Celia shrugs. 'Same here,' she says, reaching for her poncho on the coat rack. 'I'll give you a ring later this morning to see how things are shaping up.' As she drapes the woollen cloth over her arms, she looks at Alex and lets the tip of her tongue flicker over her lips, casually provocative, as if she's licking off a breakfast crumb.

Alex smiles very faintly and opens the front door for her. 'Right, bye for now,' he says, so deadpan-sober Dominic looks at him speculatively for a moment, then at Celia, his eyes narrowed to slits under their hoods. Seconds later he tips his cap at her, smirks and turns on his heel, off to the spare bedroom.

That's what Alex has been waiting for; he snatches her hand with the palm smothered in gauze and says, 'Kiss it better, shall I?'

'Mm, this feels good,' Celia sighs, inching closer to him. 'If only that assistant of yours wasn't here . . .'

Suddenly an icy blast comes whirling down the corridor from the spare room – where Dominic must have opened the windows – and joins forces with the draught from the stairwell. At the same instant his voice calls out, 'Problems, Alex?' Perhaps she merely imagines it, but his tone seems more strident than normal, with a curtness that reminds her of an other event, so similar and yet so different, years and years ago and in this very same corridor. She shivers violently. Then the bedroom door slams.

Alex folds her in his arms, wondering whether Dominic has smelt a rat. He'll sound him out afterwards, maybe drop a few unflattering remarks about Celia, just in case. As for the newly painted bathroom, he'll say her finicky specifications included doing it over a weekend when she was away – double time, of course. He quickly kisses Celia on the mouth and, before she can kiss him back, holds her a little away from him to scrutinise her face – she really has caught the sun, and there's defiance in her eyes, mixed with fear. Lifting her hair free from the poncho in one big cascading fall, he loops a few strands together under her chin, like the strings of a hat. 'That should keep you safe,' he says, 'my little mermaid.'

Celia isn't used to this kind of behaviour. Soppy and romantic, it appears to her, especially in a man. Franz would never have dreamt of saying or doing anything like that.

Without warning she kicks the front door shut behind them. Her unhurt hand makes a grab for Alex's groin – the simplest expedient, in her experience, to return a relationship to a less emotional state.

There's a sharp intake of breath, then Alex's lips brush against the crown of her head. God, she couldn't cope with being affectionate. Mechanically her hand rubs up and down, up and down. No, 'couldn't' isn't right: she *can't*, and that's the truth. Or is it possibly more a question of *not wanting*, in both senses of the word? Not yet at any rate, she decides and unbuttons his overalls. Because accepting a want would mean letting go. She has started to rub harder, nipping him gently through the jeans, the way she knows he likes it. It would mean letting go so entirely she'd be sure to drown in the process. Or get stuck forever in a bottomless mire of feelings. A tragic demise for anyone, not least a mermaid.

'No belt today?' she asks lightly as she unzips him. His tongue is nuzzling her ear now with urgent thrusts. Her index finger traces circles round the polished tip of flesh that's strained free of his underwear, round and round, towards the wet centre which has begun to ooze thick slow drops, making him groan.

She tilts up her head, smiles a pouting smile.

His tongue is inside her mouth when the door opens at the other end of the corridor. 'Alex? Ready if you are!'

Alex eases her hand away. 'Be . . . right . . . with you,' he gasps.

Celia giggles and starts to untangle the loops of hair under her chin. 'Phone me while he's out getting your mid-morning rolls,' she whispers. The kiss aimed at Alex's cheek is lost in the stubble of his Vandyke. 'Okay, Bluebeard?'

She has left before he's zipped himself up.

Outside it's frosty, an oyster sky glowing in the early sunlight. The snow has almost vanished during her trip to the Alps; scrappy and scummy, it lies under the beech hedge like the dregs of winter.

Schildi has been snoozing on a cushion of snowdrops under the ash tree; now she stretches and arches her back, gazing wistfully at the abandoned bird feeder above. 'Puss, puss, puss,' Celia coaxes. She bends to stroke the cat, feeling the softness of its fur squirm against her legs. Suddenly exuberant, she begins picking the snowdrops at her feet and smelling them – so very fragrant they are, such delicate bells of spring. Schildi is fawning around her knees with reproachful miaows. Celia has no idea who the flowers are for, not for herself anyway; they're too meek and pretty. Then it occurs to her that they might help mollify Eric after her last-minute day off. It's worth a try. Behind her some military jeeps are droning past, but for once she isn't bothered about the soldiers.

Holding the bunch of snowdrops in one hand, she checks the letter box. No squashed black tulip heads or staring passion-flowers, thankgod. Just three thick wads of her daily paper, a council circular, a letter from the bank, another from the insurance company. And, Celia catches her breath, an unstamped envelope with her name printed in block capitals dead centre.

'Morning,' a voice shouts from the street and she recoils, having to steady herself against the gatepost. Deli-Doris is pedalling past on her mountain bike, waving cheerfully.

Celia grimaces her mouth into the semblance of a smile. Then she puts the snowdrops down on the letter box and rips open the envelope. Inside is a card, yellowed at the edges.

The message is short and commanding: 'Meet me at the Hölloch – guided tour, this Tuesday lunchtime.'

Hell Cave? Today? She is expected at the office, dammit.

There's no address, no date or signature.

But the handwriting looks familiar. It's her uncle's.

Her uncle's?

The scent of the snowdrops mingles with the winter jasmine, sickeningly sweet. The apartment block opposite looms. The overhanging roof of Frau Müller's farmhouse is like a giant hat pulled low to hide a face.

Back in the flat again, Celia flings herself into the upholstered chair. Alex is nowhere in sight. She laughs and laughs. Uncle Godfrey! She is shaking with laughter. The Hölloch! Her head makes small jerky movements she has no control over. Her father has been dead more than thirty years – what's *he* got to do with this? The heels of her boots grind into the discarded silk petals on the floor without her noticing. Her hands clench and unclench and she never even feels the pain from the cuts.

Uncle Godfrey must have gone stark raving mad. Which explains his odd behaviour on Friday night. Howinhell does he hope to negotiate the slippery underground passages of a dark bloody cave? He can barely climb the stairs in his own house! And the memorial service has been arranged for this evening – they need to attend, both of them.

Celia shifts in her chair, sits up straight with sudden determination. She'll phone him. Yes! There's no reason they should drive all the way to that cave. Can't they deal with things in a more civilised fashion, like grown-ups?

NO! She crashes the receiver back down.

Perhaps she could call Lily? Lily must have received her letter by now and might be able to shed some light or offer advice.

No! Yes! No! YES! Halfway through punching out the numbers she realises she can't see what she's doing, her eyes are blind with tears.

She doesn't know anything any more. Doesn't understand either. At least that's what she wants to believe. She DOESNT-DOESNTDOESNT want to understand. DOESNTDOESNT-DOESNT want to know. Anything beyond the obvious is beyond her.

Then she feels the touch of someone's hand on her shoulder. 'Celia, what's wrong?'

Uncertainly she raises her head and Alex kisses her brow, her wet eyes. 'Won't you tell me?' He leans closer, fondles her hair. 'Won't you?'

But she only cries harder and buries her face in the roughness of his overalls to stifle the sobs. She doesn't want Dominic to hear. She couldn't bear his grin, couldn't bear that sly glance which seems to see right through her. The overalls are soaked where she's been burrowing into them; the dampness has an acrid smell of paint and industrial-strength washing powder that tingles and bites, and makes her sneeze.

She wipes her nose on the poncho, then probes her contact lenses with her fingertips because everything around her appears so bleary and stained. 'Ssssorry,' she sniffs. Alex plucks a strand of damp hair from her lips and cradles her head in the crook of his arm.

For a while neither of them speaks.

Eventually she motions towards the envelope on the telephone table. 'My uncle,' she says. 'My UNCLE! Ijustcantbelieveit.'

What happens next blurs into a sequence of film clips which flash past her as if she wasn't involved at all. As if she was a spectator watching herself and Alex act out scenes written and directed years ago.

. . . Alex fending off Dominic's unwanted attentions, asking him to carry on with the work on his own and giving the necessary instructions . . .

. . . Herself inside the Beauty Room, prising open a half-empty tin from the stack in the corner with a screwdriver, the way she'd seen Dominic do. Then seizing the nearest paint brush, dunking it up to the hilt into the puddingy greasy-looking mass. The wall getting covered in splintering strokes of azure that burst like jets of wild sea water from the doorway and make the room flounder and sway. Like a ship cut loose from its anchor. Dancing on the waves. Up and down, roundandroundandround. Dancing . . .

. . . Herself cleaned up and sitting at the kitchen table, nursing a cup of instant coffee. Alex lounging by the balcony door with his blue-eyed smile, ready to come to her rescue yet again, though the danger's over now, she won't mess around with his paint any more. She is talking to him. Telling him things – haltingly at first, in bits and pieces she has to wrench from herself, until it feels like she's bleeding and it all begins to flow – about her uncle, her mother and father, about Walter, Lily, the lock of Margaret's hair in her mother's bedside drawer, the black-tulip Valentine cards . . .

. . . Later the phone call to the office with Angelina relaying her mother's prediction that Celia will soon reach the end of the tunnel, and herself thinking: Tunnel? What damn tunnel? just as the girl adds, a little embarrassed, that her mother has the gift of seeing people's auras – and yours was very strong yesterday evening, Celia, very bright. Then the unexpected voice of Handsome Henry saying how he didn't mean to disturb her neighbours last weekend, sorry, he'd simply stopped by on the spur of the moment and, hey presto, the main door was unlocked. Finally Eric himself, clicking his tongue in concern at hearing of her family trouble and wishing her well for the memorial service tonight – and look forward to having you back with us tomorrow . . .

. . . Still later Alex ringing the tourist information to inquire whether the Hölloch is indeed open today, and do they offer a guided tour at lunchtime, which they do, at one o'clock. So, into the bedroom and on with her jeans-and-jersey outfit from the travelling bag; take her father's old map from the night table; then over to the chest of drawers and get the key from under the African violet; hunker down, a quick turn in the lock, and here are her gemstones in all their glory, the small tourmaline figurine of the naked woman like an image of herself, to be grabbed and deposited in the left breast pocket of her blouse, underneath the jersey, more than counterbalancing the map in the other. Out into the corridor with her mother's 'Arctic gear' jacket slung over one arm; don't forget the torch – it served its purpose before, didn't it? – and Alex grinning meaningfully when he sees it in her hand . . .

. . . Next thing she finds herself waiting in the passenger seat of her Golf, parked in the yard of Alex's workshop at the back of his solid grey two-storey house. She's using yet another of the small boxful of silk handkerchiefs while he is inside getting changed, her very own knight donning his shining armour to go with her to the centre of the earth.

Once they're on the motorway heading towards Zurich and the heartlands beyond, Alex relaxes. He has a shrewd notion of what's going on. There's more at stake than meets the eye, that's for sure. Celia's confidences earlier had felt like someone dismantling a room, hedgehogging the wallpaper, tearing and scraping it off to expose the holes underneath. Skeletons all right. Invisible ones. Not too difficult to pick the guilty party, as it were, with half of them dead already. At first he'd been tempted to contact Celia's uncle, but she had absolutely refused, and he didn't want to force the issue. She seems to have calmed down now, thank Christ. Still distressed, he can tell by the clumsy snuffling way in which she keeps blowing her nose. Poor little mermaid. She's certainly not in the mood for any tender-loving-care.

'You warm enough?'

She twitches her shoulders. Could mean yes or no. He slides the temperature lever up a bit, just in case. Then glances over. She is clutching her left breast and staring straight ahead. Seeing her profile in the harsh snow-brightness of the surrounding fields, he's struck for the first time by the exaggerated bone structure of her face. Like she'd been held in a vice at some point in her life. He shudders at the thought and stamps on the accelerator. The car shoots forward, past a convoy of lorries which are hammering downhill, hard at the speed limit.

He gestures towards the radio, 'All right if I put it on?'

Another twitch and the handkerchief's fluttering about her face again.

The ten o'clock news summary is just finishing. The weatherman forecasts a fair share of sunshine and 'unseasonably mild temperatures' for central areas. No more snowfalls until the weekend, Alex is relieved to hear, though the Golf is fitted with winter tyres.

This is his first real adventure in years. He has never been down a big cave before, only read about accidents occasionally. The third-largest in the world, the woman from the tourist information had said proudly. Road tunnels are different of course, no comparison. Lights at regular intervals, SOS sites, ventilation tubes, the constant rumble and hum of traffic. If he's honest with himself, well, he's kind of apprehensive – apprehensive enough to have stuffed two bars of chocolate, a smoked *Landjäger* sausage and a small bottle of Kirsch into the outer pockets of his parka.

A slow dark sandpapery voice has started up, and now the drums, melancholy brushstrokes. Blues. Not bad, but not his favourite. Nothing can beat a piece of madcap Madness. Gets into your blood, so you rip, strip and slap on the paint all the faster.

Mad, mad, mad, he thinks, mad and bad. Just like him. Chauffeuring a woman he hardly knows around the country on a hunch – while his wife and kids believe he's working his butt off for their creature comforts.

He notices Celia clutch her breast again as if she's in pain. Suffering from heartache, well and truly. What do they call this now, when the body hurts in place of the mind, *psycho*-something? At long last she must have allowed herself to acknowledge who is behind the whole business. Pretty obvious even to himself, a mere bystander, that the old man is being manipulated.

Alex switches off the radio. Under his breath he says, 'You know *who* you're going to meet, don't you?'

There's a draught of air as she nods, savagely.

'Not your uncle.'

In answer her head slumps forward and her hair swings between them like a curtain. For a moment he fears she'll begin to cry again. But she says without a whiff of teariness, 'No, not him.'

After a pause he asks, 'You sure you want to go through with this?'

Her hand shuffles among the cassettes in the glove compartment. 'Flowers is all I've received. No threats,' she says. Then she snaps a cassette into the deck, hits the play button. 'And *you*'re with me.' She turns up the volume.

Alex has heard the piece before; guitar warblings and the hoarse passion of Janis Joplin crooning and shouting. He decides to give it a rest. They should arrive well before one o'clock. Most of the journey is motorway and they're beyond Zurich now, travelling beside the lake, which resembles a strip of cobalt blue stencilled here and there with white sails.

Celia couldn't say another word. She just sits, stiff and immobile yet sort of floating, hypnotised by the engine noise and the magic of the music. She feels like that night two weeks ago, after first meeting Alex, when the full moon was all over her. Like being sucked into a vortex.

Already she is whirling towards the dead centre where *he* is waiting for her.

26

BUT SHE CAN'T see him. Hasn't he come? Celia tries to survey the slope down below, then gives up, frustrated. The snow reflects back her gaze in a kaleidoscope of blinding winks as if to make fun of her. She and Alex are all set: they've panted up the path to the hut near the cave entrance in the dazzling winter brilliance; they've bought their tickets and in return been issued with rubber boots and battered carbide lamps.

Not counting the guide with his handlebar moustache, there are six other people in their group. A discreetly elegant couple, the man with silverfox hair and loose tailored trousers folded umbrella-style round his legs, the woman a bit younger, good-looking in her red coat, soft black felt hat, black gloves and black scarf. Then a father and his two implike sons, the three of them wearing scuffed hiking boots, sheepskin jackets, red ski caps and big grins. The sixth member is ageless and colourless, his watery eyes huge behind thick glasses, his skin so transparent the veins show through.

Celia doesn't recognise anyone. Whereonearth is he? For a moment she seizes Alex round the waist and he responds by pressing his thigh against her. She isn't really listening to what the guide is saying and feels a little giddy, despite having had some lunch at the Höllgrotte Restaurant. Tonight is the memorial service for her mother – and a new moon. And over thirty-two years ago her father died in the very place where she is now.

* * *

After the sun-and-snow glare the interior of the cave seems pitch black. The guide informs them that the name Hölloch is derived from an old dialect expression meaning 'slippery' and so, here he chuckles triumphantly, has nothing whatever to do with hell.

Well, that's one interpretation, Celia muses. *Because it must have been hell for poor Father. Perhaps that's how it happened, in the end: he slipped and just kept slipping, everything wet and sliding and cold and dark, so dark. So frighteningly dark.*

At first she can't see much beyond the feeble yellow circle oozing out from her carbide lamp, only Alex's shoulders a short way in front, almost within reach. The rock underfoot feels treacherous all right. Her hair is ruffled by a faint draught that's slightly warmer than the air outside – some kind of chimney effect to do with further cave openings and apparently a clear sign there's no danger of floods. Thankgodforthat. Still, Celia can't help fumbling for the figurine below her heart to rally herself. Avoiding the map in the other breast pocket, at least for the present.

Where is he? Did he miss the tour?

The guide is walking off at a fair clip now and his lamp, attached to the orange helmet, is like a shaky star they're hastening to follow. It's a bumpy meandering experience, the rock rising and falling above their heads, the ground rutted and pitted, sometimes with long flights of rough-hewn steps, ropes or cold metal to hold on to, sometimes nothing at all.

Perhaps that's how it happened, in the end, nothing to grip?

Every so often the guide makes them stop and he switches on his torch to point out joints and bedding-planes in the rock, various types of erosion patterns, some of them big and phallic like Celia's black candle. 'No stalactites or stalagmites in this part of the cave system, I'm sorry to say.' He sounds just apologetic enough to be believable.

Or did Father die surrounded by those hard icicle beauties maybe, injured and crazy with pain, crazy with hunger and thirst, licking the water off them?

The guide's moustache jumps up and down as he talks. Celia shivers, tries not to inhale the pungent carbide smell. She's getting damper and clammier by the second. Huddling up to Alex, she wriggles her free hand into his pocket, grateful for his fingers which start to rub some warmth into her. He smiles, 'You okay?'

On another occasion the guide pokes around in the mud, then proudly opens his fist to disclose a couple of small worms. 'Genuine cave-dwellers,' he declares, and laughs.

Cave-dwellers, forgodsake! What about the dead? One dead body, to be precise? Or simply the skeleton under rotted clothes?

When the colourless man asks about accidents, the guide grows wary, and vague. Mentions their generally excellent track record and the rescue team on stand-by at all times. 'No need to be afraid,' he concludes. 'This introductory tour is absolutely safe.'

And the other passages? The ones deeper inside the mountain? What are their *secrets?* Their *dangers?*

Then the hiss and tinkle of the lamps as they all move on again.

What if the carbide gives out, or the batteries?

And where is *he*? Wherewherewhere?

Suddenly the noise of water rushing towards them. Coming from behind what looks like a boarded-up doorway that cuts off the tunnel perhaps twenty metres ahead.

'Nothing to worry about!' the guide calls out. 'Trust me. I suggest we have a short rest here. We'll douse our lamps and just listen, just *feel* the darkness. Okay?'

One by one the flames are blown out; Celia observes the elegant woman fuss a little – until a boy's puffed-out cheeks lean into view, and then there's nothing but the crash of water from the other side of the partition. Every breath smells and tastes of darkness. Thankgod she's got the torch in her pocket.

'This is as black as it gets – blacker than a moonless night,' the guide jokes, completely and complacently at his ease.

Poor, poor Father. Celia pictures his spirit trapped in an underworld of cold damp blackness, trapped in the rocky echoes of this man's self-satisfied laughter. Blinking her eyes open and shut, open and shut, open and shut, she finds it makes no difference, except for the cool draughty sensation on the skin of her eyeballs.

The tourmaline seems to nudge her breast and sends out a tiny electrical charge when she reaches for Alex's hand. Is this what affection is all about? Celia wonders, still blinking. A sense of well-being that's only ever felt in the other's presence, no matter where or how or when?

It's the wind that is causing the furious water noise, throwing itself like a battering ram against the planks. A roaring tearing wind. The instant she walks through the low narrow passage, Celia gets sucked into a force field. She is slammed about viciously, the breath knocked out of her. Nasty. She grabs hold of Alex, then wipes her eyes; they're watering from the raw violence of the onslaught.

Alex is glad to feel Celia's body up against his and wraps himself round her, shoulders hunched like someone dancing a slow number.

'Don't cry,' he murmurs, kissing her wet cheeks. 'We'll be out of here soon, I promise.'

He frowns to himself. Frankly, he's had it with caves, he is definitely more of a road-tunnel man. Without thinking, he has disengaged himself and unscrewed the metal top of his Kirsch. He offers Celia the bottle but she flinches away. 'Sure?' he asks, before taking a deep gurgling swig himself – abashed now because he didn't mean to offend her.

She doesn't answer, instead pulls out one of those large men's handkerchiefs. For a moment the fabric flares in the darkness like the wings of some weird albino bat, and he braces himself instinctively.

Up ahead the other members of the group have gained the top of an incline and are marching off, the glow of their lamps receding in a frail ragged line.

Alex is getting anxious. After a second slug of Kirsch he says with all the persuasiveness he can muster, 'We'd better hurry up. He must be waiting for you outside.'

She seems an eternity stowing away the handkerchief and his legs are beginning to tremble. Let's go please, Celia, he implores her silently. Then she lifts her lamp to gaze at him, and he sees her face.

She looks changed. As if the tears just now had washed away a layer of something, though he isn't sure what. He doesn't know her well enough. Doesn't know whether he ever will. Whether she'll ever want him to. But yes, she looks softer. More lovable. With a shadowy beauty that almost obscures the sharpness underneath.

'Celia?' He touches her on the arm. 'Let's go.'

Finally, she nods.

They have nearly caught up with the group when she sees *him* emerge from a side tunnel, a fuzzy figure in the lamp light.

'*Et voilà!*' she exclaims as his palm pushes up and outward in the splayed old gesture, at once swaggering and self-denigrating, she remembers so well. He has put on weight and the cleft in his chin seems less pronounced. His hair is grizzled now, as if sprinkled with permanent snow, but it's still thick and tightly curled. He's still handsome and she's still jealously proud at the sight of him. Despite her anger smouldering deep down.

He grins, halts a few paces away from her and Alex. 'So you did come, after all.' Said in that gravelly foreign-yet-familiar tone he'd used at the Métropole. Celia tries not to show her annoyance – for the sake of Alex, who is hovering uneasily.

'Alex, meet my brother Walter,' she says, introducing them.

'I expected as much,' Alex gabbles as they shake hands. 'How d'ye do?' He smooths down his already perfectly smooth Vandyke and, with mounting dismay, watches the lights of the group vanish round a corner.

There's an awkward pause, then Walter turns back to Celia, 'Sorry about Mother, and –'

Alex, desperate to rejoin the group, announces with sudden panache, 'I'll see you both later. I'll tell the others you'll be along shortly.' And he strides off, his lamp dangling wildly, signalling relief.

As if he'd just accomplished an important peace-keeping mission, Celia reflects. Maybe he has, more likely he hasn't. And most probably this is the last of his personal services she'll ever need.

'Your boyfriend's rather keen to get away, appears to me,' Walter taunts from a safe distance. Celia lets it pass.

She hears him gulp. 'That's me all over again, isn't it? Seriously, Cel, I'm happy you're with someone.' He takes a step towards her. 'And I'm sorry about when you phoned . . .'

Raging bull subdued into grovelling mode, she comments to herself. But she isn't ready yet to snuff that dull red glow of anger inside her, crackling to get out.

'I was bloody upset,' Walter continues, grasping her hand. 'Nothing really to do with the money. Or with you inheriting the flat. It's to do with *her*.' He gulps again. 'Ever since I left home she treated me like a traitor. As if I had abandoned her, for God's sake. I was her son, not her husband!' He spits the words out so bitterly they seem to infect the blackness around them and Celia jerks her hand away.

She is thinking of their poor father's trapped spirit. What did *he* shout or scream or whisper or whimper before he merged forever with that blackness?

'Sorry you got the brunt of it, Cel.' Now she is being hugged breathless. The zip of his jacket scrapes her cheek. The tourmaline woman is hurting her breast.

'So am I.'

Their lamps clash together and the metal rings out. The doorbell code was no secret to Walter, of course. And he couldn't resist jabbing it out as he dumped those tulips on her doorstep – Margaret's tulips. Compulsively almost, Celia's mind replays the TV clip of the Carnival Parade with him in his carmine robe standing next to Lily's mother in the crowd . . . Lily must have known he wasn't in Australia when they talked last Tuesday, damnher! And she must have warned her mother not to tell. Doubtless made excuses for Walter, *You see, Ma, he's awfully cut up about Gabrielle's death – not exactly a cosy relationship, was it?* (yes, that's how Lily would phrase it) *– so now it's all the harder for him, poor darling. He'll have to sort himself out first. A week or two* . . . Blah blah blah.

'Let go of me!' Celia struggles free, breathing lungfuls of dark carbide-tainted air. As she releases the figurine from where it got stuck under her breast, she feels an abrupt charge.

'What a fucking coward!' she shouts, aflame with anger now. 'Staying away from Mother when she needed you! Staying away from her pain! Her funeral! Didn't have the guts even to face ME! All those goddamn games! Those cranky calls and flowers! That stupidstupid mask!' For an instant the slitted eyeholes are right there again in front of her, boring into her from the stony darkness. Ignoring Walter's protests, she whips out the torch. 'Abracadabra!' A *click* and it's shining straight into his eyes, bright yellow.

He cries out, stumbles backwards, blinded, his lamp jangling, one hand raised to shield himself.

'I just couldn't,' he falters. He sidesteps the fierceness of the flash. 'And then it was too late.'

'Too late? Damn right it was TOO LATE!' She snorts. 'So you simply regressed? Is that it? Refined your childhood methods? No more dead beetles – flowers now, fake ones?' She starts playing the torch all over him, tying his body up in spirals, loops and knots of light.

'Celia, please.' He coughs. 'I don't know what came over me. It all got mixed up with Father's death . . . This time round I guess I wanted *you* to suffer . . . Because you haven't been told the whole story of how Father died.'

The beam locks on target. And, for the briefest of moments, it isn't Walter's face floating in the gloom of the tunnel but their father's. Starved and wasted. Skull-like.

'Please.' Walter looks like an animal at bay. He is tossing his head, trying to push away the glare.

Celia lowers the torch and it illuminates the drab eroded limestone surface between them. 'Carry on,' she says, her mouth suddenly dry with foreboding. A rasping pain in her throat makes her want to retch, and retch. Her lamp is sputtering.

Walter advances cautiously. 'I was with him that day. With Father. Here. The floods caught us unawares. Flash floods. We were scrambling towards a wall we needed to scale. And I got to the rope first. It was either him or me. I swear it was. The map was in my rucksack. There was no time. No time. I couldn't have –' He checks himself, hesitates, then lifts his arms in clumsy invitation.

Celia doesn't notice. She's reeling, staring at the ground unseeing. Her lamp drops with a loud clatter, flickers and goes out, thickening the darkness around them. She makes no attempt to retrieve it. Her empty hand is hanging by her side with the fingers still curved from being hooked through the ring. The other is clamped round the torch.

'He screamed at me to "get up that rope double-quick, or else . . ." I swear there was nothing I could have done. It was either him or me. Me or him. I swear. And then it was only me. I've paid for it. Mother and Uncle saw to that. With the carrot and the stick. Bribery. Smothering. Until I couldn't bear it any longer.' He glances at her.

That's when Celia wrenches the map from under her clothing and thrusts it into his face. 'You bastard! Bastard! BASTARD! You left him behind! Took his map! YOU!' She drops the map. Stamps on it. Lunges out at him with the torch. One fast swing, the beam swiping at an outcrop of rock above, and Walter's been hit squarely in the midriff. He lets out a yelp and collapses against the tunnel wall. His lamp has rolled off, the flame a mere will-o'-the-wisp before it's swallowed by blackness.

Celia feels like crumpling up herself, feels like lying down on the cold insensible stone. She's choking. Everything's upside-down. Nothing's as she thought it was. And nobody, nobody cared. Was Lily in on it too? The loyal wife, disloyal to her friend? Why hadn't she been told? Whywhywhy? Like a ghostly travesty of that hot faraway summer afternoon in the lounge, it's herself now that's holding her mother up by the ankles. Trying to shake the truth out of her. No sound can be heard, no rattling breath, no shouts exhorting to smack, and SMACK HARD.

Celia's torch casts a jagged oval of light into the bowels of the cave. The silence is almost total. There are only the faintest of tinklings from the direction in which the group disappeared, ages ago it seems, and the occasional *plop* of an invisible drop of water somewhere nearby. The darkness is beginning to oppress her, the mass of rock on all sides is crushing: already her head feels fit to burst, her flesh raw and bruised, and her bones creak, brittle enough to shatter at any moment. Is this what it's like to be entombed alive? Before the thirst, the hunger, the madness?

Suddenly there's a groan. The scuffling of feet. Another groan. Godwhathasshedone? He might be injured, might be bleeding, smearing the rocks with ruby-red blood. How cruelly pointless. The past can't be restored, nothing can bring their father back to life, no one.

She approaches him timidly, saying, 'I'm sorry, Walter. You aren't hurt or anything, are you?'

He has managed to get up. His face is in darkness but she can sense him shrug. 'Hope not.' He giggles in a funny broken way, then tries to clasp her to his chest.

She pulls away. Father's death wasn't Walter's fault, she reassures herself. It couldn't have been, could it? Or would she rather have had *him* dead?

She is getting very cold, much colder than the cave itself could make her. It's a coldness that seeps from the marrow of her bones, freezing her from the inside. A coldness that tugs at her scalp, tweaks at every single hair. Walter has taken everyone from her: her father, her mother, her best friend Lily. Here Celia stops herself. This is childish reasoning. Their parents are dead, they're just memories now, and no one, not even Walter, can take those away from her. As for Lily, she's moved on of her own free will. Maybe it's time she herself did the same.

As Celia lets Walter hug her, the tourmaline woman pinches the soft flesh of her breast. *Yes*, it urges her, *go on, you're no longer a little girl.*

Walter's voice is husky: 'Mother and Uncle wanted to protect me. They said if people got wind of me being involved, we'd be hounded. By social workers, the police, the press. Can you picture the headlines? "Boy Leaves Father to Die in Cave" – or worse? You were too young to be told what had happened, and afterwards it seemed better to let sleeping dogs lie, as Grandmother used to say. Mother made me promise to keep it a secret. "Our secret".'

But now she is dead. Dead. She's dead, the tourmaline woman repeats.

Celia feels her fingers dig into Walter's shoulders; she is dizzy with sheer exhaustion. And then the torch slips from her hand.

'NO!' She staggers away as it smashes on the ground, flicking a final crazy zigzag of light across the tunnel wall.

O-o-o-o-o, goes the echo, before losing itself in blackness.

Complete and utter blackness. Walter hasn't stirred, but she could swear his breathing has changed; it's become rapid and spluttering. As if he's drowning. Or is it herself? Is it? A terrible deafening noise fills her ears – until she can't stand it any more . . .

Seconds later she feels someone grip her and then she's being yanked roughly from side to side.

'-ia! -ey! -ia! -ey!' The voice reaches her in waves, as though from some remote underwater region.

She lashes out, she punches and kicks. She yells – without a sound.

Because her mouth is wide open, has been wide open all the time, sucking in air for what must be dear life.

Once her gasps have subsided, she can hear at last what's being said: 'Celia! Hey! Celia! It's okay!'

Walter's arms are around her and he is rocking her to and fro, to and fro. 'I've got a lighter, don't worry. Those carbide lamps can't be far.'

She unclenches her fists, wincing at the stabs of pain from the half-healed cuts. 'Thanks, I'm all right,' she says with a huffy laugh. 'I'm afraid you'll have to be my guide for now.'

'Of course.' His tone reminds her of his 'man-of-the-house' days. As he embraces her more tightly, she has a sudden vision of the snowdrops lying in a wilted heap on top of her letter box. She pretends to go limp herself – nice and compliant, like Lily would – and smirks into the all-forgiving all-encompassing darkness. 'You deserve a special bunch of flowers, Walter, nothing less would do. Just wait till we get home.' She laughs out loud and he joins in. Then she throws off his arms. 'So, let's see that lighter of yours.'

Walter mutters something that's followed by a distinct 'dammit' and the increasingly forcible fiddling with a zip.

'In any case, the group'll have to return here. There's no other way out.'

Celia's hand has slid under her jersey to trace the outline of the tourmaline figurine; the charge coming from it seems weak now, almost non-existent. Slipping a finger inside her blouse, she touches her breast. Her nipple is soft, velvety.

The abrupt sound of a zip being opened, rustlings, the retch of velcro fastenings, more zip noises, more rustlings, the jingle of keys and coins.

'AlexAlexAlex,' Celia whispers to herself, kissing the syllables with her tongue. For a moment she closes her eyes to shut out the cave blackness. But there's no surge of excitement at the thought of him. Nothing. Instead she finds herself imagining all the men in the world outside, beyond the cave. Faceless men, and still unknown. Men in the snow. In the sun. Men asleep. And awake. Herself with them. Or without them. YES!

Her hand is clutching the figurine again: YES! YES! YES! clutching it so hard the carved edges are beginning to hurt her.

'Got you!' Walter's voice breaks the spell.

Seconds later a thin wavering flame licks into the darkness.

'Happy now?' he asks.

Celia smiles to herself. Then in one swift movement she takes the lighter from him and walks off towards where she knows her lamp must be.